50

Before the Devil Knows You're Dead

ALSO BY MICHAEL LEDWIDGE

The Narrowback
Bad Connection

Before the
Devil Knows You're Dead

MICHAEL LEDWIDGE

ATRIA BOOKS

NEW YORK   LONDON   TORONTO   SYDNEY   SINGAPORE

This book is a work of fiction. Names, characters, places and incidents are products of the author's imagination or are used fictitiously. Any resemblance to actual events or locales or persons, living or dead, is entirely coincidental.

ATRIA BOOKS
1230 Avenue of the Americas
New York, NY 10020

Copyright © 2003 by Michael Ledwidge

Library of Congress Control Number: 2002105361

ISBN: 0-7434-4285-7

First Atria Books hardcover printing January 2003

10 9 8 7 6 5 4 3 2 1

ATRIA BOOKS is a trademark of Simon & Schuster, Inc.

For information regarding special discounts for bulk purchases, please contact Simon & Schuster Special Sales at 1-800-456-6798 or business@simonandschuster.com

Designed by Jaime Putorti

Printed in the U.S.A.

For Tom and Grace
With Love and Appreciation

May the road rise to meet you
May the wind be always at your back
And may you be half an hour in heaven
Before the Devil knows you're dead

—Irish Toast

Before the Devil Knows You're Dead

Chapter One

THE DRUM ROLL OF RAIN against the roof of the car paused when John Coglin drove beneath the elevated subway track and started up again as he rolled out the other side. The first parking spot he lucked upon was directly across from the precinct house, and he downshifted his beat-up hatchback, eased into it, and cut the engine. In the rearview mirror, the Bronx skyline was indistinct, the mounds of low, rain-washed buildings like huge sculptures made of clay and paper bags. The only color at all came from the notches of yellow window light in the squat police station directly behind him. He listened to the rain drill down. Then he took a breath, lifted his midnight blue uniform shirt in its dry cleaner plastic off the passenger seat, grasped the inside door latch and got ready to run.

The day sergeant talking on the phone behind the massive, raised wooden desk nodded to him gravely as he pushed through the swinging door. The multicolored, plastic chairs in the reception area before the desk were empty, but Coglin noticed a cop sitting with an elderly man in one of the anterooms, filling out a report. He watched as the old man bent slowly in his chair and started sobbing into his age-spotted hands. The cop beside him put his pen in his mouth and began patting him tentatively on the back in an awkward gesture of comfort. When he spotted Coglin through the doorway, the cop shook his head and rolled his eyes.

Coglin pulled open a steel door and went directly to the back row of battered, green metal lockers that filled the low-ceilinged room. He popped one of the locks, hung his shirt and glanced at himself in the mirror affixed to the inside of the metal door. He blinked at his wet, lean face, his darkish gray blue eyes. He passed a hand briskly through the stubble of his light brown hair, shucking water to the floor and began removing his equipment and laying it on the worn wood of the adjacent bench: heavy vest and wide leather belt, handcuffs and flashlight, mace and gloves, memo book, hat.

He had his uniform on and everything correctly strapped and stowed before he pressed down the inside lever, popping open the top compartment. He shifted slowly under the reassuring weight of the Kevlar and gear, and took out the light, black plastic Glock 17. It was already loaded, and he checked that the safety was on before he secured it in his holster. Then he removed the off-duty Smith & Wesson .38 that he wore at his ankle, placed it into the compartment where the Glock had been, and closed the small door with a click. Lastly, he retrieved a small, black velvet box from his jeans that now hung in his locker. Resisting the temptation to open it, he placed it in the breast pocket of his shirt, carefully buttoned the pocket and locked up.

Two uniformed officers, back early from the day shift,

entered the locker room as Coglin was on his way out. One of them grabbed his arm.

"What? We don't say hi anymore?" the cop said.

He was tall, slim and middle-aged and had a tan. His gray hair looked styled. His name was Martinelli and he'd been Coglin's first partner out of the academy. Coglin smiled as he clasped his extended hand.

"Jimmy!" Coglin said. "Somebody said you were already gone."

"Nah, nah. Six more months," Martinelli said, grinning. He took cigarettes out of his shirt pocket and lit one with a match. "Then all you suckers can just kiss my ass."

"Who would've thought you'd actually make the full twenty?" Coglin said, smiling and shaking his head.

"Same old Irish ballbuster," Martinelli said, punching him in the arm. "Heard we had a couple of gun collars last month. Very impressive."

Coglin looked off at the beat-up lockers and put up his hands.

"When you're taught by the best, Jimmy, how could you expect anything less?"

Martinelli rolled his eyes.

"Word is, I'm not the only one who might be leaving our sorry ranks," he said.

"Put in for Street Crimes," Coglin said. "But I haven't heard back yet."

"You got a phone call?"

Coglin nodded. "Made it already," he said. "Have to see."

"You'll get it," Martinelli said. "If there's any justice in this world, and I think there's still a little, tiny bit left, you'll get it."

"Hope you're right," Coglin said. "You're gonna have a bon voyage party, right?"

"Oh, we got major plans goin' on," Martinelli said. "Actually, tonight we're throwing a little bachelor party for Robbie at the Dew Drop. If it's slow, do drop by."

"Maybe I will," Coglin lied.

The veteran clouted him again on the shoulder and took a step farther into the room.

"Hey, just do me a favor, would ya?" he said. "When you make it down to One Police Plaza, bring your old partner back in a cushy consultant job or something."

Coglin laughed.

"If you're still breathing," he said, opening the door, "I'll see what I can do."

Out in the hall, the desk sergeant squinted down at him.

"You Coglin?" he said.

Coglin nodded.

The sergeant moved something on the unseen desktop before him with slow, angry deliberation. Then he held up a piece of paper.

Coglin stepped forward.

"This ain't a fuckin' answering service," the sergeant said as he sailed the paper down.

Coglin barely caught it. He looked up at the man's tag. Oliver. He was new. What did the day guys call him? Was it one-nut? No, Coglin thought. No-nuts. No-nuts Ned Oliver. Ride that desk, No-nuts, he thought.

Coglin smiled up at him and gave him a peppy thumbs-up.

"Welcome," he said.

He thought it was from his girlfriend, but when he looked at the sheet it said "Clarke," along with a number.

His phone call, he thought.

He turned immediately for the pay phones by the door.

"Midtown North Homicide, Clarke," a voice answered on the third ring.

"Joe," Coglin said. "Joe, how you doin'? It's John Coglin."

"John," Clarke said. "There you are. Great news. You're in. It's set."

"No," Coglin said with an uncontrollable grin. "For real?"

"Bronx Task Force. Street Crime Unit. You'll have to sit for the interview next week, but it's just a formality. I didn't even have to do anything really. It was your record. I just slid it on the right desk."

"Holy shit," Coglin said. His smile seemed cemented, permanent. Street Crimes, he thought. No more uniform. No more bullshit, where's your hat? Just pure police work: undercover, action and making collars.

"Christ. Thank you," Coglin said.

"Like I said, I . . ."

"Bullshit, Joe. I know how things work. I owe you big time."

"You want to pay me back?" Clarke said. "Be successful. Make me and the department proud. Work your way up. Do it right and you'll be working for me soon enough."

"Yeah right," Coglin said.

"Mark my words," Clarke said. "Listen, I gotta go. Congratulations and call me next week."

"Thank you."

"Take care," Clarke said and hung up.

Coglin stood unmoving, just holding the plastic receiver in his hand, relishing the moment. It was a good five years back since Coglin, then a carpenter, had installed cabinets in Lieutenant Detective Joe Clarke's Upper West Side apartment. Clarke had been interested in carpentry, and they'd struck up a friendly relationship that Coglin had kept up after he'd replaced his hammer with a gun. He thought on the randomness of their meeting, the strange way that life sometimes worked out.

He finally hung up and as he was passing the sergeant's elevated station, Coglin felt like jumping and clicking his heels together, but decided against it. Instead, to the old, gray face of the grim police clerk, Coglin just gave another thumbs-up and said, "Rock on."

The muster room down the hall was empty. Coglin went to the vending machines and then brought his coffee over to one of the tables along the wall. It was darker now beyond the arrow-slit windows, as if night had already fallen. The rain was still pouring down. He took off his hat and picked up a newspaper that somebody had left on the table.

He was finishing his coffee when his partner walked in. His name was Baker and he was black and stocky and just turned twenty-five. He took Coglin's paper away as he sat down beside him. He looked up from the sports section at the bulge in Coglin's shirt pocket and raised an eyebrow.

"Do I see something?" he said.

"What are you nuts?" Coglin said, glancing quickly over his shoulder. "Wait till we get on the roll."

Ten minutes later, the room was milling with cops. They quieted and quickly found seats when the two sergeants finally came in. One of the sergeants cleared his throat and began dispatching mechanically by precinct sector, car number and meal.

"Coglin, Baker," he bellowed after a minute. "Alpha three, thirteen-eighty-seven, nine o'clock."

They picked up their hats and stood. They retrieved their radios from the equipment room across the hall and descended the side stairwell to the garage. Once inside their patrol car, they simultaneously looked at the almost-empty fuel gauge. Outside the mouth of the garage, rain pounded down loudly on the gas pump.

Coglin took out a coin.

"Call it," he said.

"Heads," Baker said.

Coglin flipped the coin and slapped it down loudly on the back of his hand. He peeked at it.

"Lucky bastard," he said.

Five minutes later, they pulled out of the precinct lot. Coglin drove slowly by the low, old, stone buildings. Having been in the construction trade, Coglin often marveled at the hidden architectural splendor they'd happen upon. Wrought iron spiral staircases in abandoned row houses. Scorched gargoyles grinning down from the tops of burnt-out buildings. Plaster ceilings in crack houses that, beneath the grime, had animals worked into them: fairy tale unicorns, griffins, seahorses.

Without discussion, they drove to the McDonald's in their patrol sector, bought coffee at the drive-thru and idled in the corner of the lot. Across from them, on the corner, three young Hispanic males, wearing expensive ski jackets, hooded sweatshirts and baggy pants, exited a bodega.

"Check out the Puerto Rican ski team," Baker said, gesturing across the street with his chin. "Probably looking for Vail. Must've made a wrong turn."

"Are they anything like the Jamaican bob-sledders?" Coglin said as he watched one of them lean back against the colorful, product-lined window of the store, take out a box of cigars and begin to strip one of its tobacco. He would've started packing it with weed right then and there, if his friend hadn't nudged him and pointed toward their cruiser with his chin.

"Kinda," Baker said, lifting his coffee at them in a salute. "Only these guys here are in the Special Olympics."

Coglin chuckled as the kid with the cigar glared back before pushing himself up off the window and strolling away with his companions into the rain.

"OK," Baker said. "Enough play time. Let's see it already."

Coglin put down his coffee, took the box from his breast pocket and opened it. The diamond wasn't huge, but even in the gloom of the cruiser's cage, its fire was undeniable.

"Two months' pay?" Baker said.

Coglin nodded gazing at it. "Closer to three," he said.

"What's that? White gold?"

"Platinum."

"Saturday?" Baker said.

"Yep," Coglin said.

"Well, like I said before," Baker said, "good luck with it. I hope it all works out."

Coglin squinted at him.

"Fuck's that supposed to mean?"

Baker leaned back until his head was pressed against the plastic mesh of the cage.

"Nothing, man. Don't listen to me . . . it's . . . you been livin' together how long now? Six months? Been goin' out a couple more, right?"

"You bring this up now? Now?"

"When you want to hear it? When you get back from the honeymoon?"

Coglin shook his head. He was silent for a moment.

"I've known her since we were sixteen," he finally said. "I told you that. We went out in fuckin' high school."

"Knew her *when* you were both sixteen," Baker said. "Not since. There's a difference. Lot changes from high school. She's in finance, right? Wall Street? Got an apartment in the city, which, let's face it, means she makes twice as much as you and me combined. I mean, I like Karen. She seems like a sweet, sweet girl. But she's a modern woman. Full bore and hard core. I just got my doubts about your modern women."

Coglin snapped the jewelry box shut. For a second, he felt

like telling him about the promotion he was about to get. His ball-busting, prick partner couldn't just feel happy for him? Yeah, well, fuck you then, pal. I'm out of here anyway.

He took a breath. Jesus. What the hell was he thinking? Daryl was going to be stuck here with some rookie, a ninety-pound woman no doubt, that he'd have to entrust his ass to as he broke her in. Chop breaker or not, Daryl was his fucking friend. His *partner*. There was plenty of time to break that harsh news to him later.

"You trying to fuck this up for me?" Coglin said.

"No, I . . ."

"Check it out," Coglin said. "I got this ring and our child growing in the woman's belly. Two days from now, when I take her home from dinner, this ring is gonna be sitting in the cradle I built with these two fucking hands, and I'm gonna get down on my knees and ask her to marry me. I may not be the professional pimp you are, my man, but that sounds like a pretty good plan to me."

Baker shook his head.

"You fill me in on what I should do then," Coglin said.

"Forget I said anything."

"A proposal like that," Coglin continued, "and I could get the fucking sarge to say yes."

Baker smiled.

"Sarge is already spoken for, I think," he said.

Coglin looked out at the grim, rain-soaked vista for a moment. Then he, too, smiled.

"Yeah, well," Coglin said, stepping on the brake and bringing the transmission down into reverse. "What about that sweetheart at the desk there on days?"

"Oh, No-nuts?" Baker said. "That's a different story. You bust out that rock on old No-nuts and he'll go all weak at the knees."

They pulled out. They patrolled silently, advancing cautiously through the dark, rain-slicked streets. The rectangles of light that began to appear in the old buildings seemed slightly crooked through the rain, Coglin thought, a bit off plumb. On a corner, two young black men turned around quickly toward the cruiser, their wary hostility apparent even beneath the shadowed hoods of their sweatshirts.

"New spot?" Baker said.

"Ahh, the unquenchable American entrepreneurial spirit," Coglin said, slowing, letting the duo know they'd been made. "Write it down."

"Fucker's comin' this far west?" Baker said, scratching on his note pad. He glanced in his side mirror and shook his head. "This is like the nice part of town. Starbucks ain't beatin' the door down or nothin', but it's actually fuckin' habitable."

"Hey, don't worry," Coglin said. "Didn't you read the paper? Mayor said crime was way down."

"Shit, I'm sorry I didn't read it," Baker said. "Pull over then. Let's take a nap."

The first call of the night was for a car accident. It involved a city bus and a gypsy cab at an intersection a block east of the El. The bus was completely unscathed, but the cabdriver was livid at the crumpled side of his pale blue Lincoln. When Baker explained in his hackneyed Spanish that having no insurance was a capital issue, the cabby decided to drop his complaint. The fat bus driver, un-budged from the elevated seat of his vehicle throughout the incident, shrugged his shoulders down at them after the cab had departed.

"Makes no difference to me," he said. "I get paid either way."

Back in the radio car, Baker took out his notepad again. He slid a pen from his pocket and checked his watch.

"You think I should quote him there? How about, 'Bus operator asserted traffic incident failed to make significant impact upon him'?"

"Definitely," Coglin said with a laugh. "You got to write down everything. 'Corpulent civil servant made reference to his confidence in receiving proper compensation despite outcome.'"

"Well, I don't know about that," Baker said, scratching his signature at the bottom of the incident sheet. "'Corpulent civil servant?' They'll think I'm talking about one of us."

"You maybe," Coglin said. "Speak for yourself."

They pulled out. They rolled down an avenue on the southern perimeter of their patrol sector that was filled with auto body shops. Their low, bunkerlike structures seemed to Coglin as he looked them over like military buildings designed to survive the harshest environments: Antarctica, nuclear testing sites, the surfaces of other planets. He looked out at the continuous wave of graffiti that covered their steel shutters, block after block, color upon color, like some insidious, multihued moss. He looked at varying points within the mass, trying to distinguish something recognizable in the scrawled names and squiggles within it, but came up empty. Perhaps, it was like a mosaic whose meaning could only be gleaned from a distance, he thought. A message perhaps that could only be read by passing aircraft. He wondered what it would say. "YEAH, BOY!" he thought with a smile, or maybe, "BRONX IN DA HOUSE!"

Coglin looked out at one of the desolate establishments that had an electric cross erected on top of it. SIN, the red neon warned inside the cruciform, WILL FIND YOU OUT. Our Lady of the Chop Shop, some of the cops called it, or Immaculate Window Tinting. Coglin shook his head.

"You know what people in Manhattan used to call the Bronx?" Coglin said, pulling out.

"The place where you lay your rubber down after a Yankee game?" Baker said.

"They call it that now," Coglin said. "No, I'm talkin' a long time ago, a hundred years ago."

"What's that?" Baker said.

"The Great North Side," Coglin said.

Baker guffawed.

"Well, it is north," he said.

"I was watching this documentary about it on cable. See, a hundred or so years ago, all this shit was farmland and Manhattan was jammed with immigrants. After they built the subways, some nineteenth-century Donald Trump got the idea to build some housing up here. They built the buildings bigger and nicer and the apartments more spacious to attract people. They were saying some of the apartment houses on the Grand Concourse rival the nicest on Park Avenue."

"The Concourse?" Baker said, looking at him. "The Yo-check-it-somebody-just-got-stabbed-up-on-the-Concourse Grand Concourse?"

"Think about it," Coglin said. "Concourse. That's like a flowery nineteenth-century bullshit word for road. The concourse to Hades, my good sir, is paved with grand intentions. Do tell, Watson. Why did the chicken ambulate across the concourse?"

"To get to the cockfight in the back of Manny's bodega?" Baker said with a laugh. "Nineteenth century. That's like eighteen hundreds?"

"Ah, yeah," Coglin said.

"I got to watch me more TV," Baker said, crossing his eyes. "Get me some learnin'."

They were turning off the industrial strip when they heard a report of a suspicious person on the roof of a building, two and a half blocks away. It seemed no different from the chatter and feedback that had been streaming constantly from their radios as they sat there, but the proximity of the address had peaked their interest. Baker raised an eyebrow. Coglin nodded.

"Thirteen-eighty-seven responding, Dispatch," Baker called into his radio.

A muscular black man in a cut-off T-shirt was standing in the vestibule of the address, staring out at them as they came to a stop. The man extended the large palms of his hands as they approached.

"I'm the super," he said. "They're up on the roof."

He led them up five flights of stairs and pointed through the open threshold of the roof at the top landing. Coglin aimed his flashlight into the darkness and suddenly found himself bereft of speech. Huddled in the corner of the roof, instead of the rapist or crack addict or homeless person they'd expected, was a woman. A white woman in a thin nightgown that was plastered to her body by the rain. Her hair was platinum and her skin so pale, it seemed as if she emitted light. Even curled in the corner, she seemed tall, and there was an austere beauty to her middle-aged face. She put her head down, and started talking to herself.

"Damn crazy bitch," the super said. "Lives on the second floor. All the time bugging me with her nutty shit. Says people using her bathroom, eating her food. Bitch claimed I switched the electric and phone lines on her because she can hear people talkin' out the outlets."

Coglin blinked.

"She live alone?" he said.

The super looked at him.

"What do you think?" he said. "Moved in two years ago. Said she grew up in the building. Shoulda known she was gonna be trouble a week later when she asked me where her parents were.

She'd checked every room in her apartment she said, and she couldn't find them. Asked if I could pry open the wall in back of one of her closets because she needed to talk to them."

Coglin lifted his radio and called for an ambulance.

"What's her name?" he said to the super after he put it back. "Her first name?"

"Wendy," the super said.

"Wendy," Baker said. "Looks more like Tinkerbell to me."

Coglin watched the woman for a while, then looked at his partner.

"This job, Daryl," he said, taking out his gloves from his rear pocket and pulling them on, "this job we have here is special. Because you see, it's not just a job, it's also an adventure."

"I thought that was the navy," Baker said, putting on his own gloves. "Besides, I thought two-for-one deals were supposed to be good."

Coglin nodded enthusiastically.

"They are. That's the beauty of it," he said. "The adventure part is tossed in at no extra charge."

The woman stood immediately as they stepped onto the roof. Behind her, the rooftops of other buildings lay black and slick in the rain like some blasted wasteland.

"Don't take my baby," the woman suddenly cried.

Coglin exchanged a glance with his partner.

"OK," he said, trying his best to make his voice sound soothing. "Fair enough. We just want to get you out of the rain, Wendy. We don't want you to get sick."

His partner snickered.

"My baby," the woman said. She took a step toward them. As she did so, her head dropped and her shoulders began hitching, as if she were about to break down in tears. Coglin put out a hand.

"My baby," she said again softly. And then, as if some circuit tripped within her, her body stiffened and her eyes rolled up in her head as she rushed forward at them, a scream tearing from the black hole of her mouth.

Coglin wasn't quick enough to avoid her clawed hand. Skin sliced beneath his eye. He dropped his flashlight and leaned into her before she could come back at him again, and he and Baker tackled her to the wet, rough tarpaper.

Coglin almost had to break one of her arms to get her cuffed. But after a minute of Coglin sitting on her back, she finally relented, the strength and madness leaving her just as quickly as it'd come. Coglin tapped at his cheek and looked at the blood on his gloved fingertips. Fuck, he thought. Blood wasn't good.

"My babies," she cried.

"Wendy," Coglin said. "Tell you the truth, I'm starting to care less and less."

She was calm as they took her down the stairs to the lobby. She sat dripping in one of the windowsills, looking at Coglin blankly—innocently—as if she was just waiting for a friend to pick her up, as if she hadn't just tried to rip his eyes out.

"Shoo, shoo," she said, waving her hands at him. "Under a hedge."

Coglin took a deep breath and exhaled loudly out of his mouth. Baker looked at him.

"How you doing, partner? Want me to get the first aid kit?"

Coglin shook his head without taking his eyes off the woman.

"Why don't you go up to her apartment?" Baker said. "See if you can find her a coat."

Coglin took the super with him. The door was unlocked. Inside, all the lights were on, the walls bare, save for black electrical tape covering the outlets. A few paint-splattered aluminum chairs. A sheetless mattress.

He found a long coat underneath some tossed newspaper and stopped in the bathroom to see if he could find the medication she wasn't taking. He turned on the light. She had smashed the mirror of the medicine cabinet and the old-fashioned porcelain sink beneath it was filled with the bright silver shards of its glass. There was more newspaper flung about the rancid bathroom, and as he stood there, a large, brown water bug peeked over the rim of the tub—its antennae wavering softly—and then retreated.

"How . . ." Coglin said in disgust. "Fuckin' people."

He was just about to turn the light off when he noticed the open photo album on the closed lid of the toilet. On the left-hand page was a yellowed film portrait of a young girl, seven or eight, in a red velvet dress. She was pretty and blonde-haired and there was a Christmas tree on the painted background behind her, snow-covered hills, an ice-covered pond. When it dawned on him that it was the woman downstairs, he felt the anger in him cool and settle heavily like lead in his stomach. He stared into the blue eyes of the young girl, at the sink of broken glass.

"You about done?" the super called from the front hall.

Coglin turned on the tap, the jagged shards loosening with a screech under the water. He put his hands under the cold stream and patted his face. There was nothing inside the shattered cabinet. He closed it carefully and turned off the light. He found a purse and keys on the table in the kitchen and an empty pill bottle, sitting in the garbage at the top of the pail. He took all of it with him, and waited while the super locked the apartment behind them.

The ambulance had already arrived as they came back downstairs, and Coglin gave everything to the EMTs. He watched silently as they guided the woman through the rain into the back of their truck.

"How you wanna write this up?" his partner said, giving him back his handcuffs in the car after the ambulance left.

"No way," Coglin said, taking the cuffs and stowing them in their leather pouch around his back. "Grabbed her off the roof, put her in a bus."

Baker studied him.

"OK," he said. "Sure you don't want a Band-Aid or something?"

Coglin shook his head.

"Nah," he said. "It stopped bleeding. I'll live."

Baker checked his watch.

"Seems like it's mealtime to me, partner. Whataya think?" he said. "On second thought, stow what you think. We're gonna grab some food."

Chapter Two

THE PLACE THEY WENT to eat called itself a diner, but it was little more than a large coffee shop. It was empty except for the old Spanish cook and the middle-aged waitress, his daughter, who turned from where she sat smoking at the front counter.

"Oh no, you again," she said. It was what she always said.

They sat in the deepest booth and put their radios up on the table top next to the ketchup. They ordered burgers and ate them slowly. Nobody came in or out. The waitress took their empty plates and went for coffee. Baker shifted in the silence.

"If it's about what I said about Karen," he said.

"No," Coglin said, looking out into the rain through the plate glass. "It ain't that."

"What then? That EDP? The lady?

Coglin turned from the rain to his partner.

"You notice how pretty she was?" he said.

Baker nodded.

"Now that you mention it."

"Well, there was a picture of her in her apartment, when she was a kid. She looked like an angel, like a little girl in a fairy tale."

"And?" Baker said.

Coglin placed his hands on the table in front of him and stared down between them as if some answer lay there in the paled swirls of worn linoleum.

"I guess I never really thought about how fucked up it is to be crazy like that," he said quietly, "so alone and fucked up."

Baker looked at him in shock. He was at a complete loss for a response.

"Does this have anything to do with that fancy TV you're watching now?" he said.

Coglin gave him the finger as he looked back out the window. When the waitress brought the check, Baker grabbed it.

"Gotta try something radical to cheer your ass up," he said, taking out his wallet.

A thin, hunched form appeared up the block, pushing a shopping cart as they exited the coffee shop. As the figure passed under a streetlight, Coglin could see that he was an older black man with a messed-up face: his nose a swollen bag; his eyes purple, puffed slits; his lips split.

"Is that Smilin' Ronnie?" Baker said.

"Hey, Smilin'!" Coglin called, taking a step toward him. "Hey, Smilin'! What happened?"

The old man slowed for a moment, his pulverized face turning vaguely toward the sound of Coglin's voice. Then he began to step quickly. The metal rattling of his cart off the breaks in the sidewalk was suddenly more rapid, like the clatter of a train skipping a stop.

"What the hell happened to him?" Baker said. "Took a spill?"

"Off a roof, maybe," Coglin said.

"Ream knocked him out," said a voice behind them.

They both turned. There was a recessed window in the old, dark building beside the coffee shop, and behind its rusting bars stood a small Hispanic boy of no more than seven. He gripped the bars with his little fists like a miniature, irate inmate. Blue television light flashed from the room behind.

"C'mon," Coglin said. "You saw it? A little guy like you?"

"Shit, yeah," the child said proudly. "Only happened right there on the corner. Ream and his crew, out drinkin' forties, see the bum roll up, so they play them some Knockout."

Coglin exchanged glances with his partner.

"Knockout," Baker said. "What's that?"

The kid rolled his eyes and shook his head with a "where the fuck you been?" expression.

"'Knockout,'" he explained slowly. "It's when you coldcock some sucka in his cranium an' try an' knock his ass out with one punch."

"What happens after you knock 'im out?" Baker asked. "You rob him?"

"Straight up. Stomp his sorry ass, too. But they didn't vic no bum." The kid rolled his eyes again. "What they gonna take? His cans? Shit."

"They stomped on him, though, huh?" Coglin said.

"Word," the kid said. "Beat his old ass." The dark child laughed for a second, the sound chilling for the unlikely innocence in it, a tickled baby.

"And they pissed on 'im. He was lyin' on the ground and they whipped their shits out and showered the stinky old fuck."

Coglin checked his desire to reach through the bars and wrap his hands around the kid's throat.

"Little man," Coglin said "I don't believe a word of your bullshit. You believe him, Daryl?"

"He's spittin' lies," Baker said.

"Hey, I seen it," the kid whined. "I seen it right there."

"Who did it then?" Baker said. "Who knocked him out?"

"Ream did it. Ream turned that old nigga's fuckin' lights out."

"Who the fuck's Ream?"

"Ream deals rock in the park across from Tubman. Ask anybody. Tall ass nigga with a red Lex. Got silver loops in his ears."

"Yeah, we'll see," Coglin said, pushing himself off the wall.

"You playin' us," Baker said, "and we're gonna be comin' back."

The kid kicked the bars with his small, sneakered foot.

"Dang," he called after them, offended. "Why the *fuck* would I be lying?"

Back in the car, Coglin looked off in the direction the bum had gone, a tightness spreading through his body. Adrenaline injecting into his bloodstream at the anticipation of contact. He rolled his neck, his thoughts racing back to the crazy woman.

Maybe there were some problems that he or anybody couldn't do anything about.

But luckily some punk kids torturing an old defenseless man wasn't one of them.

"Whataya say we take a little spin by the park?" he said, starting the car. He stomped on the gas, making the engine roar.

Baker smiled and nodded his approval.

"Now, that's my Coglin," he said, grasping the dash as the car shot forward. "Let's see how much Mr. Ream likes havin' his own cranium cracked."

The drug spot was empty when they pulled in front of the Harriet Tubman projects five minutes later. Normally, the wooden benches facing the street in the adjacent park would be filled with the dealers, circles of hooded young men glancing constantly about like some strange order of cautious persecuted monks.

"I think Harriet would have skipped this stop on the ol' Underground Railroad, don't you?" Baker said. "I think she would have taken the express right on past if she had the choice. Business is slow with this rain."

Coglin took a deep breath and looked out at the desolate complex of dark stone high-rises, the pale cement paths criss-crossing the mud between.

"Yeah," he said. "I've seen that red Lex around, though."

"Me, too," Baker said.

A train blasted past on the El two blocks away, and its electric spark's soft blue glow lit up the dismal brick for a moment.

"You think it was what? Some kind of gang thing?" Coglin said.

"Yeah. Some kind of sick initiation," Baker said. "At least the LA gangs have the decency to beat the fuck out of each other."

They sat in silence.

"Fuck it," Baker said after a while. "We're gonna cross paths with the animal sooner or later. Hopefully sooner in one of these hallways with the back of his head opened up for him."

He checked his watch. "It's time anyway. We gotta get back."

Coglin turned to his partner.

"Smilin' ever show you his union card?"

"Used to be a plumber, right?"

"Steamfitter," Coglin said. "He told me he used to be the house steamfitter at the Plaza hotel till he got fired."

Baker shook his head grimly.

"Pissed on him, Daryl," Coglin said. "Who does that? What species?"

"I agree," Baker said. "That's some bothersome prehistoric shit. But it's still time."

Coglin glanced out at the dark, desolate façades of the buildings. He blew out a pent-up breath loudly.

"You're right," he said quietly, shifting the transmission down into drive.

They pulled out and drove in silence, the rain on the roof a low, constant rattle.

"I just wish he'd been there," Coglin said after a few blocks.

"Me, too, man," Baker said. "Me, too."

Back at the precinct house, they parked the radio car in the garage, handed in their paperwork and went up to the locker room. It took Coglin less than ten minutes to put away the belt and gear, change out of his uniform, and exchange his service automatic for his off-duty .38. He closed his locker and sat down next to Baker, who was still getting dressed.

"So you want me to bring the cradle tomorrow, right?" Baker said.

Coglin nodded.

"I appreciate you letting me use your basement to work on it," he said.

Baker shook his head.

"You know I was just fuckin' with you about Karen," he said.

"No," Coglin said. "I don't know that. But I think I know what you were getting at. Don't worry about it."

"You gonna be OK," Baker said with a grin, "or you want me to call the rubber-gun squad for you, maybe? Ask if they got any openings?"

"You're a sensitive motherfucker," Coglin said, shaking his head with a slight smile. "I ever tell you that? A real warm individual. It's easy to share with you."

Baker smiled widely.

"Glad to see you're feeling better, partner," he said.

"Shoo, shoo," Coglin told him as he rose. "Under a hedge."

Coglin left the locker room, walked out through the musty stationhouse and crossed the street to his car. He turned the engine over and waited, letting it warm. He glanced at the precinct, its narrow windows still burning with their grim but steady yellow light. He backed out.

He was passing under the elevated track on his way to the highway when he saw them: a group of teens—a half dozen or more—crowded in the roofed stairwell leading up to the El. At first, the older man in their midst seemed to be a friend of theirs, a concerned father maybe taking his son home. Then a forty-ounce malt liquor bottle crashed across the side of his head, and he buckled and fell.

Coglin was out in the rain and running almost before his fishtailing car had stopped completely. He was less than twenty feet away and closing when they noticed him. Young, hooded bodies spilled over the black-painted stair rail, through the thin opening, up the stairs. He caught the last one out—a squat, over-weight punk—with a slap that set him down on the pavement. The kid managed to push himself to his feet and then ran off.

The victim was middle-aged and Hispanic. He was wearing a suit that was wet and soiled, and he raised his bloodied head with a moan. Coglin looked up the stairs in time to see the sneaker soles of one of the pack gain the top landing. He helped the man into a sitting position and reached at his side for his radio that wasn't there. The man spit a stringy gob of blood onto the worn metal rim of one of the stairs.

Coglin stepped over him, started up the stairs.

"Stay there," he called back. "Wait for an ambulance. Don't move."

He sprinted up the long flight of stairs, across the wooden

boards at the top of the landing and burst through the station door. It was empty. Being one of the last stops on the line, there was no token-booth clerk, just a barred, revolving turnstile that required a token he didn't have. He pressed against the bars scanning the platform beside the tracks, but he couldn't see anything. Then he heard something clatter above his head.

He ran back out the door to the top landing's outside stair rail. Blinking up through the rain, he made out a drainpipe that snaked upward to the eave of the station's sloped terra cotta roof. He squinted down at the sidewalk thirty feet below and listened for a moment to the ceaseless pounding of the rain. Then he leaned out and grasped the drainpipe.

By the time he swung himself onto the roof, he was completely soaked. He drew his gun from his ankle holster with a Velcro rip, looked around, but there was nothing. When he gained the crest of the roof, he was just in time to see a figure drop off the other side onto the platform.

He'd started down quickly and had almost reached the other eave, when he slipped. His left boot shot out from under him on some slick piece of flashing, and then the right one, and his face slapped against the wet stone. His gun flew out of his hand, slid away with a clatter and dropped off the eave. He was only a second behind it.

The platform smacked him hard and his breath was gone. Through his shock he registered that he'd landed on something hard and metal that might've cracked a rib.

Once, as a small kid, he'd caught a line drive in the chest while standing in foul territory at a men's softball game, and he felt that same sensation now. The same torturously slow suffocation, same dancing spots of black and malignant nausea, dreamy death like a lead blanket swaddled around his chest.

Frozen needles of rain dashed unheeded off his unprotected

face as he couldn't breathe and couldn't breathe and couldn't breathe.

Then the rain suddenly stopped.

The face of the figure that stared down at him from an impossible height above was young and black and had eyes cold and glistening as the silver hoops in his ears. A chunky multifinger ring of gold, billboard-huge from where Coglin lay, was sprawled across the wide fist of his right hand.

R-E-A-M.

Coglin's breath came back in a loud wheeze. Backbeat by his pumping heart, a single refrain began to play in his head as he unsuccessfully tried to move.

I should've stayed a carpenter I should've stayed a carpenter I should've stayed a carpenter.

He felt his wallet come free from the front pocket of his jeans. His badge flashed in front of his face.

"Five-O, bitch," the dealer whispered in his ear. "'Gainst the wall."

Coglin managed to jerk up slightly when the man went into his breast pocket for the engagement ring. The blow that fell an instant later crackled white fuzz across the insides of Coglin's eyelids. The back of his head bounced up off the cement. Blood ran over his teeth, dripping down his throat in a copper stream.

Hurricane storm clouds of black arrived now, swirling above even blacker, crashing waves.

As Coglin was about to pass out completely, he felt a shudder that he feared was the final tremble of something vital failing in his body. He felt it again, this time accompanied by a far-off bleat, like an alarm clock through a dream. He wished the noise would stop, so he could get his much-needed rest. It dulled for a moment.

The platform shook again with the enormous weight of the approaching subway train. Its horn issued another short blast.

Ream was lifting Coglin's legs when he managed to crack open his left eye.

"Yeahhh, bitch," Ream said, starting to drag him across the cement.

"Train's a comin, bitch," he said.

And it was. Coglin could hear the wheels of the subway car clearly now, the rising metal screech of its approach like the sharpening of a thousand knives.

"Chugga, chugga, woo, woo," Ream said, smiling. Even dazed, Coglin could see he was a handsome kid.

"Chugga, chugga, woo, woo."

He's going to throw me in front of the train, Coglin thought with the astonishing simplicity of panic. When he opened his mouth to protest, he found he couldn't speak.

It took Coglin another second to notice that the piece of metal he landed on was moving with him. It was his gun. He raised himself off it slightly and managed to hook it with his elbow, dragging it along with him.

The rumble and horn of the train mounted an unbelievable notch higher, like an unstoppable tornado now down in the front yard. Ream stopped abruptly. He pulled Coglin parallel to the edge of the platform and dropped his feet. Coglin could feel the humming power of the train reverberating through the wet cement at his cheek. He stared down at the silver rail tops below.

He reached out blindly with his right hand and wrapped it around the hard rubber handle of his gun beneath his other elbow. He fumbled at the checkered metal safety with his thumb. It wouldn't come. His thumb wasn't working. His hand was too cold. He was too weak. Too weak to live. Please. No. Then the safety finally flicked down with an almost imperceptible snick.

Ream stepped away for a moment as if suddenly deciding to

stop this insanity. Then Coglin felt the sole of his sneaker begin to push at his back, inching him off the platform. He passed the gun across his body, found the metal filament of the trigger with his finger and squeezed.

The shot was only a slight, muffled pop against the now rising roar of the train, but it caught Ream in the foot. The pusher looked down slowly at the mess that had blossomed across the flawless white leather of his Reeboks.

Coglin pulled the trigger of the suddenly heavy gun again, and the bullet bit out a piece of the platform between Ream's feet with a whine.

Ream looked down at Coglin with puzzled annoyance, as if perturbed by the distraction from his newly interesting foot. Then Coglin squeezed and shot again, and the round went through Ream's knee, and he dropped.

The driver of the train had the horn pulled in a constant scream as Coglin rolled himself away from the edge. When he looked back he saw Ream, a few yards away, gripping feebly at the platform, his bloody legs hanging over the space above the tracks. In the brightening light of the oncoming train, Ream's expression had softened to a look of childish regret as he reached out a hand toward Coglin.

Then the train hit him.

One moment, he was there and the next instant, there was a sound, a kind of hollow sickening bump and like a magic trick, the dealer was gone, replaced by the flying metal wall of the train. Staring at the blurring steel with the darkness coming for him again, Coglin suddenly thought of the ring. He had to have it for Saturday. He patted at the wet concrete around him, probing the pocked cement blindly with his fingertips. Then he toppled over and passed out.

It was still dark and still raining when Coglin opened his

eyes, but the train had stopped. It was sitting there at the station, right in front of him, with its doors open and its bright light spilling onto the platform. A black man in a transit uniform was stepping in and out of the doors, clenching and unclenching his hands. He was crying.

"Johnny! Johnny! Wake the fuck up!"

Coglin turned up to his left toward the voice. It took him a moment to recognize the face out of uniform. It was Martinelli. Martinelli, his first partner. His old friend.

"Are you shot?" Martinelli said.

Coglin shook his head.

"Who's the kid under the train?"

"Saw him beatin' an old man," Coglin mumbled. "Chased him."

"Did you shoot him?"

Coglin blinked, nodded slowly.

"Goddamn," Martinelli said. "Goddamn . . . Here, sit up."

Martinelli pulled him off his back. Coglin sat and wrapped his hands around his knees. There was blood on the sleeve of his coat. He looked up as Martinelli took a white handkerchief out of his coat pocket. He thought he was going to give it to him to stanch some wound, then he saw there was something in it. Black and heavy, gleaming with oil. A small automatic.

Coglin squinted at him, confused.

"Gotta drop it," Martinelli explained somberly.

"What?"

"On the kid. The kid," Martinelli said, annoyed now. "It's the only way."

"No," Coglin said weakly. "That's not the way it happened."

Martinelli put a hand behind Coglin's head and pulled him in until their foreheads touched. Coglin could smell the alcohol on his breath.

"You think that matters? That don't mean shit. I got you covered, kid."

Martinelli let go of him and walked quickly down the platform.

Coglin sat there watching him. At the front of the train, Martinelli stopped and took out the handkerchief.

"No," Coglin said quietly as he watched the gun fall toward the tracks, tiny and black and irretrievable. He heard it click on the street below. A small, but portentous sound. Like the last punch on the timecard of a man clocking out on his very last day.

Chapter Three

IT WAS MORNING AS THEY drove down the Grand Concourse. Though not yet nine, already the heat was rising, the bright, dusty streets beginning to cook. Coglin sat in the back seat of the taxi, sweating, in his stiff suit.

"Can't you cool it down back here?" his lawyer, Mulvane, called up to the driver. "We're fucking melting."

"Broke," the driver called back with a Caribbean accent. "A/C broke."

"Goddamn, fuck it all to hell," Mulvane mumbled, exasperated.

From the opposite side of Coglin, his mother leaned forward and glared at the lawyer.

Mulvane put his hands up.

"Sorry, Ma'am," he said. "Excuse me."

Coglin pulled at his collar with a finger and looked out at the street.

People flashed by in front of the crumbling, majestic buildings: a super hosing down a sidewalk, a girl—sixteen at most—pushing a baby in a stroller, men and women waiting at a bus stop, screaming children hanging from a jungle gym. People doing errands, attending to their lives. They blasted past them all.

The cab driver kept looking back at Coglin. He was a very dark, young black man, and every few blocks or so, his eyes would drift into the rearview and regard Coglin with cold interest. Coglin had gotten plenty of unwanted attention in the four months following the incident. In the last two and a half weeks since the trial's inception, with the constant newspaper and television coverage, he'd achieved a kind of celebrity status. He might've said he was getting used to it by now, if it were something that was possible to get used to. But it was as if all the world had suddenly been gifted with X-ray vision, and what they saw at his core was something that made them sick.

Even before the courthouse came into view, Coglin could see the commotion: the double-parked television vans and the crowd. He felt light-headed for a moment as the bottom of his stomach seemed to drop away. His mother placed her hand over the top of his arm, and her small, strong fingers locked into his like a vise. He looked over at her, at the fear and resolve wrestling in her eyes and he smiled.

"I'm sorry I told you not to come, Ma," he said after a moment. "Who the hell am I kidding? You're tougher than me."

Ahead, above the avenue's anemic trees, the east side of the huge courthouse was white as alabaster in the rising sun. When they crossed the intersection at 161st Street, Coglin turned to look at the stage that had been erected in the park across the street. A person was pushing some cases of bottled water up onto the structure, while someone else set up chairs. SOMETHING JUSTICE COALITION was spray-painted in red on a bedsheet strung along the back of it.

As Coglin had left the courthouse the day before, a large, well-dressed black man with a bullhorn was addressing the crowd. Coglin had stopped on the courthouse steps when he saw the unmistakable face of a famous movie actress seated on the stage behind the man. She'd looked at Coglin sternly in disgust and tapped at the back of the rabble-rouser, alerting him to Coglin's presence. The big man had stopped what he was saying and immediately pointed at Coglin from across the street. The crowd had turned with the sweep of his hand.

"Speak of the devil!" he'd said.

Maybe they'd just hang him there, Coglin thought. Rig up a noose, cut out a drop in the stage and push him through.

He closed his eyes. *No,* he thought. *Things were going to work out.* Even with all the insanity. All the setbacks. The truth would come out, rise to the top of all the bullshit. He was innocent, he reminded himself, gathering strength from that simple fact. He'd been doing his job. Finally, here at the end of the trial, he'd have the opportunity to speak for himself, allow the jury to hear his voice and they would know.

Coglin opened his eyes as the cab slowed by the main entrance of the courthouse. He looked up at the scenes carved in the stone above the brass revolving doors. Famous events concerning justice from Greek tragedy, maybe, or the Bible. Depictions of throngs, only slightly dissimilar to the present one on the sidewalk below, TV cameras and reporters replacing togas and livestock. Coglin looked up at the city seal chiseled above the doors of the building, the same antiquated coat of arms flanked by Dutchman and Indian that had been on the badge they'd taken away from him.

There was a collective movement in the crowd as reporters and photographers craned their necks at the cab.

"Around the corner," Mulvane said to the driver. "Quick! Around the side."

Mulvane popped open his door even before the car had stopped on the sidestreet. He stood on the curb going through his pockets.

"I got it," Coglin said to him, following his mother out the other door.

On the street, Coglin counted out fifteen for the ten-dollar fare, and handed it through the window. He held the driver's cold gaze.

"I didn't kill him," he said. "It was self-defense."

The driver's face seemed to soften. He motioned Coglin closer with a jerk of his head. As Coglin stepped forward, the driver leaned across his seat and hit a switch on the dashboard. Frigid air blasted Coglin's face. The driver was still holding the bills Coglin had given him, and he tilted them downward, letting the five drop unheeded out the window. Coglin looked down at the bill lying on the asphalt.

"Think of me when they give you the injection," the driver said in his low, musical, voice. Then he hit the gas and the car shot away from the curb, missing Coglin's toes by a centimeter. The five sat on the street for a split second before it was sucked down the block in the car's wake.

The guy obviously didn't read the paper too closely, Coglin thought, as he stepped onto the sidewalk. The district attorney's office had to apply for the death penalty before a murder trial started, and in this case, they'd opted not to. The only consoling fact in the whole affair.

The first reporters and photographers were already coming down the stairs at him as he started to climb them. He leveled his eyes directly ahead as the flashbulbs began popping. Out of the corner of his eye, he saw the cameramen racing each other around the corner. They looked ridiculous with their jeans and T-shirts and their bulky gear slapping noisily about them. Like electricians in a company picnic race. They flicked the lights of their shoulder-mounted cameras at him on the fly. Even in the warm air, Coglin could feel the heat of those lights on the skin of his face and neck. Some reporter, who was jabbering loudly in his ear, was pushed from behind, and he poked Coglin in the side of the head with his pen before he fell back. Clenching his fists, Coglin barely controlled the urge to start swinging and throwing people down the stairs.

Court officers stood between the building's massive columns, and as he reached the top of the steps, they ushered him through the revolving doors while blocking the reporters. Coglin stopped just inside, breathing in the cool air of the high-ceilinged, marble foyer.

"There's a mark on you," his mother said, touching his cheek.

Coglin licked his thumb and rubbed at it.

"Ink," he said.

His mother looked out the glass doors. Photographers were still taking pictures through it, the flashes lighting her lined face in the dim hall.

"Bastards," she said softly. She looked over at Coglin. "Too bad Karen couldn't be here for all the fun."

His girlfriend had come for the first two weeks of the trial, but her vacation time ran out and she had returned to work.

"Gee, Mom. Thanks for bringing that up," Coglin said, ushering her farther into the hall. "I really need something else to think about right now."

They passed through the metal detectors and took the elevator to the seventh floor. The courtroom's ornate wooden doors were locked when they arrived before them, so they sat on one of the benches lining the walls of the wide hall. A man on the bench across from them was reading the paper.

Coglin looked over at his own black and white picture on the front page under the headline, "DANCE, BOY!" COP TO FINISH STORY. It'd been taken the day before, out in front of the courthouse, and there was a smug looking sneer on his face, an expression he'd made right after a huge monster of a cameraman had stomped on his foot. He wondered how long the photographer had waited to capture the moment. Probably paid the cameraman to do it on purpose, he thought.

He looked down at the polished tile floor. When he looked up, he noticed that there was a small crowd waiting to get into the courtroom. Their stares felt like the heat from the cameras' lights.

"You want something?" Mulvane said. "You wanna go over anything again?"

"No, I'm OK. How about you, Ma? You want something?"

His mother sat with her gnarled hands folded primly in her lap.

"Not a thing," she said.

Coglin stood. The spectators in the hall stilled, tensed like birds debating to fly away or not. He checked his watch.

"I gotta make a call," he said.

Mulvane started pulling his cell phone out of his suit jacket.

"Don't worry about it," Coglin said. "One of these pricks is probably pointing a microphone at us. I'll use a payphone."

He stepped down the hall, past the spectators' gallery, and turned the corner. Three payphones in old-fashioned wooden and glass booths stood against the marble wall. He went to the last one and shut the door. He dropped a quarter, lifted the receiver and dialed a number written on a piece of paper he'd taken from his pocket.

He'd managed to wheedle the number out of his reluctant sergeant, only after he'd promised that he wouldn't say where he'd gotten it.

Baker answered on the second ring.

"Hello?"

"Hey, Daryl," Coglin said. "Hope I didn't wake you. I would've called sooner, but you forgot to tell me you changed your number."

There was a long stretch of silence from the other end.

"What can I do for you?"

"Nothing now, Daryl. Before, maybe you could've helped keep my ass outta jail, but not now. Did you think I was going to ask you to testify? How about just showing up and sitting behind me? I'm out here in the cold, Daryl. You were supposed to watch my back and you left me all alone."

"You done?" his partner said.

Coglin gripped the receiver. He could feel the heat in his face, the anger flowing, bubbling up.

"Who got to you, Daryl? Was it Reverend Smalls from TV? The African Knights? You know they got a rally set up across the street. Maybe you can go to that instead."

His partner sighed.

"You think you're the only one Martinelli ever showed that piece of shit throwdown to? You were after that kid from the beginning of the night, in case you don't remember. I don't think you want them talking to me, John."

"We were both after him," Coglin said loudly. "We were supposed to be after him!"

"I'm not the one who fucked up, John," his partner said.

Coglin closed his eyes tightly. They felt hot, filled with acid.

"Yeah, you keep tellin' yourself that," he said, and he slammed down the receiver.

Coglin stood with his reddened face away from the hall and took several breaths before he dropped another quarter.

"Midtown North Homicide."

"Joe?" Coglin said. "That you?"

"John," Clarke said somberly. "How's it goin'?"

"Been better, Joe. I'm about to go in."

"How's that Mulvane treating you?"

"He's terrific under the circumstances, Joe. Thanks for pointing me in the right direction."

"I can't tell you how sick I am about how things worked out," Clarke said. "About everything getting all fucked up."

From the moment after the shooting, Clarke had come forward to help him. He'd counseled Coglin to steer clear of the bargain-basement lawyers the union supplied and urged him to retain Mulvane, a veteran Bronx court defense lawyer and old, trusted friend. After the grand jury indictment, he'd even called and told Coglin that he'd been able to pull some strings.

He told Coglin that after much discussion with the higher-ups, an unspoken arrangement had been made. The deal was Coglin would plead not guilty and appeal to get the trial moved out of the Bronx to upstate where the jury might be a little less historically suspicious of the police. The case would then be directed before one of the more conservative, pro-law-enforcement judges in the appellate court and the motion would be granted.

But the whole thing had fallen through. Their sympathetic judge had taken ill at the last minute and the case had come before a crusading liberal judge who'd halted the appeal in its tracks. Coglin could almost still hear the righteous contempt in the judge's whiny voice as he made his pronouncement. Crimes committed in the County of the Bronx were to be tried in the County of the Bronx, he'd said. Media or no media, those were the rules.

The rules, Coglin thought.

"Shit happens," Coglin said into the phone. "At least you tried. My only other option was going with the union lawyer. His bright idea was to plead fuckin' guilty and cut a deal. At least Mulvane has balls."

"The whole thing is so fuckin' unfair," Clarke said tiredly.

"I won't argue with you there," Coglin said. "At least you've been in my corner from the get-go, Joe. I just wanted to call and thank you for that. For all you've done for me. Mulvane. Everything. You've been like a father to me. Even before all this."

"Ah, Jesus, kid. Thanks, but cheer up, huh? Would you? You sound like a man at his own funeral. Jury ain't in yet."

"You're right," Coglin said, passing a hand through his short hair. "You're right. I'm testifying today. And I don't care what everybody's been saying, all that Bronx jury crap. I know these people. I've served in this community for the last three years. I think I can get them to listen to me. I really do."

"Exactly, John. Look them right in the eye and tell them the truth," Clarke said. "Person to person. It'll cut right through all this media bullshit. And let's say worst-case scenario, which is not gonna happen mind you, but let's just say you're convicted. Mulvane wins on appeal, because half an hour after it's over, the fuckin' liberal media lice running the lynch mob out there will be onto the next travesty. You'd be out in three or four months, and then you sue fuckin' everybody. The department, the union. The TV stations. But like I said, that's not even gonna happen."

"Man, it's good to hear a friendly voice," Coglin said. "Glad I called. Anyway, I gotta get going. Thanks again."

"Hang in there. Mulvane is good. Trust him, OK? We're gonna win."

Coglin took a breath.

"I know. I know. Talk to you," Coglin said. "Take care."

After he hung up, Coglin went back down the hall and sat with his mother and Mulvane. The courtroom doors were still closed. Beside them, a heavy, white-shirted court officer stood beside another smaller door: the jury entrance. Every few minutes, members would arrive, their faces going slack once they spotted Coglin.

After a while, the jury door opened and a second, slimmer court officer walked directly toward Coglin. He stopped, extending his hand.

"John," he said. "Long time, no see."

Coglin looked up at him warily. The man had black hair and a pale, lean face. Coglin suddenly recognized him from his old neighborhood. His name was Sullivan, and he was the younger brother of an old high school friend.

"Mrs. Coglin," Sullivan said with a nod.

"Hello, Timmy," she said.

"How you been, John?" Sullivan said.

Coglin looked down the hall at the group of reporters and spectators and rubbed at an eye socket with the heel of his hand.

"Better," he said.

Sullivan looked uncomfortable for a moment, like a visitor at a wake.

"Guy called in sick today. I'm gonna be working your case."

Sullivan looked up and down the hall, leaned in close to Coglin and put a hand on his shoulder.

"Just wanted to come over, and letcha know, I gotcha back, aright? It ain't right, what they're doin to you. I'm not the only one who feels that way either."

Coglin looked at him for a long moment, the young man's friendly face bringing back good memories: Little League and Irish football, schoolyard basketball, high school dances, keg parties.

He'd been without support for so long, he'd almost forgotten what it felt like.

Coglin took a long breath, then smiled.

"I appreciate it, Timmy," Coglin said. "Nice of you to come over. Tell your brother I said hi."

"You got it," Sullivan said. "I will. Anything you need in there, Mrs. Coglin—water or whatever—you wave me over, OK?"

"That's nice of you, Timmy," she said.

See, Coglin thought, watching Sullivan walk over and unlock the courtroom doors. There were people who supported him. It wasn't completely hopeless.

Inside, Coglin set his mother in the front bench on the right and crossed through the low, wooden gate to the defendant's table.

The courtroom was enormous. Everything but the intricate coffered plaster ceiling was paneled in acres of old, dark oak. Coglin rubbed his hand across the glass-smooth walnut finish of the defendant's table as he sat. He leaned back in his padded banker's chair and looked around, trying to let the circumspect majesty of the place console him. Out a copper rimmed window to his right, the distant shining sprawl of Manhattan lay like a subject in a portrait.

How, he thought, could anything but truth be uncovered here?

But it had come to this, Coglin thought, clasping the polished wood of his arm rests. Unfair didn't even begin to describe it.

It had started out well enough. The initial interview after the shooting had actually gone well. Save for omitting the tossed gun, he told them the absolute truth. Everyone present—assistant DA, investigating detective, Internal Affairs investigator and Mulvane—seemed to accept it. He thought he'd sensed relief among them at the end of his account. That the shooting seemed "good." The grand jury scheduled for a week later was more a formality than anything else, the ADA had said.

But there were problems.

Two days before the grand jury, an investigative reporter from one of the television network affiliates had visited the neighborhood. There was a piece on the six o'clock news that featured the reporter canvassing the neighborhood, speaking about the community's unrest and historical distrust of the police. The piece turned into a two-parter, once a witness was found. The witness, dramatically shot in silhouette with his voice disguised, said that he'd seen everything from the window of his apartment. He made the outrageous claim that he'd seen Coglin and heard him tell the boy to dance before he shot him and pushed him in front of the train. The next morning, it took the grand jury two hours to hand back an indictment, and before the day was out, the district attorney had charged him with murder in the second degree.

The mayor, terrified of even the possibility of a riot under his watch, had back-pedaled away from him immediately at a speed that would've made Allen Iverson jealous. The new police commissioner had kept his distance with complete silence. Some asshole real estate developer had put a full-page "advertorial" in the *Times* about the savageness of the police department, citing him personally as incontrovertible evidence. Even the Cardinal, the fucking Cardinal of the Archdiocese of New York, for whom Coglin had served as an altar boy in grammar school, had come

forward to ease tensions by voicing skepticism of Coglin's innocence. His own union, that he'd paid dues to for this very con-
tingency, had shown little enthusiasm for his plight. A sparse
contingent had come to the first couple of days of the trial, but
even they had petered away.

The whole thing was heinous, Mulvane had told him. Monstrously wrong. Political forces were using the whole thing to get
their faces on television, bolster their chances for future elec-
tions and reelections. The media, in the midst of a slow news
month, was more than happy to oblige. But he would be vindicated, Mulvane had promised.

Coglin looked over at the empty jury box and listened to the
commotion behind him as the spectators found their seats.

He would be vindicated, he thought to himself. Vindicated.
Vindicated.

He'd been on desk duty for the last four months since being
charged. They'd already confiscated the off-duty gun he'd shot
Ream with, and before taking a leave to attend the trial, he'd been
made to hand over his service weapon and badge. You'll get them
back if you're acquitted, his new boss, Lieutenant Pencil Pusher,
had told him, hefting them smugly in his hand as if they were
Coglin's very nuts. If, the man had made sure to skeptically
stress, not when.

After a minute, the prosecuting attorney arrived with his
assistant and sat at the table to the left. He was a little blob of a
man: short, his black hair balding. Without a glance toward the
defendant's side of the courtroom, he unfastened his briefcase,
took out some papers and started going over the plans of
Coglin's destruction with his colleague in a low whisper.

Coglin had been charged with murder in the second degree.
Capital M fucking Murder. They were saying that he'd shot
Ream, or the young Reginald Mason as they were now calling

him, with the sole, cold-blooded intent to end his life. That he'd actually had a choice *not* to shoot him, but decided instead, out of boredom perhaps, that he'd rather kill him and throw him in front of a train. This, from the same prosecutor who'd refused to indict a man who, earlier in the year, had pushed a uniformed officer of the law out a window during a domestic dispute, crippling him for life.

Coglin passed his hands over his face.

He could not lose faith now.

After a moment, the court clerk entered the room from a door to the right side of the judge's bench and asked them all to rise. The assembly stood loudly as the judge stepped in. He was a small, stern-looking man with silver-rimmed spectacles. He climbed to his red leather chair at the top of the raised bench and sat.

"Please be seated," he said.

Above his black robe, his face was thin and lined and weatherbeaten, an austere manly face that hinted of the outdoors, Coglin thought, horses maybe, or hunting.

"Bailiff?" he said. Sullivan stood from a chair against the right-hand wall.

"Are all the members of the jury here?"

"Present and accounted for, Your Honor," Sullivan said.

"See them in, would you?"

Sullivan went in through another door to the left of the judge's bench and brought in the jury. Four black women, three black men, two Hispanic women, two Hispanic men, and one white woman. As he always did when they entered, Coglin tried to make eye contact with each member, hoping to evoke some compassion from them. One of the Hispanic women—the older one—gave him a small smile of greeting. He'd detected warmth from her before. As he thought about it, he recalled detecting other small signs of empathy during his brief testimony the day before, wistful looks of concern, slight nods.

Maybe, he thought, watching them be seated, maybe he'd gotten through to them a little. Maybe they wouldn't vote only on emotion. Maybe they wouldn't ignore the facts. People who would take the time to respond to jury duty had to be somewhat together, didn't they? All he needed was to be heard by reasonable people.

The judge greeted the jury warmly and then turned to Coglin's lawyer.

"Counselor, would you like to pick it up from yesterday?" he said.

"Yes, Your Honor," said Mulvane.

Coglin stood. He stepped across the marble to the witness chair beside the jury box and sat.

"Please, Mr. Coglin, if you would continue telling us the events of the night in question."

A pitcher of water and a glass sat on a little shelf before Coglin. He lifted the pitcher and poured the glass full.

He continued with his testimony, telling them about the injured homeless man he and his partner had encountered, and about the boy who'd witnessed his beating. He told them how they'd gone in search of the assailant but were unable to find him.

"Is it common," Mulvane asked, "to pursue a suspect without a complainant?"

Coglin leaned forward into the microphone.

"Smilin' Ronnie was pretty beat up," he said. "I wanted to see if we could prevent anyone else from getting hurt."

Mulvane nodded.

"Could you tell us what happened after, when your shift was over?"

Coglin lifted the water and drank. The glass made a click when he placed it back down on the shelf.

He explained it to them: the group beating on the man in the subway stairs, how he'd gotten out of his car and ran after them, how he'd fallen from the wet train station roof. He took another drink of water and told them how Ream had hovered over him as he lay motionless and robbed him of his wallet and the engagement ring he'd just bought. He told them what Ream had said, and how he was dragged to the edge of the tracks, about the sound of the approaching train.

"And is that when you shot him?" Mulvane asked.

"Yes," Coglin said.

"When he took your wallet and ring, why didn't he take your gun?"

"It had dropped when I fell, and I had landed on it. It was under me."

"You shot him in the knee and foot. Why?"

"I was dazed," Coglin said. "I just lifted the gun in his direction and pulled the trigger."

"How many times did you shoot?"

"They tell me three. That seems about right."

"At any time did you tell Reginald Mason to dance?"

"No," Coglin said.

"Why do you think a witness would say that?"

"I have no idea," Coglin said.

"How did you feel when you pulled the trigger?"

Coglin looked down at the glass of water on its little shelf, again hearing the train, again feeling the foot at his back.

"I was never so afraid in my life."

His lawyer peered at the jury and nodded slowly for a moment. Then he looked up at the judge.

"Defense res . . . Oh, did they ever find the ring?"

Coglin looked down.

"No," he said. "No they didn't."

Mulvane frowned and gave an almost imperceptible shake of his head like a man in deep mourning. Clarke was right, Coglin thought. Mulvane was very good.

"That's all, Your Honor," Mulvane said, turning to the judge. "Defense rests."

"Prosecutor?" the judge said.

Coglin rolled his neck as the ADA stood.

"Briefly, Your Honor," he said. "Mr. Coglin, did you know that Reginald Mason was armed?"

Coglin felt a tightening in his stomach, alarm bells seemed to go off in the back of his head. *The gun,* he thought.

"No, I didn't."

"Did he pull a gun out at any point? Maybe wave it at you?"

"No," Coglin said.

He stared fixedly at the prosecutor.

"He was too busy trying to throw me under the train," he said.

"But a gun was recovered?"

Why hadn't he told on that idiot Martinelli? Coglin thought. He knew he should have protected himself from the idiot's supposed help that night but he hadn't wanted to get the retiring moron in trouble. Yeah, he thought. Who was in trouble now? Why hadn't he gotten out in front of it?

"That's what they tell me," Coglin said.

"They tell you a lot of things, don't they, Mr. Coglin?"

"Objection," Mulvane said.

"Sustained," the judge said.

"Sorry, Your Honor. That's all for this witness."

Coglin exchanged baffled looks with his lawyer. He was expecting a barrage of questions.

Even the judge looked a little surprised as he turned toward Coglin.

"You may step down," he said.

The prosecutor was still standing at his table as Coglin passed by.

"The State would like to recall Officer James Martinelli."

Knew it, Coglin thought as Mulvane shot up from his seat. I knew it would come back to bite me in the ass.

"Objection," Coglin's lawyer said.

"Sidebar, Your Honor?" the prosecutor said.

The judge nodded wearily.

"Alright, alright," he said.

The prosecutor, his assistant, the court stenographer, the court clerk, Mulvane and Coglin all stepped over. They stood in a close huddle around the side of the judge's bench, opposite the jury. Coglin's attorney spoke first.

"How the heck can he call a witness he's already questioned? One of my witnesses?"

"The witness approached us yesterday with a confession. New evidence has come to light, Your Honor. New perspective in this case that needs to be addressed."

"He had his chance," Mulvane said. "What's this? A do-over?"

The judge sat with his head down. He seemed to be studying his fingers intertwined on the dark wood surface before him.

"I'm going to allow it," he said.

"What?" Mulvane said, his voice rising.

The judge looked up.

"Are you hard of hearing, Counsel?" he said.

"You're going to allow it?" Mulvane said in the same high voice.

"I see. Perhaps some time in one of the cells downstairs might correct your deficiency."

Mulvane was squinting off into space. A disgusted look slowly crossed his face.

"You'd do that, too, wouldn't you?" Mulvane said. "This whole thing is bullshit." He leaned toward the stenographer, who was typing away with his head down.

"You getting all that? Defense attorney, Mulvane, says this whole thing is a crock." He turned toward the stunned judge. "I thought the prosecution and the media were in charge of this railroad. I guess I was wrong. You're driving the fucking train!"

The judge seemed unable to speak. His tanned face had turned a hot, dangerous red. The gel that slicked his hair looked as if it was about to start sizzling. The intake of his breath, a split second later, sounded like an industrial vacuum, as if he were attempting to suck every cubic foot of oxygen from the room. He exhaled in a great gust, glanced at the stenographer and paused.

"You know what, Counselor? I'm going to ignore that. This has been an emotional case for everyone involved. Proceed."

The huddle dispersed. Coglin stepped unsteadily back to his seat with his lawyer.

"How bad is this going to be?" Mulvane whispered as they sat.

Coglin looked at him without speaking, then looked away.

Mulvane snuffed, threw his pen across the pad before him.

"Alrightee, then," he said.

For the second time during the trial, the clerk called for Martinelli and a moment later, Coglin's old partner entered the courtroom. He wore a double-breasted suit and a bright tie, but his expression was grave. Coglin stared at the side of his face as he passed, oddly curious at exactly how the man could put one foot in front of the other without looking his way.

He'd been Coglin's first partner. They'd protected each other out in the world, and it had come down to this? Coglin took a breath, trying to look calm for the jury. His knuckles turned white as he squeezed the arms of his chair. He was doing his best to figure out exactly what was about to occur, but his mind dulled under the weight of possibilities.

"Do you promise to tell the truth, the whole truth, and nothing but the truth, so help you God?" the clerk said.

"Rat!" someone called from the back.

Coglin turned to the gallery, seeking his anonymous ally among the blank faces as the judge banged down his gavel. Martinelli flinched as it struck above his head. He swallowed.

"I do," he said.

The prosecutor rose from behind his table and stood before the jury. He began by reviewing Martinelli's previous testimony about his career as a police officer. After Martinelli confirmed the information, the prosecutor asked him if he was there the night the boy was killed.

"I arrived right after," Martinelli said.

"Were you on duty?"

"No," Martinelli said. "I work the day shift, but I came back for a party for another officer in a place down the block."

"This party was for what? A retirement?"

"No, it was a bachelor party, actually."

"Oh, a bachelor party," the lawyer said. "They can get a little crazy, can't they? A lot of drinking goes on?"

"Objection," Mulvane said. "Relevance?"

The judge turned toward him.

"Hmm. Relevance, huh? Thanks for the help on which particular point of law you want me to rule on," the judge said to Mulvane. "Been watching reruns of *LA Law*, Counselor?"

There were chuckles from the audience and the jury.

"Overruled," the judge said.

"Yes," Martinelli said. "It was pretty wild."

"Were there any uniformed officers at this party?"

"Yes," Martinelli said. "There were a few."

"Men who were supposed to be on duty?"

"Yes."

"Was Officer Coglin one of those officers?"

"I don't know. It was pretty crowded."

"But he could've been?"

"Yes."

Coglin squinted, abject disbelief starting to crack his mask of calm.

"You testify that you were outside, smoking a cigarette, when you heard a train horn and shots coming from the train station down the block and you went to investigate."

"That's right."

"You testify that when you got to the top of the landing, you found Officer Coglin unconscious and that you revived him. Did you notice anything else that you might've failed to mention in your other testimony?"

"Yes."

"What was that?"

"Officer Coglin smelled like alcohol, as if he'd been drinking."

Coglin's chair scraped loudly off the marble tile of the floor and he found himself on his feet.

"You lying sack of shit!" he yelled.

The judge was banging his gavel savagely. He rose from his chair.

"Sit down!" he commanded, pointing at Coglin.

Mulvane pushed at his shoulders from behind, trying to reseat him. Sullivan and other white-shirted court officers appeared in front of the table in a loud jangle of keys. Coglin sat reluctantly, not taking his eyes from where they were riveted on Martinelli's down-turned face.

"Officer," the judge said. "You do that again and I will have you put in shackles. Damn me, if I won't!"

"Continue," he barked at the prosecutor.

"So the concussion that Mr. Coglin received at the incident could've been the result of a drunken fall?"

"I guess," Martinelli said.

"Please continue," the prosecutor said.

"I saw the motorman walking around and acting oddly. I thought he might be in shock, so I went to see if I could help him."

"And?" the prosecutor said.

"While I was trying to calm him, I looked back to see where I'd left Officer Coglin, but he was up near the front of the train. And then I saw him toss something. Something black. It was heavy, because I heard it hit the street below."

The prosecutor wheeled around, took something from his briefcase and held it up with a theatrical flourish. It was a gun. The small automatic Coglin had tossed. The one Martinelli had given him.

"Your Honor, the prosecution would like to enter this gun found at the scene as state's evidence."

The judge swiveled his chair toward Coglin's table and sat watching Mulvane.

"Objec . . ." Mulvane began.

"Overruled," the judge said, cutting him off. "Continue," the judge said to the prosecutor.

"Was it this gun?" the lawyer said, handing the weapon to Martinelli.

Coglin watched his old partner handle it gingerly, peering at it closely, as if he'd never seen it before.

They must've caught him for something, Coglin thought. Threatened to fire him, take away his pension, because he was killing him now. Saying that Coglin had planted a gun erased his whole version of the events. If he'd lied once, then he'd lied about everything else, the jury would think. Why don't you just shoot me, you Judas motherfucker? Coglin thought. Would have been kinder if you'd just shot me in the back of the head that first day we stepped out together on the street.

"Maybe," Martinelli said. "He was pretty far away."

"This gun was found on the street beneath the front of the train. Would that be where you saw Officer Coglin toss the heavy, black object?"

"Yes," Martinelli said.

"That's all I have for this witness."

Mulvane was already up and approaching Martinelli, before the judge indicated that it was his turn.

"Are you currently under criminal investigation, Mr. Martinelli?"

"No," Martinelli said.

Mulvane looked panicked for a moment, then he held up a finger and smiled.

"Were you under criminal investigation prior to agreeing to testify today?"

Martinelli looked over at the prosecutor, whose eyes were glued to the notepad on the desk in front of him.

"Yes," he said.

"I see," Mulvane said. "So in other words, your testimony today against my client will help you to avoid criminal prosecution?"

"I guess so," Martinelli said.

"You were my client's first partner, weren't you?" Mulvane said.

Martinelli had had his eyes downcast throughout his testimony, but now his head fell even lower as he nodded in acknowledgment.

"Yes," he said quietly.

"Officer Martinelli, someone called you a rat as you stepped into court today. How do you feel about that?"

"Objection," the prosecutor said.

"Sustained," the judge said. "Don't answer that," he said to Martinelli.

"That's all I have for this . . . this . . . witness," Mulvane said.

"Redirect?" the judge asked the prosecutor.

The prosecutor shook his head.

"Thank you, sir. You're dismissed."

Martinelli stepped down. His movements seemed slower, more careful, as if he'd aged in the time he'd been in the witness box. Coglin stilled as Martinelli approached the defense table. Mulvane leaned in close to Coglin.

"Don't you say a fucking word," he said.

Martinelli passed through the gate.

"Any more witnesses?" the judge said.

"No, Your Honor," the prosecutor said.

The judge banged down his gavel.

"We'll break for lunch and then hear closing arguments at one."

Coglin heard the people rising behind him, the hungry crowd rushing out to get a snack. He sat there numb, immobile. He watched the jury depart. The Hispanic grandmother was the last one out, and he tried unsuccessfully to get her to meet his gaze.

Mulvane stood and began to gather his things.

"Thanks, John," he said, as he stepped from the table. "Appreciate you helping me not to look like an ass out there, for being so upfront."

Coglin just sat there.

Vindicated, he thought.

He didn't feel hungry at all.

After a minute, he felt a tap on his back.

"It's not looking too good is it, John?" his mother behind him said.

"No, Ma," Coglin said. "No, it ain't."

She came through the gate and sat down next to him. He smiled at her. If she died while he was inside, would he get to go to her funeral? She leaned in toward him and brushed something off his lapel.

They watched the clock and the door that led to the jury room. After a while, the beeper he wore at his belt went off. It was his own home phone number. *Karen?* he thought. *Wasn't she supposed to be at work?*

Karen. And she'd thought becoming pregnant was the biggest shock they'd have to face. And what the fuck were they going to do now? Get married the day before his sentencing? There hadn't even been time to figure it out. He envisioned her in the waiting room at Riker's, among the inmates groping their wives and girlfriends, with their baby on her knee.

Fuck that. No way. *Give up hope when all hope is gone,* he thought. Not a second before.

He rose slowly.

"Be right back," he told his mother.

Safely back inside the old phone booth again, he dialed home. Karen answered, sobbing, on the first ring.

"Oh, John," she said.

She'd been attacked, Coglin thought quickly. She'd been recognized and assaulted by somebody on the street.

"What is it?" he said. "Jesus Christ! What's wrong?"

"The baby, John. I was at work and I started bleeding and . . . Oh, God, John. The baby. I lost the baby."

Coglin closed his eyes slowly as the floor, the walls, the world around him wavered, dissolved. His head sank until it was pressed against the cold, metal faceplate of the payphone. *Dear God*, he thought. *Please. Not more.*

"Jesus, Karen," he finally managed to say. "Are you OK?"

"I'm fine. I'm fine. It was a girl, John," she sobbed. "The doctor said she was a little baby girl."

The stress, Coglin thought, stunned. The constant hounding and embarrassment. How could anyone withstand it? He glanced quickly out the smudged plastic door at the lawyers and reporters filing busily by. *They'd done it,* he thought. Every one of them had played a fucking part.

"Did you go to the hospital?"

"No, I went right in to Dr. Morris."

"I'm sorry," he said again. "Are you sure you're OK? Can your mother come?"

"Just come home as soon as you can," she said.

"OK."

He hung up and called the doctor. Karen was alright, he told him. These things happened. Coglin hung up. Baby girl, he thought, blowing into a closed fist. Baby girl. He thought of the cradle he'd made. Wouldn't need that now, would they?

He called Karen back.

"Karen Horgan's office."

"Oh, hi, Janet," he said to Karen's secretary. "I'm sorry, it's John. I dialed wrong. Were you with Karen when it happened?"

"When what happened, Mr. Coglin?"

"When Karen got sick. When she started bleeding."

"Started bleeding? I'm sorry, Mr. Coglin, I don't know what you're talking about. I know Karen called in sick. Is she OK?"

Called in sick? Coglin thought. He almost dropped the receiver.

"Mr. Coglin?"

He hung up and sat in the cramped booth, holding his shaking hands. It was no accident. Without telling him, Karen had gone and done it. Stripped herself of all connection to him before the worst of it started. Wiped the slate clean. Got the doctor to go along with her. Four and a half months pregnant, he thought. A little baby girl. Or did she make that up, too?

His beeper went off again. He stared at his home number in the box for a long moment then clicked it off. Then he slammed open the door of the booth and began to move quickly, head down, through the hall.

THE PROSECUTION'S CLOSING ARGUMENT lasted an hour. The corpulent ADA stalked the floor before the jury box, emphasizing each pertinent point of the state's case by loudly slapping the back of one plump hand into the palm of the other. He referred to Coglin as a drunken cop—a cowboy, he called him—who thought it might be funny to make a man dance. He alluded to the party that Coglin hadn't attended.

"We all know what they're about, don't we?" the lawyer bellowed, backhanding his meaty palm.

"Fired-up cops, fueled with alcohol and frustration, looking to prove their manhood. Reginald Mason was unlucky enough to fall into the path of one of them. A boy in the wrong place at the wrong time. Officer Coglin talks about a beating, but no victim was ever found. He says he fell from a roof, chasing a suspect, while he was off duty. Isn't it more likely that he fell while drunk? Officer Martinelli has testified to smelling alcohol on his breath."

Slap, slap, slap went the lawyer's hands. *He was really beating the fuck out of them,* Coglin thought. He could imagine him practicing at home in front of the bathroom mirror trying to get the sound just right. *Had to be the fat,* Coglin thought, distracted. If you slapped his jowls, you'd probably shatter a fuckin' window. If he ever got the chance, Coglin decided, he'd have to give it a shot and see.

"These facts matter," the lawyer said. "These are serious issues. A young man is dead.

"The defense brought up the victim's prior record: a few busts for pot, a few assaults. Perhaps he wasn't a choirboy. Who among us is? Does having an arrest record mean we deserve to be shot? Does an arrest record mean we can be pushed in front of an eight-hundred-thousand-pound train? We've seen the pictures, ladies and gentlemen. I'll let the pictures speak for themselves.

"Even police will admit that there are a few rotten apples in their ranks. From the facts of this case, I think we've found a very bad one. I hope you see it as well and that you send out a message to the other Neanderthals in blue who think they can terrorize and murder the honest citizens of our community. Come back with a verdict of guilty. Thank you."

Mulvane waited for the prosecutor to take his seat before he stood. He walked slowly toward the jury box and stood before them, looking down at the floor in silence. Then he looked up.

"My client has been a police officer for five and a half years. Up until that night, four months ago, he'd never fired his gun. The prosecutor says he was at a party, that he drank on duty, and that he shot a kid for fun. But he has no proof that my client was even there, no proof that my client had even one drink. See? He needs to put that in your mind, because without these fabrications, my client has as much motive to shoot someone on his way home from work as you or I do. I propose that my client wanted to do what you or I want to do after a hard day's work: go home, take a shower and get into bed.

"But he didn't do that. He saw someone being attacked on the side of the road, and he stopped. He could've just as easily ignored the person. But he didn't. Was it duty that made him stop? Perhaps. I, who know this man, don't think so. What I think, is simply that he saw another human being in trouble and he felt he needed to help.

"In attempting to apprehend one of the perpetrators—who, despite his youth, was a recorded violent felon—Mr. Coglin slipped and fell. As he lay helpless, the perpetrator, Mr. Mason, tried to push Officer Coglin onto the tracks in front of an oncoming train. In order to save his life, Officer Coglin shot him, and the perpetrator himself fell to the tracks. That is what happened.

"A witness testifies that he heard Mr. Coglin tell Mason to dance. As I have shown, the distance from his apartment to the track would have made it difficult to see Mr. Coglin, let alone hear what he was saying. And if he did see and hear these incredible events, why did he go to the media, not the police? Another officer testified that he saw Officer Coglin toss a gun down on the perpetrator, in order to make his story look good. Granted a gun was found down the block, but should we listen to a man who's trading his testimony for leniency? Also, Officer Coglin's badge was found on the perpetrator's body under the train. Did he climb down and plant that as well?"

Mulvane paused.

"This is a beautiful room, isn't it?" he said, gesturing with his arms. "This whole courthouse, in fact, is an incredible structure. The great pillars outside. The statues. There's a reason for it. This is the place where something is produced that only human beings can create. Justice. Carved in stone somewhere on the side of this building, it says that justice is mankind's greatest endeavor. To right what is wrong. I can't do that. Although he tries to pretend that he can, the prosecutor can't do it either. Even the judge there in his robes can't do it. Only you can. We're only here to help you find it.

"Logic, reason itself, favors my client's version of what happened that tragic night. And I believe that you know, deep in your hearts, that what I say is true."

Mulvane turned, walked back to the defense table and sat. The courtroom was completely silent. The jury members seemed to be sitting up a little straighter. The judge started instructing them on the charges.

Coglin patted his lawyer on the shoulder.

"Thank you," he said.

Mulvane shrugged his shoulders.

"I don't know how much it's gonna help us," he said.

"The way you told it, at least we got a shot," Coglin said.

Mulvane looked at him. "I thought cops were supposed to be cynical," he said.

"At least you told them," Coglin said, watching the jury depart. "It's on them, whatever happens next."

They sat silently. Some of the people in the gallery stood and left, but most of them stayed seated. From their faces, many of them seemed torn, as if they wanted to leave but didn't want to miss the grand finale. Coglin kept glancing up at the clock on the wall, but it didn't seem to be working. There were two hours left until four, when court would adjourn. Two hours, Coglin thought, rubbing his temples with his fingers. Might as well be two days.

For a while, Coglin tried to convince himself that every moment that passed was in his favor, time spent by one or two of the jury who didn't want to convict him, trying to calm the emotions of the others. Then he panicked, thinking it could just as easily be the other way around.

One of the court officers left the room and after some time, another one came back in. He was a big man and he eyed Coglin coldly as he passed the defense table and stood beside the copper-trimmed window. Coglin sat up quickly in his chair, realizing that he was the bull they used to take guilty defendants into custody. Had the jury reached a verdict already? Mulvane touched him on the arm.

"Doesn't mean anything," he said, indicating the big officer with his chin. "Standard procedure. I know this is hard. Why don't you go splash some water on your face or something?"

Coglin closed his eyes and rubbed at the bridge of his nose with his fingertips.

"Alright," he said standing.

He nodded to his mother as he stepped through the gate. He was too on edge to be upset by the scores of eyes behind her that followed his every move.

He was at the bathroom sink, splashing cold water on the back of his neck, when the door to the hall opened and Sullivan came in. He began checking the stalls. When he seemed satisfied that they were all empty, he stepped back to the door and locked it with a key from the huge ring on his belt. Coglin turned from the sink and looked over at him.

"They're going to convict you," Sullivan said.

Coglin flinched. The sudden finality of it like a shaft of ice speared through his heart. He closed his eyes and thought, this isn't happening. This isn't happening.

"They're back already?" he finally said. His voice sounded strange, far away. "You're sure?"

"No, they haven't come back yet," the bailiff said. "But I'm sure."

Coglin opened his eyes.

"I don't understand. If they're not back yet, how do you know?"

"I listened at the door," he said. "Howd'ya think?"

Coglin blinked at him as he absorbed the information.

"Guilty?" he said.

"Guilty," Sullivan said. "Unanimous. They didn't even have to recount once. They're going to wait to give the verdict tomorrow, so they can be ready for the cameras. Can you believe it? They ain't dressed up enough, the bastards said. You're goin' to jail. Probably after lunch tomorrow. Pricks probably want to get that last free meal in, is my bet."

"Guilty?" Coglin said again.

"You're fucked," Sullivan said. "I don't know who you pissed off. Your mouthpiece's speech about justice—me and the fellas had to try hard not to laugh out loud. Your partner was the first cop on the stand that I've ever seen one of these juries believe. And I been here four years."

Coglin leaned with his hands back against the sink. All of a sudden, he didn't trust his legs.

"Thank you," he said weakly.

Sullivan clapped him on the shoulder.

"No problem," he said. He stepped to the door and unlocked it. "Thought you should know. Take it easy."

Coglin stood there. The full weight of everything falling and falling and falling upon him. He still hadn't moved when the door opened again. It was the courtroom sketch artist. He blocked the man's path, his eyes burning.

"Lookin for another angle, you cocksucker?" he said.

The man turned immediately on his heels.

When Coglin stepped back into the courtroom, the gallery was still three-quarters full. Sorry, he felt like saying to them as he took his seat. Sorry for the inconvenience, but the lynching is going to be postponed until tomorrow. The judge whispered to the court clerk to the right of the bench, and then they started laughing.

Funny shit, huh? Coglin thought. He clenched his shaking hands. Some funny, funny shit.

Coglin sat there. His knowledge of what was to come seemed to have unfrozen the clock. After a while, more people started to leave. His lawyer went out and came back in. There was a commotion and he turned and saw the movie actress who'd been seated at the rally the day before, standing along the back wall. He shook his head and bent and held it in his hands.

What would happen next? he thought. The jury would come back out dressed like a deck of cards and the judge would say, "off with his head"? Maybe the whole trial was a movie. Maybe in a moment the director would yell "cut" and he could get up and leave. He waited, listening for it.

After another twenty minutes, Sullivan appeared from the jury room door with a slip of paper and handed it up to the judge. The judge looked at the paper and cleared his throat.

"The jury has not reached a verdict and will be sequestered. We'll pick it up tomorrow at ten."

He banged down his gavel.

"Court adjourned," he said.

Coglin felt light-headed, oxygen depleted, as he stood. He grabbed his mother and they made their way out. The hall was filled with reporters. Mulvane was out in front blocking, trying to carve some sort of path. Questions were fired at Coglin left and right, but he could barely hear them in the commotion. They sounded like insults being hurled at him. They took the elevator down to the gilded lobby and made their way outside.

He'd forgotten how hot it was. Immediately, the heat again

clung to his skin. In a moment, there seemed to be a film of sweat over every inch of his body. From the top of the court-house steps, he could see motes of dust and car exhaust hanging in the thick yellow air over the traffic and buildings. The little, gritty particles began to collect on his skin as the television teams that hadn't been allowed inside, ran up and encircled them.

A boom mike dropped in front of Coglin's face, and as he started down the steps, its rough sponge covering brushed against his lips. He grabbed it and pulled it free from whomever was holding it, and let it drop. He heard it snap when he stepped on it.

"This is impossible," Mulvane yelled at him. "I'll make some type of statement. You guys go around back and grab a cab. I'll beep you later."

Coglin pulled his mother away. All the cameramen but one remained with the lawyer. It was the bastard who'd crushed his foot the day before. Coglin stopped on the sidewalk and stared at him.

"Do you have a mother?" he said to the lower part of the man's face that stuck out beneath the huge bore of the lens.

The cameraman filmed silently for another few seconds.

"Hey, nothing personal," he said, and then retreated back toward the courtroom steps where Mulvane was starting his address.

Coglin walked quickly along the back end of the courthouse. Correction vans were backed up perpendicular to the building, ferrying prisoners back and forth to court. He would've been on one of them right now, if there had been a huge bail that he couldn't afford. Mulvane had taken care of that, at least. But he'd be on one sure enough tomorrow, he thought. He began to walk faster.

"Yo, cop!" came a low voice from inside one of the caged rear windows as they passed. He glanced back. It was dark inside, but he could see two large hands gripping at the steel mesh.

"Betta smuggle yo' badge an' gun up yo' ass when they put you in here with me, racist pig," the deep, faceless voice called after him. "Because you gonna need those mothafuckas."

His celebrity status had even infiltrated prison walls, Coglin thought, almost beginning to run now. Wasn't that just the best?

They weren't yet at the corner when Coglin heard the bull-horn. He'd almost forgotten about the rally. How could he get past that? A gypsy cab was approaching and he almost dove in front of it as he flagged it down. He opened the door and ush-ered his mother in first, then he sank into the soft velour.

"Where?" the driver said, after Coglin slammed the door. Coglin looked forward at the driver thinking about his death-wishing Carribean chauffeur from the morning. He was His-panic, he saw with relief. Maybe they'd make it out alive.

Coglin looked out as a flock of pigeons flew from the corner of an old building behind the courthouse, a wad of grayish specks shooting like buckshot across the late afternoon, pale blue summer sky.

"North," Coglin said, as he loosened his tie. "Away from here. Just move."

Chapter Four

COGLIN HADN'T BEEN TO HIS MOTHER'S apartment in a long while, and as they pulled up to his old building fifteen minutes after the courthouse pandemonium, he felt guilty about it. Even before all the bullshit started, he hadn't been by that often, and he felt bad now that he'd neglected her.

As they got out of the taxi, an unmarked police car pulled to the curb across from his mother's building, and the two plain-clothesmen, Internal Affairs most likely, sitting in the front seat stared at him blankly. He stopped in the street and nodded his head at them and mouthed, "Scumbags."

He looked out over his mother's small, neat living room as she locked the door behind them. The little ceramic knick-knacks, the books on the shelves. He sank into the stiff love seat.

His mother put a hand on the back of his head.

"I'll put on coffee," she said.

It was too hot for coffee, but he didn't say that. He listened to her moving things around in the kitchen. The clock ticked.

It had often been like this, hadn't it? he thought. The quiet and just the two of them. His father had died in Vietnam before he was born. There was a picture of him on the mantel. Some dark-haired, twenty-year-old stranger who'd had the luck to be shot dead on some nameless mountain during the Tet Offensive. His mother had told him often that they shared the same eyes, but as he looked over at him now, he wondered if that wasn't the only thing they shared.

He stood and went into his room. It was pretty much as he had left it. The bed made, the bookcase he had built, the padded bench and the weights in the milk crate in the corner. He stepped to the window and opened it up. There was a fire escape outside it and through its worn, thin metal bars, he looked down at the overgrown stand of tall weeds beyond the building's rusted back-yard fence.

There'd been railroad tracks there years ago, but the line had been discontinued, and the rails had been pulled up and hauled away. He remembered evenings spent sitting in this very windowsill as a teenager, staring north up those tracks where they curved away into the trees of Van Cortlandt Park, wondering on paths, imagining journeys.

His mother came in carrying a mug. She left the coffee on the sill, turned and left, closing the door behind her.

He left the coffee where it sat and wiped sweat off his forehead with his hand. He looked at the cars flashing past on the highway beyond the weeds and at the backs of the other old buildings across the highway.

They hadn't always lived here. Until he was fifteen, they'd lived in a house farther north in a nice part of Yonkers. It'd been his paternal grandfather's house, but when the old man died, they'd found out his grandmother was a lot less happy with the arrangement, so they had to move down here.

It had been an adjustment. His mother had to get a secretary job downtown and he'd had to change schools. At his grandfather's insistence, he'd been attending a Catholic prep school and playing football, but with him gone, the tuition was out of the question, and Coglin had to transfer to public school.

Coglin felt his pager start vibrating and he pressed it off without looking at it. Karen had been beeping him steadily since he left the courthouse, but he wasn't about to call her back. Not now.

She was a girl, John, a little baby girl.

Not fuckin' ever.

He remembered meeting her in high school. She'd come from Minnesota, following some job of her long-haul, truck-driving stepfather. If there was anyone more out of place than himself that first year in the inner city public school, it was Karen. The second day of class, he'd pulled her away from a welcoming committee of female Latin Kings who had surrounded her, calling her a stuck-up white bitch. From that day to the one where she'd left again that summer, they were inseparable.

He remembered skipping class those mornings. The holy quiet as she led him by the hand into her mother and stepfather's apartment after they'd gone to work. The clinging warmth of her young body, a generosity he could never repay.

And then she'd just left. No good-bye kiss, no letter. He'd come by her apartment one morning and she and her parents were just gone. That's why when he saw her a year ago, walking down Fifth Avenue in a business suit, he'd run across the street and almost tackled her. It had seemed that in that moment his world had finally, impossibly come full circle. As if all that had been lost was found again.

He glanced down at his beeper: 911, she'd put. Yeah, right. Emergency. She should have put 10–13. Officer in dire need of assistance. Officer down.

His partner, scumbag though he was, had turned out to be right, hadn't he? Coglin thought. He had said Karen was a modern woman, and if by modern he meant that she was possessed with an unknowable depth of duplicity, he was dead fucking on.

When his mother came back in, she had a pack of cigarettes and a lighter in her hand.

He squinted at her.

"I thought you quit," he said.

She took one of them out, lit it and blew out smoke. She stepped next to him and tapped ash out the window.

"I did," she said.

He looked at the pack for a moment. *What the fuck,* he thought. *What the fuck?* He took the pack from her hand, got one out for himself and got it lit. He hadn't smoked in five years, and he coughed and closed his eyes at the headrush. Going to need something to kill the mountains of time they were about to pile on top of him.

He cleared his throat.

"I'm going in," he said.

"Jury's still out," his mother said. "Don't panic till you have a reason."

"I do, Mom," Coglin said. "Sullivan told me. He overheard the jury. They're convicting me. They're just waiting overnight to make it look good."

His mother turned toward him slowly, her unheeded cigarette burning like a slow fuse between her fingers. A subtle change came over her posture, a tremor in the usual square of her shoulders as if some internal structure had just given way. Her free hand came up covering her mouth.

"How long?" she said.

"Last offer DA put on the table was manslaughter. Maybe I can still take it. Mulvane said with this judge, count on a definite ten."

"Ten years?" his mother said. "You'll be forty."

Coglin looked out the window. The highway cars sparkled in the light. He took another drag of his cigarette.

"Forty-one," he said.

"And that's it? They convict you and you go to jail and that's it?"

"Just like that," Coglin said.

"But it's wrong. You didn't murder that boy or commit manslaughter. You were doing your job."

"That's what I thought," Coglin said. He shrugged. "I guess it doesn't have to do with right and wrong."

"Can't you appeal?"

"Maybe," Coglin said. "I wasn't at that party like they said I was. I could probably prove that. Clarke said it would be a lot easier because there'd be less media attention, but who knows? I'll be inside until that happens."

"But they'll know who you are in jail. They'll know you're a cop. They'll come after you."

Coglin looked out for a long while at the overgrown path. A small bird darted from the top of a branch to the top of the rusted fence, then flew away north into the trees.

"It'll be an adjustment," he said. "I'll be alright."

His mother stood looking at him. Her cigarette was just one long ash now. She flicked it out the window. She stared down after it.

Coglin touched her shoulder.

"I'll be fine," he said.

She went back out and after a minute he heard water running

in the kitchen. He flicked out his cigarette and took out another and got it lit. *Hey, this is kind of addictive,* he thought. He closed his eyes.

"Betta smuggle yo' badge an' gun up yo' ass when they put you in here with me, pig," he heard the voice from the van say again. *"Because you gonna need those mothafuckas."*

Yeah, Mom, he thought, opening his eyes and taking in another lungful of smoke. *I'll be just fine.*

He thought about the people on the jury. Even knowing what they were about to do to him, he couldn't make himself angry with them. They were just regular people: bus drivers, secretaries, waitresses. They'd never been made to understand how exacting they had to be to determine what had happened. The event itself, any event, was subtle. The way it had been explained to them by the prosecution and the media, though inaccurate, was easy and cheap, and they'd swallowed it. The evil cop was an exciting, brainless idea, one they were familiar with from TV, so they were all over it.

No. It wasn't their fault. It was the media's fault and the system's fault.

But it really wasn't their fault either, was it? he thought. Ultimately, really, it was his own. No matter what'd been done to him, it was being done only to him. He couldn't help thinking, had he been smarter or somebody else, had made more allies perhaps, protected himself more completely in some fundamental way, none of this would have happened to him at all.

So what now? he thought, looking out his window. *Seek out Martinelli? Go to his apartment and have it out with his girl? Get drunk?*

Across the highway, he saw the beckoning green neon in the tiny, blacked-out window of a corner bar.

No, he thought. He'd gotten it backwards. First, get drunk, then have it out with his girl, then seek out Martinelli.

Ah, there you go, he thought, flicking ash with his thumb. Finally, he was beginning to think straight.

The phone rang in the kitchen as he stood. He heard his mother answer it. When he walked in she was looking down at the floor nervously and cupping the mouthpiece.

"What?" Coglin said. "Who is it?"

She handed the receiver to him without speaking.

"Hello?" he said.

"Yes, hello," a voice with an Irish accent said with mock formality. "I'd like to speak with public enemy number one, please."

"Aidan?" Coglin said. Good Christ, his uncle, he thought. No wonder his mother had looked shocked. How long had it been since they'd heard from him? Twelve, fifteen years?

"I'd ask how yer doin, John," his uncle said in his brogue. "But I got the news on right now, so I think I can guess. Nice suit, though the tie's got to go, I think. They did get your best side. Especially Channel Six."

Yep, Coglin thought. It was Aidan. The same sarcastic bastard who'd come over from Ireland and stayed with them for a year and a half before cutting out one morning without another word or call. Aidan, his sole surviving family.

"Forgive me if I'm wrong, unc," Coglin said. "But aren't long-lost, flat-leaving relatives supposed to come out of the woodwork when you hit Lotto?"

"I don't know about Lotto," Aidan said. "But you certainly hit some type of jackpot. And what are you talking about flat-leaving? Didn't you get my card?"

"For what?"

"Christmas," Aidan said.

"Like to narrow it down to a decade?" Coglin said.

"Eighties," Aidan said. "Late."

"Oh, yeah. I remember it now. On the front, it had a Santa Claus or a Christmas tree or maybe it was a baby in a manger?"

"All three," Aidan said. "You did get it. Terrific."

"Did you get my thank you?" Coglin said.

"White card? The word 'thanks' on the front of it?" Aidan said.

"Right. Except inside I wrote, 'for nothing.'"

"Ouch," Aidan said. "I wasn't aware I was that missed."

Coglin was about to say that he wasn't, but he'd definitely been hurt when the man had left.

He was fourteen and on his way to fucking up pretty severely the summer Aidan had showed up on their doorstep. Pissed off and lost in this new crappy place his mother had brought him to, Coglin was ready to righteously and immediately do whatever the fuck he wanted to. What he settled on was getting doped up with this really cool, tattooed thirteen-year-old he'd seen setting off blockbusters on the tracks behind their building. Sometimes, the thirteen-year-old's dad would come home, and instead of kicking the shit out of both of them, he'd get high with them, too. It was the coolest. "Baba O'Riley," Pink Floyd *The Wall*, fuckin' teenage wasteland. Was, until one day a week later as they were sitting around high, watching *Planet of the Apes* in the thirteen-year-old's apartment and Aidan came in through the window.

He remembered the greasy, pony-tailed dad getting up slowly from the rancid couch, mouth opening in dulled protest, when Aidan pulled the gun out. The man sat right back down.

"Hey, fellas," Aidan had said with a smile. "Havin' fun, are we?"

Coglin had sat there wide-eyed, thinking at first he was hallucinating, that the weed they'd smoked had been laced with goofballs or something, as Aidan urged him to stand, waving him toward the window.

"Oh, and by the way," Aidan had said amiably to the thirteen-year-old and his dad as Coglin climbed wobbly out onto the bright fire escape. "If I even see you *talkin'* to my nephew again, I'll murder you both in your sleep. Enjoy the rest of the movie now. You're gonna love the ending."

His uncle didn't mention the incident and Coglin never mentioned the gun. That night, sobered up, he'd gotten it out of his mother that his uncle had been involved in "the troubles" back in their native Belfast. With that information added to the gun he'd seen, Coglin summed up that his uncle was a former member of the IRA, a bad ass of global dimension.

He remembered waiting the next day outside the building like a puppy dog for Aidan to come home from the carpentry job he scored. They'd do things. Bowl. Shoot pool. He'd even taught Coglin how to fight that summer, setting up a heavy bag in the hell-hot boiler room of their building. Tortuous lessons he'd be forced to apply later on that September when he started public high school. Aidan had been a mysterious and strong benevolent male figure when he was in dire need of one. But then, as seemed to be the continuing theme of his life with those he'd become close to, one morning Coglin found painfully that his uncle had departed just as quickly as he'd come.

"You ever make it to California like you wanted to?" Coglin said now into the phone.

"Unfortunately," Aidan said.

"Where, LA? San Francisco?"

"There was a 'San' at the front of it," Aidan said. "'San Quentin,' I think it was called."

"No," Coglin said finally.

"Way," Aidan said.

"For what?"

"Use your imagination," he said.

"Assault?" Coglin said.

"Something like that."

"With intent to kill?"

"You've fond memories of me, eh?" Aidan said.

"Nothing but," Coglin said. "You still in?"

"No," Aidan said. "I left that cunt of a state behind six months ago. I'm living in Pennsylvania now. Up in the glorious sanctity of the woods. Not too far away from you guys, actually. Couple of hours. That's why I'm callin'. I'm wondering if you'd like to come out and pay your old uncle a visit."

"You saw the news," Coglin said. "I'm a little busy."

"I been there," his uncle said, a kind of soft compasionate intensity coming into his voice. "That's why I called I guess. You're gonna need a plan if they convict. Lord knows I could have used one when the gates clanged shut behind me. I was gonna come to see you today myself, but me car's fucked. Alternator finally went I think. Why don't you come out and see me?"

Drive the hell out to Pennsylvania, Coglin thought. His uncle had been cool to him and everything but fuck that.

"I'm not allowed to leave the state," Coglin said lamely.

"You're charged with murder, aren'tcha?" Aidan said. "What more can they possibly do? Come out, boy. Honestly. At the very least a trip'll take your mind off things."

Betta smuggle yo' badge an' gun up yo' ass when they put you in here with me, pig, Coglin thought yet again. Delivered the way it was from behind steel mesh, it had become an irritatingly memorable line.

He could definitely use not thinking for a while, he had to

admit. Sitting here could, it was true, drive him mad. And what pressing concerns did he have hanging around here anyway? a voice asked him. Getting monumentally fucked up?

"You still drink?" Coglin said.

"I've been known to," Aidan said. "On special occasions."

Coglin closed his eyes.

Fuck it, he could drink with him instead, couldn't he? They could have a pleasant evening of drink and going over his family's bloody history while reviewing the finer points of how not to get shanked. Sounded like a plan.

Get him the fuck out of here for the time being anyway.

Oh, God, John. The baby, he heard Karen say again. *I lost the baby.*

He opened his eyes.

"Two hours away?" Coglin said.

"Hour and a half, if you hurry."

"You buying?" Coglin said.

Aidan laughed.

"I'm buying," he said.

"Then you better hit the cash machine," Coglin said. "'Cause I'm on my way."

"Grand," Aidan said. "We'll make an evening of it. My address is . . ."

"Wait up," Coglin said. "Let me get a pen."

Coglin wrote down all the information and said good-bye. He realized the real reason he was going the second after he hung up the phone.

He no longer had a friend in the world.

At first, his mother disapproved of his going to see her brother. But when he'd told her of his intention to ditch the cops out in front by his car by out-racing them, she'd relented with a sigh, and handed him her keys.

"My car's across from the park," she told him. "Better sneak out the back and use the path."

"Thanks, Ma Barker," he said, giving her a hug by the door. "Don't wait up."

Two minutes later, Coglin stepped into the empty cement backyard of the building with his uncle's address in his pocket and his mother's car keys in his hand. He stood for a moment.

Evening sunlight was flaring now. It lay golden on the faded brick faces of the other buildings and made gold links at the top of the rusted fence. There was a lull in the incessant swish of traffic on the highway, and he could hear unseen birds calling to one another, singing in the warm air.

He was a lot bigger now than the last time he'd squeezed through the hole in the back fence, but he managed it. He made his way through the thick, tall overgrowth north toward the park. He stumbled once over a half-buried trestle and fell hard, the scratchy knees of his slacks sinking into a mound of soft, dry black earth. Small bugs attacked his sweating face, annoyed his eyes, buzzed in his ears. The tops of the vegetation alongside the path seemed to tower above him. For a second, his swimming head told him to turn his tired, forlorn ass around and go home, or at least keep it down in this hidden place until the vicious sun descended. Instead, he blinked the sweat out of his eyes, passed the scratchy arm of his suit jacket across his brow, regained his feet, and began to slowly continue up the path.

His mother's car was an old boxlike, black Plymouth that had splotches of rust on the body below its doors. He'd bought it for her at a police auction a couple of years ago, and though it didn't look like much, the engine refused to die. After he emerged from the undergrowth of the park and unlocked its door, he sensed a car slowing on the asphalt beside him. He glanced over his shoulder, expecting to see the two watchdog cops rolling up, but it was just some pretty lady in a small car with a lot of kids in it, her indicator on, waiting for the spot.

The sweat on the back of his neck stuck against the hot vinyl of the seat as he slid behind the wheel. He thought about getting out again and taking off his suit jacket, but then decided to hell with it. He turned the engine over, rolled the window down and pulled out.

Chapter Five

THOUGH THE EXIT INDICATED on the map his mother had given him was only the third from the Pennsylvania state line, it took thirty minutes to reach it. Coglin slowed at the end of the long, single-lane exit and stopped.

The intersection, like the rest of the mountain country he'd been passing through for the last twenty minutes, was completely desolate. He lifted the beer can between his knees, his third from the ringed six-pack in the wheel well and took a long pull.

He'd stopped to get gas at a station outside of Monroe, New York, about forty minutes before and, after a glance at the frosty cooler along the wall, ended up spontaneously adding a six-pack of tallboys to his bill. He lit a cigarette from one of the two packs he'd also purchased at the minimart, took a deep satisfying drag, relishing in his recently unearthed vice and consulted his map.

He looked up after a minute and surveyed the road before him. It was long and lonely and as he watched the boughs of the trees on both sides started swaying slightly back and forth like huge waving hands. He took another sip of beer, warm and metallic tasting now, put on his clicker and made the turn.

The road was treacherous. Yellow-and-black arrow signs that warned of dangerous curves sprung up every few hundred yards off the corkscrew road like some strange, local species of tree. The infrequent houses he passed were small, no more than bungalows. There seemed to be an inordinate amount of cars in each dirt driveway, but he didn't see any people. On a straightaway, his headlights flashed briefly on an old dumptruck, immense and orange, that sat on a patch of roadside grass with a FOR SALE sign on its windshield. Coglin blinked his eyes and shook his head.

"Funny, I'm looking for a forty-year-old dump truck, too," he said out loud, "but wouldn't you know? It's gotta be green."

Soon the grade of the route began to increase dramatically. The two-lane road narrowed even more, the canopy and thickset trunks of the trees on each side like the roof and walls of some misplaced tunnel.

It was another twenty minutes before he found the turnoff for his uncle's place. He stopped to check one of the roadside mailboxes and realized he'd gone too far, so he made a U-turn. He had to get out of the car and use his headlights to make out his uncle's address scratched inexpertly on a rusted mailbox. The dirt road beside it wound down among dark trees into a type of hollow, but there was no house in sight.

He got back into the car and pulled it onto the rutted drive, his headlights probing the thick overgrowth. He rode the brakes hard on the way down, thinking he might rip a tire on a jutting rock, but it was surprisingly smooth. Twenty yards down, the path turned sharply into the trees to the left and leveled. Coglin stopped in the clearing before a trailer.

A shoebox-shaped structure of once white aluminum with cinderblock stairs before a low door in its exact middle. How they'd gotten it down here was a mystery. Yellow light burned in its small windows. Against the surrounding blackness of the forest, the illumination seemed like fires set far back in a cave. To the side of the clearing, there were two parked cars: a jacked up pickup, and a small, late-model Toyota or Hyundai.

Did his uncle collect cars? Coglin wondered, lifting his beer. Maybe he was having company.

The clacking that went off in his left ear a moment later made him drop his beer.

He recoiled to his right toward the passenger seat, away from the sound. He turned, flinching, toward the window. The enormous, wide, black single bore of a shotgun rested on the ledge of his open window, a large silhouette behind it. He threw his hands up.

"Wait! Don't shoot! I'm looking for my uncle!" finally spilled from his mouth. "Aidan O'Donnell. I'm looking for my uncle, Aidan!"

The faceless form holding the shotgun remained silent. Coglin could hear the beer he'd dropped hissing on the carpet of the passenger side foot well.

"Private property," the menacing shape finally said.

The voice was rough, rasping. Coglin was praying it would have an Irish accent, but it was American. Southern. Backwoods.

"My fault," Coglin managed to get out. "I'm sorry. Just let me get turned around, I'll get outta here, OK?"

He was bobbing as he spoke, trying to move his head away from the enormous maw of the gun, but the barrel shifted with him, trained right in the middle of his head.

"It's alright, Travis," another voice said. Coglin recognized the Irish accent immediately, the interrogative inflection at the end. His mother's Northern Irish accent had dulled considerably in the years since she'd left Belfast, but in times of anger, he would hear the same exact, incredibly harsh yet somehow musical tone.

The shotgun still hadn't moved.

"I said it's alright, Travis," sang the Irish voice again. "Go back on in."

The gun stayed for a moment more and then retreated reluctantly into the dark. The man with the shotgun stepped into the glow of the headlights. Long-haired and bearded, wearing camouflage pants and a black T-shirt with designs down its long sleeves. Coglin watched him swing the shotgun expertly down in front of him as he climbed the cinderblock stairs, opened the small trailer door, and stepped in.

Coglin turned as the interior light of the car went on and the passenger door swung open.

Chapter Six

AS HIS HEART BATTERED the inside of his chest and his mind spun, trying to reconcile the fact that he wasn't going to be shot and buried in the middle of nowhere, Coglin looked over his long-lost relative.

Still stocky with the same shoulder-length thick, black hair, Aidan looked impossibly like he was still in his early forties though a decade and a half had passed since Coglin had first met him. The lines cut in the leathery surface of his weather-beaten face were a little deeper, but the strange, faded blue eyes that sparkled out from his stony visage were no different. The pale, almost metallic light in them seemed to dance as he smiled. He extended a wide hand in a slow, cordial gesture.

"John," the Irishman said in the confident singsong of his accent. "How the fuck ya been, kid? Thanks for coming out."

Coglin shook the wide hand reflexively, released it.

A moth fluttered through Coglin's window and began battering itself against the dome light. His uncle shut his door with a short, violent yank and the light went out.

"Some guard dog you got there," Coglin said, finally recovering.

Aidan laughed.

"Aye," he said, bending and righting Coglin's displaced beer can and handing it back. "Tends to run a little paranoid, Travis does. How's Katie?"

Coglin leaned back and sipped at the warm beer. There was only a swallow left. He killed it and chucked it in the back.

"Katie's doin' alright," he said. "Considering the circumstances, Mom's doin' alright. Pass me another one, would ya? Have one. There's a couple somewhere there under your seat."

His uncle fished them out, crunched the pop-tops, and handed one to Coglin.

Coglin tipped his beer to his uncle's.

"To family," he said awkwardly.

The Irishman drank, wiped his mouth with his free hand.

"So," his uncle said. "Whatcha lookin' at with your situation? Twenty to?"

"Plead manslaughter." Coglin said, putting the can to his forehead. "Maybe ten."

"Katie wrote you didn't do it. That it was self-defense."

Coglin drank.

"Katie was right," he said.

Coglin took out his cigarettes and offered them. His uncle nodded his thanks and slid one out of the pack. Coglin lit them both. They smoked.

"State?" Aidan asked.

"State," Coglin said.

"They'll come after ya," Aidan said.

"I figured."

Aidan took a drag of his cigarette and tapped the plastic dashboard loudly with his free hand.

"Keep your eyes open," he said. His voice was soft, barely a whisper, but there was an intensity in it that made Coglin lean in toward him.

"They'll do it right quick when you hit population. Cop is bad enough. The racial thing twice so. They'll come at you hard right in the beginning when they figure you're too stunned to know what's going on. Feign like you're scared won't be too hard. But be ready, first one you have to make an example out of. Might be better if he lives."

Aidan nodded to himself. He was looking off into the trees beyond the windshield, mentally weighing the matter.

"I'd take his eyes," he said.

"For real?" Coglin said, sitting up.

Aidan looked at him. He took a drink from the can and shook his head at Coglin slowly.

"My second day," he said, "I was approached by an individual who informed me that he liked me in a romantic way. He was going to have sex with me with or without my consent, he said, but it would be easier on both of us if I agreed. I said I'd let him know. This prisoner was very large. I'd been watchin' the way things worked, how the race gangs looked after one another, so I walked across the yard and approached the head of the white one with the request to join. I told him my dilemma.

"His response was brief. He pulled out a butcher knife from somewhere inside his coveralls, put it in my hand and told me to either kill the motherfucker or punk out. My choice. Luckily, my suitor at the other end of the yard didn't think he'd be getting my answer back so soon, so I managed to sneak up on him."

His uncle paused. Took a drag of his cigarette.

"I missed his heart by an inch," he said. "But it ended the courtship. That's jail. Except in your case, with your jacket, it'll be more like kill the ten motherfuckers or punk out. If you were nobody, you could probably stay out of the radar. But you're not nobody. You're a fuckin' star. Let no slight go unanswered is my advice. And," his uncle said, "take the first one's eyes."

Coglin opened his mouth and closed it. He knew his uncle was going to say something like this. He'd transported prisoners to Riker's before. Jail was a zoo, only with all the animals in one cage. No telling what happens to the unlucky keeper who falls in. He looked out at the trailer.

"Not that it's any of my business," Coglin said. "But if jail's so bad, why you rooming with ol' Double Barrel?"

Aidan looked at him. "You're right," he said. "It isn't any of your business."

Coglin nodded.

"So besides all this shit," Aidan said with a grin, "what have you been doin' since the last time I saw ya? That punk kid and his father leave you alone like I told them to?"

Coglin smiled.

"I guess they didn't feel like getting whacked. They steered pretty clear away," Coglin said.

"You've been a cop for how long? Four years or something?" Aidan said.

"Five," Coglin said. "In the carpenters before that. You know the drill."

"Fuckin' Sheetrock," Aidan said. "If I never have to smell that dust again, I'll die a happy man. Didn't take too kindly to it yourself, did ya?"

"Can't say that I did," Coglin said. "Maybe if I had, I wouldn't be in so much trouble now."

"You?" Aidan said, grinning. "Don't worry. You would've found some way or another to fuck up."

"Wow, that's really comforting," Coglin said. "Makes my trip out here seem really worthwhile."

"One thing I think I told you a long time ago, Johnnyboy," Aidan said, "feeling sorry for yourself is a shitty luxury to allow yourself in normal circumstances. It'll be lethal where you're headed."

Coglin finished his beer and dropped it. Did he honestly need to hear this crap? Like he didn't fully realize the fucking mess he was in. He needed to hear lectures about it from his dear old faith-and-begorrah Irish uncle?

Fuck that, he thought, extending his hand.

"Well, Aidan. Unc. It was nice seeing you. Even with almost getting my head blown off. I appreciate you sittin' down to talk with me. I gotta get back."

Aidan let Coglin's hand hang in the air as he studied him. He flicked his own cigarette out the open window and tapped a finger to his mouth as if mulling something over. He stopped and checked his watch in the dashboard light.

"Not so fast," he said. "You have some time. Why don't you come out for a proper drink? A farewell drink."

Coglin checked the clock on his beeper. It was after nine. When he pressed the button for beeps, it said: OUT OF RANGE. *Thank god,* he thought.

"Nah, that's alright," Coglin said, looking up. "It's late. Besides, you got company."

"Who? Oh, 'Double Barrel'? Fuck Double Barrel."

"Nah," Coglin said. "It's OK."

"Gimme a fuckin' break," Aidan said. "I'll lay off the ball bustin', alright. I'm sorry. What the fuck am I thinking? You don't need to hear that. OK? Scout's honor."

In the dark, his uncle's metal-colored eyes again seemed to gleam. Coglin realized that the man was smiling.

"Let your old Uncle Aidan buy you a fuckin' drink," he said. "Maybe when we come back we'll smoke a little weed and watch *Planet of the Apes.*"

Coglin succumbed to the smile that forced its way onto his face.

"You should have said that before," he said. "Twist my arm."

Chapter Seven

COGLIN WAITED IN THE FRONT SEAT of the Plymouth while his uncle got out and went into the trailer. There were other guests beside Travis, his uncle had admitted, and he needed a chance to explain things to them before he introduced Coglin. After a minute or two, there were some loud voices he couldn't decipher, and then his uncle reappeared in the low doorway and waved at Coglin to come in.

He looked at his uncle through the windshield, debating whether or not to just put it in reverse. Wasn't he in enough trouble without all this? Driving drunk, getting guns pointed in his face. He'd already gotten what he'd come for, received his uncle's predictably grim advice. Blind the first person who messes with you, check. Instead of all this bullshit, he should be on the phone right now to his lawyer begging him to cut some sort of deal with the DA.

He found himself cutting the engine.

When he mounted the concrete block steps, his uncle, still standing in the door, put his arm around his shoulder and ushered him in. The trailer seemed bigger inside. A sizeable kitchen with a table sat to the right of the front door, and there was a living room with a couch and a TV to the left.

Travis was on the couch, his shotgun nowhere to be found. A skinny young Hispanic kid with dyed blond hair slouched on the couch beside Travis, and a pretty woman in her late twenties sat at the kitchen table. The woman was small and tan and had a short bob of dark brown hair and green eyes. She tapped the tabletop with a plastic lighter, took out a cigarette and lit it.

"John," his uncle said, gesturing toward his companions, "this is everybody. Everybody, this is my nephew, John."

Travis snorted and looked down at the floor. With the trailer light illuminating his weather-beaten face, Coglin could see that he was older than he'd first gauged him. Late forties, early fifties maybe. What Coglin had thought were sleeves, he could see now, were tattoos: scantily clad women hugging the huge quadriceps of sword-wielding barbarians, skulls gazing out through flames, an eight ball, an ace of spades. His black army boots, Coglin noted with unaccountable unease, held a high, glossy shine.

The gold in the Hispanic kid's mouth flashed briefly as he smiled at Coglin. It matched the copious amount he wore at his throat, his wrists, his fingers. The woman in the kitchen silently smoked her cigarette. Sitting away from the two rough looking men, she looked like a princess captured by trolls.

Coglin couldn't pinpoint what the unlikely group reminded him of. Some type of circus sideshow or something: sword swallowers, fire-eaters. Maybe the girl would flip out of her seat in a second and start walking on her hands. His uncle would put on a top hat, pull a megaphone out from behind the couch.

Shoulda backed out, Coglin mentally chastised himself. *Shoulda put that fucker in reverse while he'd had the chance.*

The bleach-blond Hispanic nudged Travis in the ribs with a sharp elbow.

"Fuck, yo," he said. "I smell bacon."

He turned to Coglin.

"Hey, Officer. How you doin' tonight? Arigh'?"

The girl in the kitchen stared levelly at Coglin with her big eyes. His uncle regarded him with a quizzical interest, waiting for Coglin's response.

Coglin looked back at the kid sympathetically. He could almost feel the familiar pull of the gear and Kevlar on his body as he slipped into cop mode. It was like flicking on a switch. People couldn't help but fuck with him tonight, could they? He smiled at the youth and beamed a hard look dead center into his pupils.

"Doin' great, Mr. T," he said. "How you feelin'?"

The kid scowled as Aidan laughed.

"Dog be lookin' familiar," the kid said.

"He's the cop from TV, you moron," Travis said in his clipped drawl. "One on trial, ain't he, O'Donnell?"

Aidan shrugged his shoulders. He went into the kitchen and took down a bottle of scotch and a couple of plastic glasses from a cabinet and placed them on the table.

"Ho shit!" the kid said, his mouth opening as he looked at Coglin more closely.

"Go Bronx!" he said. "Shot ma dog down! No justice, no peace. People oughta string your ass up!"

Coglin's smile widened.

"Think so, huh? TV happen to mention your boy was beatin' on an old man? Coulda been your fucking *abuelo.* How he liked to knock people out and piss on 'em?"

"Tssst," the kid said as he shook his head slowly. "Didn't say nothin' like that, pig."

"No, huh?" Coglin said, feeling his anger bubble up. Everyone so sure at what happened because some asshole reporter had said so.

"You seem pretty sure about the whole thing. There was a whole bunch of punks there when I showed up. Maybe you were one of them. Maybe we could call you as a witness."

"No, mothafucka," the kid said, his voice turning instantly cold. "You know I wasn't there because I was, it woulda been your ass under the train."

Coglin nodded.

"Think so?" he said.

"I know so, cop," the kid said. His glassy brown eyes were glaring at him now. "So do you."

"Well, I know something, peroxide," Coglin said, unbuttoning his jacket casually. "If I'd chucked you off the platform, you wouldn't have had to worry about the train so much as the fall to the street, because your skinny ass would've fallen through the space in the track."

Everybody laughed at that, even the girl in the kitchen.

The kid was instantly off the couch, fists at the ends of his condor-wing-length arms clenched.

"Sit your fuckin' ass down!" Aidan barked.

"I don't give a fuck he family, Irish."

"Don't like the taste of what you dish out, Angel," Aidan said tightly, "then keep yer mouth the fuck shut."

The young Hispanic kept his stare trained at Coglin. Then he lowered his gaze in the silence and sat.

Coglin took out a cigarette and lit it. He moved into the kitchen and sat down opposite the girl.

The two on the couch were, without a doubt, criminals,

prison pals of his uncle, he thought. But the girl seemed normal. *Hell, better than normal,* Coglin thought, looking her over. He thought about the shotgun Travis had stuck in his ear. Out on night patrol or some insanity. *Drugs,* he concluded. Out here in the middle of nowhere. Something with drugs. Had to be.

What he had yet to figure was how he fit in. His uncle might have been a crook, but he'd done him a good turn when he was a kid. Had given a fuck about him. Would he wait a decade until Coglin was facing the harshest shit of his life only to somehow fuck with him? He didn't know, but he didn't think so.

Like how you didn't think they'd go through with the prosecution? he thought. *Like how you didn't think the jury would convict?*

True, his judgement wasn't exactly infallible these days, now was it. Still, what was the alternative? Drive home and go to bed early for jail?

He stared into the woman's eyes as his uncle placed a cup down in front of him and poured in a measure of Blue Label scotch. The amber of it matched the little flecks in the green of the woman's eyes.

Amber waves of grain, he thought as she looked away.

Coglin took a long sip.

"Now," Aidan said, "We're going to take my nephew here out for a little farewell celebration up the road."

It sounded more like a demand than a suggestion.

Coglin raised his glass at his uncle. As he winked back at him, he searched his dark Irish, worn features for some trait they shared, but after a moment, came up empty. Coglin shrugged and tilted his head back. He closed his eyes and drank.

Chapter Eight

THEY DECIDED TO TAKE TWO CARS. He and his uncle and the girl took her Hyundai, Travis and Angel following in the pickup. His uncle had explained that he and the two other men had someplace to go to later straight from the bar, so the girl could drive him back to get his car. Coglin shrugged again from the backseat.

You're not the only one who's gotta be someplace, Unc, he thought, stretching out in the backseat. Through the side window, he could see stars, actual stars, burning pinpricks high and bright above the dark of the trees.

He watched the girl drive. Her compact was a manual, and he watched as she slid the shift in and out of gear effortlessly, flawlessly, not one time riding the clutch. She spun a little dirt at the top of the drive by the road, but Coglin thought she'd done it on purpose, kicked up a little dust for Travis and Angel to eat.

"Lisa's from the city, too, aren'tcha, Lees," his uncle said after a little while.

"Small fuckin' world," Coglin said. He took out his cigarettes. *It felt good riding,* he thought, lighting one. Comfortable, cruising along, buzzing from the beers, the scotch. He leaned back, pretending he was a teenager again, hangin' out with his friends, goin' out.

"Where abouts?" he said.

"Brooklyn," she said.

Coglin nodded. She reminded him of the dangerously pretty Italian girls he'd see sitting on the hoods of their boyfriends' IROCs in the parking lots of high school dances when he was a kid. Except she didn't wear the makeup and high hair anymore, and it had been a long time since she needed someone to drive her around.

"How about you?" she said.

"Bronx," Coglin said.

"My husband used to take me out to eat on Arthur Avenue," she said.

Husband, Coglin thought. He leaned forward slightly to look for a ring on her hand, but the seat blocked his view.

"Best cannoli in the city," he said.

She glanced at him in the rearview mirror.

"Can I ask you a question?" she said.

"Fire away."

"If you're in so much trouble, why are you all the way out here? Don't you have to be in court tomorrow?"

"Well," Coglin said. "I came out to see my uncle here. Have a kind of reunion. I don't know. I needed to take a ride. Or in other words, I guess you could say I'm basically through givin' a fuck."

She laughed.

"Basically, huh?" she said.

"Yep," Coglin said. He rolled down the window. "I'm all done."

"How about you?" he said. "Bensonhurst is a little ways off from here, isn't it?"

She smiled in the mirror.

"Maybe I'm into older men," she said, nudging Aidan as she changed gears.

"Oh, you're a nurse," Coglin said. "An RN or an LLRN? I always get those two mixed up."

She began laughing.

"Fuck ya both," Aidan said.

Ten minutes later, they pulled into the near-empty gravel parking lot of a roadhouse sheathed in black tarpaper. If he had to gauge the present year by the beat-up American pickups and cars scattered about the lot, he would have called it at 1986. The first strains of Lynyrd Skynyrd's "Sweet Home Alabama" began to blare from somewhere inside.

"Nice," Lisa said to Aidan. "Real classy. Now you're sure we're allowed to just walk in? There's gotta be a list at the door."

She turned to Aidan, her face humorless.

"I mean, when are you gonna gimme a break already with this bullshit, O'Donnell? Time is running out. This is not part of the plan."

Plan? Coglin thought.

"Lisa," Aidan said, raising a finger, "like I told you before. You'll have to trust me."

"Trust you?" she said.

Not even curious, Coglin thought, tugging at the doorlatch.

"I'm going inside," he said.

"No, that's OK," Lisa said angrily as she opened the door and got out. "Let's all go in and get rip-roaring drunk."

Aidan turned, watching her storm off toward the bar. He winked at Coglin.

"If she insists," he said.

Angel and Travis were already waiting for them in the gravel before the establishment's battered wood door. Inside was very dark and smoky and cool. Several rough looking, bearded men lined the old, gray wooden bar on the left-hand wall. They stared with unanimous bald shock at their party as they stepped by.

They sat at a rear booth beyond a pool table crowded with more tattered looking men. There was an open space in front of the booth that had Christmas lights stapled to the thick, wooden beams above. The dance floor, Coglin surmised. Lynyrd Skynyrd died and some country rock song started up on the jukebox in a jangle of electric guitars. The place smelled. A strong stench that Coglin couldn't quite place: beer, tobacco, sweat and something sharp and acrid, used to tan hides maybe. Lisa must have smelled it, too, because she was wrinkling her nose. Angel had his shirt up around his face.

"Travis, wha's that smell?" he said. "These hicks bring their sheep out on a date here before they fuck them or wha'?"

"Why don't you get your Spanglish-speakin' ass up there and ask them, Angel. I'm sure those boys be more than happy to let you know."

Coglin stood.

"Beers?" he asked.

"No, no. We're taking you out," Aidan said, starting to rise.

"I got this round," Coglin said, walking off.

Coglin threaded a careful path through the throng of men at the pool table and stepped into a space at the bar. The bartender appeared before him.

"Five Budweisers," Coglin said.

The bartender stood unmoving for a moment as if he hadn't

heard him. He was old and bald and wore wire-rimmed glasses. He pushed the glasses up on his nose with his thumb and peered into Coglin's face, studying him.

"Do I know you?" the bartender said.

Coglin looked back at him warily. The old man was wearing a clean white apron over a cleaner starched white shirt, and there was a pale spot below the little hair he had at his temples as if he'd just gotten it cut. He seemed strangely overdressed, too well groomed for the rundown place.

"Don't think so," Coglin said. He took a twenty out of his wallet and laid it on the bar. "Five Buds," he repeated.

The bartender smirked at him before stepping back. He slid open a cooler and lifted out a bottle. He popped its top with a tiny, crisp explosion on the underside of the old bar and placed it in front of Coglin. He did this five times. By the time he'd finished, the puzzlement had left his features.

"You're that cop who shot the nigger, ain't ye?" he said softly with a wink.

Coglin looked down. He recalled what the black cabdriver had said to him earlier that morning, about how he should think of him as he got the injection. Of these two stomach-churning confidences, Coglin decided he preferred the first. What was up with the geezer's accent? It didn't seem even southern really. More European, German maybe, or Dutch. Backwoods Amish Nazi, he thought.

"Don't know what the fuck you're talking about," Coglin said.

"Now, now," the bartender said. "I ain't gonna bother you."

He reached out quickly across the bar and grasped Coglin's hand firmly and began shaking it.

"I aim to thank you for strikin' a blow," he said, leaning his face in toward Coglin's. Coglin tried to pull away, but the hand that grasped his was stronger than he thought.

"For preservin' the race," the old man said. "Preservin' the intention of God."

Coglin finally ripped his hand away and backed up a step, scrubbing his palm on his pantleg as if it were contaminated.

"Fuckin' hands off me," he said.

"It's OK," the bartender chastised softly. "You're among friends."

The bartender brushed the twenty on the bar back at Coglin with his skeletal hand.

"On me," he said. "On the house."

Coglin immediately clattered the five bottles together in both hands and turned around, leaving the money where it lay.

He managed to get the drinks back through the crowd to the booth without dropping one. He placed them down in the center of the worn, wooden table, grabbed one and sat down beside his uncle.

Aidan picked up a beer and lifted it to the weak flash of the cheap, tiny lights above.

"John," he said. "Good luck. We'll miss ya."

Coglin drank. He'd been thinking about not drinking it on account of what the evil old motherfucker had said, but he paid for it.

They drank their beers and Aidan went up and returned with a bottle of scotch and some shot glasses. Coglin did a shot and poured another immediately after. He remembered going out with Karen and her friends from work in the neighborhood around their Kips Bay apartment. The reproachful looks she'd shoot across the table at him if he had a third glass of wine, embarrassing her. The flashes of surprise that would go across their soft-office-fat faces when she'd tell them what he did for a living.

Fuck her and her shiny, happy asshole work friends, he thought, lifting the glass to his lips. Finally, fuck them all and let them die. He knocked it back. His uncle clapped him consolingly on the shoulder.

They sat and drank. His uncle tried to cajole him into teaming up against the bedraggled locals at pool, but he declined.

"Just leave the bottle," Coglin said. "I'll be fine."

Angel took up the offer. He and Aidan rose. Coglin looked over at the girl. She stood as well.

"I gotta make a phone call," she said.

Coglin joined the rest of the bar in watching her walk off. When he glanced across the table at Travis, his eyes were drawn to the colorful multitude of tattoos on his arms. They reminded him of something he couldn't place. How many hours had gone into painting them? he thought. A month's worth? A year's? There was one on the front of the man's left forearm that Coglin recognized. He pointed at it.

"Third Marines," Coglin said. "You were a marine?"

"*Am* a marine," Travis said forcefully. "Third Marine Recon. Sixty-eight, sixty-nine Vietnam."

"Get outta here," Coglin said. "My father was in the Second Marines. He got killed outside of Quang Tri during the Tet Offensive. Or so they told us."

Travis peered at him for a long moment, reassessing.

"Quang Tri? No shit?" he said.

"That's what it said on the paper they sent," Coglin said.

"Was he on a firebase?" Travis asked.

"Echo," Coglin said, nodding. "Firebase Echo."

"Ho-lee fuck," Travis said. "That can't be. I was there once."

Coglin felt a brush of cold up his spine.

"Firebase Echo," Travis said. "We had to come back through there one time. What was your dad's name?"

"Timothy," Coglin said. "Timothy Coglin."

"Have a nickname?" Travis said. "Everybody had nick-names."

Coglin shook his head.

"I don't know."

"How old was he?"

"Nineteen."

"Hell, him and everybody else," Travis said. He lit a cigarette with a silver Zippo lighter. The loud, oiled snap and click of it like something dangerous, Coglin thought, a blade flicking open, the loading of a gun. The Southerner's eyes were unreadable, seemingly colorless in the yellowed glow of its flame. He snapped it shut.

"You musta been real little when he died," he said.

"Wasn't even born yet," Coglin said.

The Southerner's cigarette pulsed in the dark.

"Get out!"

"It's true," Coglin said. "My mom was pregnant before he left, and he never came back."

"Died before you were born," Travis said. "That's something else altogether."

Coglin watched the veteran closely. When he was fourteen, he'd seen movies about Vietnam, read books, made an attempt to reconcile his father's death, but he'd never spoken to any veter-ans, too awed by the enormity of what they'd done to bring up so personal a subject. Now here was someone who'd actually been where his father had been. Maybe seen him months or weeks before his death.

"What was it like?" Coglin said solemnly. "Firebase Echo. It's just a name to me."

Travis poured himself a shot, sipped it.

"Hmm," he said. "Firebase was like a fort they'd build out in the middle of the jungle. Foxholes, sandbags, barbed wire. There wasn't no front to the war, so they'd set up firebases as a type of target to draw out the enemy. Once they came out, they'd call in air support on them."

Travis took a drag of his cigarette. The jukebox was in between songs and in the silence, pool balls clacked together like a sudden pistol shot.

"Firebase was like a worm on the end of a hook," Travis continued. "Seen one get overrun one time. We were comin' back in from a long-range patrol and got stuck behind an NVA regiment that was in a pitched battle with some company in the Third Infantry. There was only eight on our team, with the enemy all around us, so all we could do was hunker down and watch them get pounded. They were heavily outnumbered and the NVA came through the wire.

"Five minutes later, this huge, fat-assed motherfucker of a twin-bladed Chinook comes in low over the trees like Dumbo the elephant. It was just a pop-up target. You could see the tracers just straight on licking into it from all around. I don't know what kinda men were on that chopper, but they were some kind, because they put that fat bird down on the top of the hill as pretty as you please, opened up its belly and started hauling in the wounded and the rest. They didn't have time to close the belly of that thing up with the heavy fire, so they just pulled up.

"Wouldn't you know it, though, that a gook—one lousy gook—in a tree beside the landing zone just drops down and fires an RPG dead right up into the open bottom of the thing."

Travis held up his glass without drinking. Though he was looking directly at Coglin, it seemed he was seeing something else, some mesmerizing event occurring presently in the distance.

"I'll never forget the flash of light that came from the windows of that aircraft, like somebody taking a picture inside a house. Then you could see that the helicopter wasn't rising anymore, just struggling there, trying desperately to stay aloft, and then it started to go over.

"As it fell, there was a whine from the helicopter that we could hear from where we were hiding. The front tipped completely up like a rocket about to launch, and people started sliding out the back, the living and the dying and the dead falling without a sound to the earth below. Then it just slid over to the right, away from the LZ, and exploded.

"It was a thing to see. I seen the film of the Hindenburg crashing, and it reminded me of that. The slowness of it, like something that seemed you could reach out and stop with your hand, but you just couldn't. I talked to an army door gunner later about what I seen, and he explained that the chopper had risen up and dumped the people in an effort to save them."

Travis stopped suddenly. His tattooed form seemed somewhat formal now, somber. He was sweating despite the cool. He finished his drink and shook his head.

"Talking my fool head off," he said. He poured another shot for himself and reached the bottle over and filled Coglin's glass.

"To your old man," Travis said, raising his cup. "For giving his full measure."

Coglin lifted his shot glass. It seemed suddenly heavy. He clicked it to Travis's and drank.

They sat in the darkness. Coglin had always thought of the death of his father in war as something somewhat glorious, heroic. But sitting now in the wake of Travis's story, he caught, for the first time, an inkling of how truly horrible it must've been. Was death itself a relief? he thought suddenly. What horror. And for what?

For answering his draft notice, Coglin thought, for doing what they told him.

So it was, came a snatch of something to him, scripture maybe, some quote. *So it shall be again.*

"How do know my uncle?" Coglin said.

Travis sat back suddenly, his sense of decorum dissipating with his ramrod posture.

"See, now you're starting to sound like a cop."

Coglin shook his head.

"What do you think? I'm investigating you guys? I'm goin' to jail tomorrow. Aidan fuckin' invited me."

"So you say," Travis said. A tension gripped the man, taut lines at his temples, new fault lines beneath the colored ink of his arms.

"Tell me, why would anyone want to be a cop anyway? Like to tell a motherfucker what to do, like your better than them or something? You think you're fuckin' better than me?"

Coglin looked at the veteran. It was a valid question. One, as he thought on it now, he'd never given too much consideration. Why had he become a cop?

He'd always thought the reason was that he'd been a carpenter, and one day he'd looked around at the hardworking, dusty men drinking their lunch beside him and decided it wasn't enough, but maybe it wasn't as simple as that.

The only motivation he could extract from memory was the way he'd been forced to deal with the street toughs at his high school when he moved into the city as a teenager. How he'd fought, faced his fear, became a man. He'd been proud of himself for that. Maybe in some way, that's what he was looking for when he found himself taking the cop test. Try to get back that feeling of pride that slapping up Sheetrock just didn't offer.

He thought about the last six months. The methodical way

in which his life had been ripped apart, piece by agonizing piece.

He looked at Travis sitting there, at his cold eyes boring through the smoky dimness between them.

"Nah, I'm not better than you," Coglin said finally. He drank some scotch this time, not even bothering to wash it back. "I'm just dumber."

Angel came back and sat down. On the other side of the dance floor, Aidan hovered over the pool table setting up the break, clacking the bright balls together in the plastic triangle.

"Shitty hillbilly sticks all crooked," Angel complained. "I'm goin' outside for a smoke. You comin', redneck?"

Travis took his heavy gaze off Coglin, placed it on Angel and shook his head.

"Don't let none of the locals see you smokin' that funky shit neither. We don't want the sheriff payin' us a visit."

Angel flashed his gold smile.

"What you think? I'm stupid?"

"I won't even answer that," Travis said, watching the kid walk off.

"Killed his parents," Travis said.

"What was that?" Coglin said, leaning forward.

Travis indicated the departing youth with a tilt of his chin.

"His parents," he said loudly. "He killed them both. His old man was a welterweight ranked, so he says. Seemed daddy mistook *madre* for a heavy bag come Friday nights after a few *cervezas.* Angel waited until he was fourteen before he stepped in and called the perpetual bout with the .38 dad kept in his sock drawer. Thing was, bullet didn't stop in daddy's heart, as black and hard as it was. The round passed on through, ricocheted off the man's spine, and caught Angel's beloved mother, standing behind him, in the eye. Whataya think of that?"

Coglin shrugged. "Don't know," he said honestly. "That's fucked up."

"Surely is. Whatever happens, don't go callin' him Ricochet Rabbit."

"Ricochet Rabbit," Coglin said. "That's really fucked up."

"No, I'm serious. Don't call him that," Travis said. "Some joker did one time and the next thing, they found him dead near the showers, shanked about eighty-seven times."

Coglin nodded slowly.

Travis laughed.

"Nope, not the regular Thursday night crowd for you tonight, Officer," Travis said. "But you're not too proud to hang with killers, are ya? Seeing as you're one yourself and all."

Coglin looked down at the tabletop. He put a thumb to the dark liquid puddled in the darkened grain of the wood.

"Like I said before," Coglin said. He could feel the alcohol coming on him, the vague weight of it not full yet but getting there, like a large back-ordered delivery due to arrive soon. He was out of drinking practice and already out of his league.

"I'm no better than you or anyone," he said.

Across the room, Lisa was returning from her phone call. Some fat, toothless goon at the bar reached out and pulled her toward him, whispering something in her ear. Instead of trying to knee him in the balls like Coglin thought she would, she laid her slim hand on his hairy arm and looked into his face, smiling. She said something into his ear, and he laughed and let her go.

"How about her?" Coglin asked Travis, as he watched her approaching them. "She ever kill anybody?"

Travis laughed.

"Not yet," he said, as Lisa sat down next to him.

Coglin looked away from her to where his uncle was playing pool. His skill was obvious. The middle-aged Irishman seemed to flow around the table, chalking his cue nimbly, his blue eyes intent on the lay of the game before him. He quickly ran his last four balls and called the eight ball in the top right-hand pocket with a point of his cue. It was a long shot, the eight halfway up the table and the cue down at the bottom. He chalked, bent and shot. The eight ball rolled, direct and slow, between two of his opponents and dropped softly in the called hole, a split second before the spinning, rebounding cue ball fell in the side.

Coglin watched as his uncle took some bills out of his wallet and handed them over to one of the rougher looking men. His uncle said something then, and the locals seemed still for a moment. Then the one he'd handed the bills to started laughing and the rest followed suit.

"Scratch," Lisa said as Aidan returned. "That's a good omen."

Aidan sat and lifted his beer.

"It was done on purpose, Lees," he said with a smile. "So I could sit back down here with the pretty likes of you."

"Me and your nephew tellin' war stories, O'Donnell," Travis said. "Why don't you share one with us, ya goddamned terrorist."

Coglin looked over at his uncle smiling, expectant.

Aidan poured himself a shot. He looked down at the cup solemnly as if there was something special in it. Like a celebrant at mass. He drank.

"Nothing to share," he said, shrugging his shoulders.

Travis elbowed Coglin in the ribs.

"Sure, crazy Irish fucker," he said, "anything you say."

Coglin leaned back.

Just then, the front door of the establishment opened and a young, rough looking tattooed man with a completely shaved head entered. Aidan and Travis exchanged a long glance. Aidan nodded finally. He looked at Coglin.

"OK, John," he said quickly. "We're gonna have to cut this party short now. Lees, you take him back. Oh, and tell Angel to come back in, would ya?"

Aidan stood with Coglin. He put an arm across his back.

"It was a pleasure seeing ya, Johnny, and I mean that, right."

Huh? Coglin thought. *That was it? Come out for a few drinks and see you later?* It seemed so anticlimatic. Whatever, he thought. He put an arm across his uncle's broad shoulders. He might've been long in the tooth, but he was a stocky little fucker still.

"I'm glad I came out," he said.

Aidan smiled grimly.

"You're gonna do fine, OK, boy? It'll be hard in the beginning, but you got balls. Where you're going that's all it's about. Tell Katie I said hi."

"You got it," Coglin said. "Thanks again, Aidan. Take care. Travis, thanks for the story and ah, for not blowing my head off."

The Southerner wiped at his long mustache with a hand and smiled.

"My pleasure," he said.

Lisa tapped Coglin on the shoulder.

"We leaving or what?" she said.

Coglin followed the girl across the lamely lit dance floor past the pool table. As they approached the bar, Lisa waved at the big man who'd grabbed her, and he gave her a little wave back, looking down at the floor shyly. The ragged men at the bar seemed less dangerous now, Coglin thought, passing by them. Sunburned and longhaired in their cut-off T-shirts and tie-dyed gimme caps, they looked like people who worked hard outdoors and didn't receive too much in exchange.

The lone exception was the skinhead, now ordering a drink at the end of the bar beside the door. Coglin looked at his shined combat boots and suspenders, the elaborate gothic letters tattooed on his thin chest beneath his tank top. The wiry youth squinted back at him with a confident hostility.

The old bartender over the skinhead's shoulder gave Coglin a patient, grandfatherly smile. For a second, the desire to hit the racist youth shot through Coglin like a deep hunger. He wanted to smash his mouth in and watch him fly back bleeding, knocking over barstools. Coglin's right hand clenched slowly into a fist as he neared. But then Lisa called to him from the open door, and he found himself moving forward, passing through the dark and smoke following her out into the night.

Chapter Nine

AFTER THE COOL OF THE BAR, the humid air in the dark parking lot felt viscous, clinging like a layer of lotion smeared on Coglin's exposed skin. She was a healthy woman, he concluded, following Lisa deeper into the lot toward her car, equally as solid and nice to look at from the back as the front.

"Don't you be checkin' out my Italian princess," said a voice off to his left. Coglin turned. Angel sat in the front of the parked pickup, cackling, blowing out smoke.

"You can relax yourself now, tough guy," Coglin said, walking toward him. "I'm outta here."

"Aidan said you goin' for a tumble?" the kid said. He seemed calmer now. The lids of his red eyes were half-closed, and he seemed almost friendly. The cab of the truck stunk like the inside of a bong.

"What it looks like," Coglin said.

The kid extended a fist out the window, a grave expression taking away his smile.

"Peace, man," he said in a quiet voice. "Wouldn't wish that shit even on you."

Coglin looked at the fist. He remembered Travis's tale. He thought of the little Spanish kid from half a year ago, the one in the caged window who'd directed him toward Ream. After a second, he tapped it with his own.

"'Preciate it," he said. "I think they need you inside."

The kid opened the door of the truck and stepped out.

"Here, take it," he said, offering the joint.

"Nah, I'm alright," Coglin said.

"You kiddin' me? I was you, I'd show up so high, they'd have to roll my shit in the van. I'd make the mo'fuckas carry me."

Coglin took the joint. Its pungent smoke was barely rising in the thick, heavy air, its noxious blue swirl just hovering.

Fuck it, he thought, raising it to his lips. No more random drug tests to worry about now.

Teenage wasteland, he thought, sucking smoke. Only teenage wasteland.

He could feel it immediately after the first toke. A lightness that spread quickly through his body, a hollowness from the back of his neck to his feet. His spine seemed to expand like a balloon. He wondered if it was laced. He dropped it to the dusty gravel.

When he looked up, Lisa was staring at him from the front seat of her idling car, waiting.

"Don't let me rush you," she said.

Coglin stepped carefully over to the car, opened the door, sat. He lost his balance and almost fell out when he leaned to shut the door, but he managed to catch himself. He slammed it shut.

"You weren't kidding about being through giving a fuck, were you?" Lisa said, pulling out.

"If you were me," Coglin said, bracing his hands on the dash, "take my word for it, neither would you."

Coglin looked at her, the fine side of her face in the dashboard light. She flicked on the A/C, pulled up her dark hair with a hand and turned her slim neck toward the vent. Coglin watched her without moving. She caught him watching and then shut off the A/C.

Coglin draped his head against the door frame as they drove, feeling the wind. It felt good not caring, as if everything still lay untouched before him, as if he hadn't fucked it all up yet. He could feel an exaggerated pull on his body whenever the car turned into a curve. With the warm wind, it reminded him of a carnival ride. He closed his eyes and could almost smell the sugar and grease from the fairway, the gasoline from the ride that threw him around and around.

He could feel himself nodding off, and he forced his eyes open. He turned on the radio. Dance music blasted. It was scratchy, the signal from the city radio station too weak to be picked up clearly all the way up here. He shut it off.

"Can I ask you a question?" he said. Even to him his voice sounded sleepy.

She smiled.

"Pretty wasted, huh?" she said.

"Do you remember a song when you were in high school that was like all the vowels?" he continued.

"What?" she said, looking over at him. "Are you awake?"

"Remember? 'A, E, AEIOU U U'?"

"'And sometimes Y,'" she sang. "Of course," she said, laughing. "It was a dance song."

"Yeah," he said, sitting up a little. "How about, 'All Night Passion'?"

She laughed again.

"They'd mix them both together. Toss in a little Chaka Khan. The strobe lights flashing on the gym floor. Oh, those were fun. Those were some fun times."

"Did you have high hair?"

"Oh, gawd," she said, speaking in thicker Brooklynese. "It was as high as a house. The makeup, the fingernails, the whole package. I was like the Guidette Queen."

"Did you have a boyfriend who said things like, 'feggedaboudit'?" Coglin said. "Mighta drove, oh, I don't know, a Monte Carlo maybe?"

"I had a husband like that," she said.

Coglin looked over at her with a grin.

"What happened?" he said with a smile. "He get whacked? Cement shoes?"

There was an extended beat of silence.

"As a matter of fact, yeah, he did," she finally said. "He was murdered four months ago in prison."

Good one, Einstein, he thought.

"Jesus, that's horrible," he said after a minute. "Murdered. I'm sorry. I'm an ass."

"Don't worry about it," she said. "How about you?" she said, changing the subject. "Married? Divorced?"

"I was gonna get married until all this . . . uh . . . legal trouble started, but I'm not anymore. My girl crapped out on me. Exit stage right."

Lisa frowned, nodded. She could sympathize. She grinned after a moment.

"Did she have high hair back in high school?" she said.

"No," Coglin said. "She was from Michigan. Her hair was low. She had very low hair."

They drove. Coglin could make out flowers among the roadside grass before the treeline. Keep on driving he thought. How he wanted that. Just pretend it all didn't happen and start fresh tomorrow, a clean slate. Wake up with just the rest of the summer and the open road before him, everything behind erased from memory.

"My uncle seems like a pretty nice guy," Coglin said. "He seem like a nice guy to you?"

"Sure, he's a sweetheart," Lisa said. "For a complete psychopath."

Coglin looked at her.

"Why the hell are you here?" he said finally. "The kid and the hick are prison buddies of my uncle, that's obvious. But how are you involved with them?"

"That's a long story," she said. She down shifted and Coglin was thrown toward her suddenly as she turned into his uncle's steep drive. She pulled to a stop in a plume of dust in the clearing before the trailer.

"And you know what? I don't think you have the time," she said.

He was still close to her. She was wearing a subtle scent, some type of flower, the hint of something delicate, clean and cool.

"I'll make some," he said.

He tried to lean in even closer. She put a hand on his chest.

"Thanks, Officer," she said. "But I don't think so."

She threw open her door and got out.

"Take care now," she said. "You want me to start your car for you or do you think you can manage it?"

Coglin got out on the other side and closed the door.

"Thanks, Lees," he said in his uncle's Irish accent. "But I think I can handle it from here."

He could hear her laughing as she walked off. He stood still smelling her, looking after her, trying to decide whether he should follow or not.

He took a slight step back to steady himself and his ass found the door of his mother's Plymouth. He opened it and sat.

Just watch her leave now, he thought. Don't ruin it. Take the image with him, a still life. *Pretty, black-haired woman in tight, faded jeans and a tank top walking off into the summer night.*

She turned back as he flicked on his lights. Then the screen door banged to a close and she was gone. He watched the light come on in the two windows. He glanced at St. Patrick on the dashboard. In the dark, he didn't look so saintly anymore, more sinister, an evil wizard with a wand.

"I know, Paddy," he said to it. "I know. My moves are double fuckin' smooth."

It took him a little time to get situated. Put key in ignition, turn engine over, click on seat belt. When he looked out again through the windshield, the quality of the light seemed to have changed. Whether it was the weed he'd smoked or the humidity or the light from the car itself or all three, he didn't know. The headlights seemed diffused, the trailer and trees beyond foggy and almost yellow, as if seen through thick liquid. He debated whether to leave or to wait and sober up, but it seemed the longer he sat, the more fucked up he became.

"I better get on the road and rush home, Paddy," he told the statue with a smile. "Before I pass the fuck out."

He lit a cigarette. He rolled down the windows and turned on the anemic A/C, hoping the cool air would keep his eyelids from closing. He was sober enough to realize the challenge it would be to get his car out of the hollow, but too drunk to decide not to try. He dropped it in reverse and the car jolted violently as it struck a tree. He put it in drive and turned furiously pulling it forward, frantically aiming his yellow headlights between the thin space in the trees.

It took him five minutes to get on the road. He'd made it up the hill, but the tires kept spinning in the dirt before the lip of the blacktop. He finally solved the problem in a rush of insight by putting the transmission into low and easing the car out.

He yelled and flicked his cigarette out the window as its forgotten tip burned the fingers of his left hand. He stopped the car a hundred yards up the road from his uncle's turnoff and turned it off completely to light another. He put the cigarette in his mouth, probing the end of it with his finger to ensure that it wasn't the filter. *Score,* he said, feeling the crumbly tobacco end, and he lit it up.

Drunk driving was easy, he thought, taking a deep drag. You just had to concentrate on the thing at hand.

He was just about to turn the ignition over again when he saw the headlights in his rear view mirror. He sat there, waiting for the car to pass so he wouldn't be tailgated the whole way down the mountain. The headlights got steadily bigger, brighter. Part of him hoped it was his uncle returning early, back to tell him to hang out a little longer. He smiled as the closing headlights seemed to slow by his uncle's turnoff. Then the headlights went out suddenly, and the now dark vehicle turned slowly into his uncle's drive.

Strange, Coglin thought. It hadn't looked like Travis's pickup, more like a van.

His uncle's business, a voice told him. *Shouldn't be concerned.*

He sat up a little straighter in his seat and rubbed at his face. He tried reasoning out why he was so bothered by the vehicle, but thinking was becoming steadily more difficult, like staying on a path that was quickly being covered by a thick fog.

The lights, he thought suddenly. Why the hell would somebody turn off their lights?

He thought of the girl down in the trailer by herself. Then he found himself searching desperately for the door latch. He finally grasped it, pulled the door open and stepped out onto the dark shoulder of the road.

Chapter Ten

HE MANAGED TO CLOSE the car door quietly and stood looking into the forest, trying to make out the trailer's lights, but he couldn't see anything. Through the blackness and trees, he could hear insects now, their soft, continually fluctuating chatter in the overgrowth like some alluring, diabolical whisper. He took a breath.

On summer nights at his grandfather's house, he remembered standing with the other neighborhood kids, staring at the darkening parkland just beyond the last house in the development. From the relative safety of their dead-end street, they'd look into its thick and ominous forest and dare each other to sleep there overnight. Neighborhood legend had it there was a duo of killers named Pimples and Slash who roamed the park after dark. And even if they didn't get you, everybody knew the satanic cult (who his next-door neighbor, Jimmy O'Leary, swore on his mother that he saw kill a chicken one night by the big rocks) would. No matter how much imaginary money was offered, no takers were ever found.

Pimples and Slash, he thought, nodding to himself in the dark. Anytime was a great time for a trip down memory lane, he supposed. If only he had his gun. Check that. Both of them, and several extra clips. Hey, why not his handcuffs and pepper spray? Fuck it. If only he had his cruiser and a partner and some back up. Ten–sixty-nine, Dispatch, he thought. Drunk and stoned officer needs assistance in Pennsylvania wilderness.

He squeezed his fists and closed his eyes. Then he opened them and reluctantly started walking down into the trees.

The slope of the forest floor was steep, and the undergrowth was thick. Coglin tried unsuccessfully to avoid the thorn bushes that caught and scratched at his socks and pant legs. He stepped on small, rotted logs so dry they seemed to burst underfoot, and he kept walking into invisible strands of cobwebs that stuck instantly to his sweat-filled face.

He kept his eyes trained rigidly off to his right for any sign of light, trying to ignore the vague, stoned terror brought on by the sight of the endless trunks of the dark, enveloping trees. It wasn't so much that he actually believed anyone was out there, just unsettled by even the tiny possibility. What if somebody stepped out behind that tree? Or that one? Or even more horrifying, both at once? What did you do then? What would you actually fuckin' do?

Coglin thought about his father. How the fuck had he managed? At nineteen, he'd been plopped down in the middle of a fucking jungle, an actual jungle with tigers and bugs and who knew what the fuck else. And a crafty enemy set intently on killing him or worse. He'd had only sixty-five days remaining on his tour when they got him. Coglin used to think how ironic it'd been that his father had almost gotten out. Now, he realized, looking out at the dark, the really fucking incredible thing about it was that he'd actually gotten through the first three hundred.

As I walk in the valley of the shadow of death, I shall fear no evil, Coglin thought, stepping forward. It was a snatch of psalm remembered from a Vietnam movie he'd seen once.

You are my rod and my staff, he thought, his breath laboring loudly in his ears.

My salvation. My cup runneth over.

His pants caught again on some pricker bushes. He ripped the fabric free, scratching his leg in the process. He walked on.

Mercy shall follow me all the days of my life, he prayed softly to himself, *and I shall dwell in the house of the Lord forever.*

He was just about to decide he was lost and turn back when he spotted some illumination far ahead between the tree trunks. He stopped stock still, thinking at first that it was a small candle. Then he slowly began inching forward and he could make out the window of the trailer. After couple of minutes at a crouched crawl, Coglin spied the rest of the trailer and the van parked sideways behind Lisa's car, blocking it in.

A moment later, he sensed a flash of movement to his left through the trees behind the trailer and then heard a voice to his right by the van give a hushed call.

"Back of the trailer. Go. Around back!"

After a split second, two shapes darted out from around the back of the van and began moving quickly into the trees toward him.

"Shit," he whispered.

He turned toward his left and saw Lisa's white tank top. She was headed in his direction, falling and picking herself up, and scrambling forward again. He couldn't call to her, so he stood from where he was crouching and began barreling down the slope toward her at a run.

She gave out a short yell when he tackled her and clawed at his eyes. He managed to get a hand over her mouth. She looked up at him, terrified. He put a finger to his lips as he let his hand up from her mouth.

"Jesus, God, we gotta get outta here," she said. "It's . . . C'mon. Let's go."

Coglin looked over his right shoulder. The shapes that had come from the back of the van were still a ways off at the bottom of the wooded hill, but they seemed to be moving more quickly now. Coglin knew they couldn't make it back to his car. He quickly took off his dark coat and wrapped it over Lisa's shoulders, covering her white shirt. He pulled her behind a tree, pressed her close to the ground, and put his keys in her hand.

"Lay here for five minutes, then move straight up that hill. My car's up on the road. Get the fuck out of here."

"What are you going to do?"

But Coglin was already moving away from her, running full out toward the dark shapes, putting distance between himself and the girl as fast as he could.

"Alright!" he called at them.

He sounded to himself like a kid quitting a game. Ring-a-leavio maybe or kick-the-can. He threw his hands into the air.

"You got me!"

He watched as the figures up ahead stopped dead. There was a muffled clatter as they leaned into trees and swung up with guns, shotguns, or rifles up to their shoulders. There were two twin metallic clicks.

Coglin knelt on the ground with his hands still up, fighting the desire to look back over his shoulder where he'd hid Lisa.

"Relax, fellas," he said. "You win. What do you want?"

One of them moved forward, lowering his gun, while the other one stayed, gun trained. Coglin could see the man approaching was young, pale, thin, a scraggly beard without a mustache fuzzing his jaw. The ghost of a young Abe Lincoln, Coglin thought, his terrified mind racing. Wandering through the Pennsylvania woods, restlessly searching for Gettysburg to give his famous address again.

The youth came closer and strapped before him, Coglin saw, with a freezing stab of new terror, was the sharp, unmistakable form of an M-16.

He swallowed.

"You boys lookin' for something?" he said, but even he could hear the weakness that had crept into his voice.

As if in answer, Honest Abe raised the gun back and hit him in the side of the head with the hard plastic butt of the rifle. Coglin found himself sprawled on his back. When the kid squatted down on his haunches next to his face, Coglin could see he had pimples on his face.

"How about for two million?" he could hear his freckle-faced neighbor say. "Two million dollars for one night in the park."

"Not for all the money in the world, O'Leary," Coglin said to the maniac hovering above him. After a moment, Abe became the drug dealer he'd shot on the platform and Coglin searched at his elbow for his gun, but it wasn't there. And then everything went black.

Chapter
Eleven

WHEN COGLIN FIRST AWOKE, he thought he was back at his mother's house. He was seated in a hard-backed chair, and he thought he might've gotten drunk and fallen asleep at the kitchen table. When he heard the clank of pots off to his right, he figured it was his mother putting on the kettle. Then the pain at the side of his head flared up, and it dawned on him that he was definitely *not* at his mother's house. No, he realized with his head down, he was far, far away.

He looked up.

The bald man looking directly back at him from the sink of his uncle's trailer didn't seem real for several logical reasons. He was too big for one. He seemed to stoop beneath the ceiling of the trailer, hover over the low sink like an adult at a child's toy. If he were real, Coglin figured, he'd have to be six-six, six-seven. And with his shirt off, he was apparently a muscular three hundred pounds, bigger than a football player. More like a WWF wrestler. Freak-show huge. Compelling reason number two was the man's face, which held the smooth boyishness and symmetry of a mannequin. A monstrously huge, big-and-tall store mannequin, he thought crazily.

"Is it me?" the bald man said in a voice, all the more bizarre for the hint of intelligence in it. "Or is it hot in here?"

He wafted a huge palm past his strange, pale face.

It was simple, Coglin concluded. The weed he'd smoked had been laced. Angel dust or LSD. Some bad strain of Ecstasy maybe. Call it Agony.

Coglin closed his eyes and shook his head slightly, willing himself to wake up.

"Not even if you click your heels together three times," he heard the giant say.

Coglin opened his eyes very reluctantly back up.

"Ah," the giant said, taking something out of the kitchen drawer and holding it up. "Here it is."

It was a thin metal bar with a black handle. Coglin thought he was going to use it to pummel him, but then he lifted up the butcher knife lying on the counter next to the sink and began drawing it up and down the sharpening steel with slow, scraping strokes.

Slash, Coglin thought. He'd seen Pimples outside and here was his partner. He looked down at the floor again, trying his best not to hyperventilate.

They were real, they were real, they were real.

Click, clack went the knife. The man wiped his brow with the back of his knife hand. He held up the blade to the light and nodded his head, seemingly satisfied. He dropped the sharpening steel into the sink with a clatter.

He stepped to the kitchen table and pulled it over with a

screech beside Coglin. He took a chair, turned it around and sat. The back of it hardly seemed to come up to his solar plex. He reached for the cigarettes and lighter on the table and took one out. He offered it to Coglin's lips and Coglin accepted it. When he pulled his hand away, he brushed his fingertips across Coglin's face in a slow, sensual gesture. The cigarette in Coglin's mouth shook visibly as the man offered the light. Coglin dragged, coughed, dragged again. The man smiled. His vast, pale nakedness seemed to block out everything else in the room.

Please, Coglin wanted to say, please put on a shirt. No shoes no shirt no service, he thought crazily.

Coglin took another drag, squinting at the smoke, and remembered when he was a kid how he and a friend, not O'Leary, but a Spanish kid, Vinny Alvarez, got their hands on some firecrackers one summer around the Fourth of July. They decided to set some off in the crack of an old, dead tree in an abandoned lot by the park. Soon other kids came by to watch, and a teenager took out an M-80 and set it off. The moment after the explosion, ants—tens of thousands, maybe a million of them—began to pour forth from the crack like black syrup. And among the ants, here and there, were the see-through, snot-colored blobs of their larvae. The torso of the man before him was the same color, he thought, same color, same horror, same thing.

When Coglin tried to stand, he found he couldn't. His arms were tied tightly around his back with an electrical cord that cut sharply into the flesh of his arms like strings on a roast beef.

The man smiled. Jesus Christ, he had a lot of teeth. No, it was his mouth, Coglin saw, it was abnormally large. Toad mouth, Coglin thought.

Coglin swallowed. On the kitchen table were the two plastic cups he and his uncle had used. He could see little, brown flecks of liquor on their sides. They seemed important as he sat there.

Evidence that the world had once not consisted of this man and his knife.

Coglin snapped his head around toward the front door of the trailer as it suddenly creaked open.

"What the fuck are you doing in here?" the bald giant said angrily over Coglin's shoulder.

Coglin heard a hissing sound from behind him, an outtake of breath. He could picture the pimple-faced Lincoln lookalike looking dejectedly at the floor.

"Just that me and Otis flipped for it," said a coarse, southern sounding voice, "and I'm next, is all. After you, of course, I mean, sir."

Next, Coglin thought. His stomach rolled, a nauseous feeling of falling down into something dark and cramped and wet.

"Now, don't you think you could've told me that *after I was done?*" the giant screamed. *"Get your shit-caked ass back out there and hold the perimeter!"*

The door clattered again.

"Now," the large man said, lifting the newly sharpened blade. "Where were we?"

When a muffled sputter started outside, it made no sense to Coglin at first. Then, the deafening snap of machine-gun fire followed outside the trailer, and he winced and sat up.

"Otis!" called the voice of Lincoln from outside. Another impossibly loud burst of gunfire followed.

"Otis!!!"

Abe must have switched the gun onto auto now because there was just one continuous stream of gunfire. Threading through it came again the far-off sputter. The nearby M-16 was suddenly cut short.

Coglin looked at the giant. He was still sitting, holding the knife, bug-eyed shock as bald as his head, plain in his face.

Then the soft clacking started up again and the window blew in.

Glass shattered. Machine-gun rounds splintered the counter top, chomped holes out of the cabinets, clanged off the metal of the sink. Coglin threw his weight back and tipped himself to the floor. He looked up in time to see the blinds atop the kitchen window burst forward and fly across the room like a broken bird.

The giant was up and moving backward away from the fire, out of the kitchen and into the living room. The trailer shook under the heavy falls of his feet. He bumped into the kitchen drawer he'd left open, and then smashed a fist down into it, sending utensils flying.

The bullets stopped for a moment, and then the clacking flutter started up again and the living room window on the left-hand side of the trailer burst inward. Bullets whined off the top of the television, imploding it with a hissing blast. Neat, little holes clicked through the aluminum wall above the couch. The other set of blinds dropped, broken, to the cheap linoleum.

A twin set of fluorescent lights on the living room ceiling illuminated the entire trailer, and the giant raised his fists and smashed them out.

"Shoot me now, you sniping Irish fuck," Coglin heard him say in the dark.

For a third time, the soft, repetitive snapping of gunfire began and the rounds ripped into the door. Coglin kicked his legs, trying to move under the table. The bullets seemed to be hitting the floor. Then the bottom hinge of the door popped outward with a clang and the door groaned.

There was a long pause. Coglin could hear the hairless giant breathing heavily. He looked over at him, crouching low in the moonlit darkness between the living room window and the door. In the dark, he could see something silver in his hand. A pistol.

Coglin searched desperately behind him for the forgotten knife to cut himself free. He thought he felt the handle of the knife, and he was able to grab it. His heart sank as he realized it was just a flashlight.

When the gunfire started up again, it was louder, closer, and the top hinge of the door was decimated. The door hung for a second in its frame and then dropped as if some enormous hand had ripped it free. It fell into the dark front yard, banging loudly off the concrete steps.

The gunfire stopped. Coglin looked fearfully back into the living room where the big, bald man was staring at him, a look of anger beyond all reason and fairness scorching like nuclear fire in his dark eyes. He raised his gun. Coglin yanked himself as hard as he could to the side as the big man fired. A hole appeared in the linoleum where his head had been.

"Stay still, you piece of shit," the giant said, shooting again. Coglin sensed the round flying past as it barely missed his face.

"You suck," Coglin cried, a strange exhilaration giving his voice volume. "Fuck you! You suck, you ugly, frog-faced freak!"

"We'll see if I miss!" the big man said, beginning to move, his heavy feet stomping toward him. "When I put it in your *filthy mouth!*"

Coglin gave the giant a second more and then rolled, bringing around the flashlight he held behind his back, and flicked it on.

The beam hit the big man's pale chest dead center as he was passing through the open doorway. He flapped his hand at it as if trying to brush it away.

The gunfire that started up a split-second later came from just outside the door, a loud, unstoppably violent crackling, ice water poured into super hot grease. The beam of light flickered, followed by a series of thunks. The big man's arm and side seemed to ripple, and he fell out of the light as if he had been yanked with a cord.

Coglin had hardly registered that the big man had been shot when he crashed onto him. His breath left instantly and he lay gasping. The weight of the man didn't seem human, Coglin thought. It seemed more like a horse had fallen on top of him or a brick wall.

When he managed to inhale some oxygen, he realized there was something warm and wet on his face. It was blood, and he thought that maybe he'd been shot after all, but then he felt it dripping slowly onto his cheek and realized it was the lunatic's. He tried to wriggle out from beneath him, but with his arms and legs tied to the chair, it was impossible to budge the dead weight. He pressed his lips tightly together as the blood started migrating toward his mouth.

He was going to die anyway, he thought. The mad man's prison-house, disease-ridden blood would infect him.

He heard a step at the doorway.

"Nnnnnn," he sounded through his nose.

"Nnnnnnnnnnn."

He felt the big man's weight slide off him, and he looked up at his uncle. He was wearing black clothes and a black watch cap and his pale eyes were burning like blue diamonds in his black-smeared face. He had his own M-16 strapped in front of his chest, a slight ghost of smoke still rising from its barrel. He bent and lifted the butcher knife from under the table and cut Coglin free.

Coglin struggled up and rushed past him to the kitchen sink and opened the faucets. He put his face under the cool stream and reached out and grabbed some dish powder and scrubbed at his face until it felt raw and sore. Then he shut off the faucet and reached through a bullet-ridden cabinet for the bottle of scotch.

It was remarkably unscathed, and he unscrewed the top and took a long sip. He held the liquor in his mouth, letting it burn until he could no longer stand it.

Aidan was standing over the huge corpse, staring down at it. He hacked up something in his throat and spit.

"Never was able to get that butcher knife back ta ya," he said down to it. "But how's about a couple of fuckin' bullets in yer head instead, ya fuckin' monster?"

There was a loud whistle from outside.

"*Clear!*" Aidan called out the open doorway.

Coglin looked at the paper towel. It was dark with blood.

"Woulda killed me," Coglin said, shuddering, his teeth beginning to chatter.

"You," he said slowly at his uncle, trying unsuccessfully to regain his composure. "You saved my life."

His uncle made a shooing noise.

There was a sound, and Travis and Angel walked in, bearing a thin body between them. They dumped him on top of the big man and stepped back out the door. Coglin noticed that they, too, had M-16s.

"When did the war start?" Coglin said.

Aidan stepped to a small chest of drawers in the corner and took out a black T-shirt and chucked it at Coglin.

"Your shirt's a mess," he said. He stepped outside.

Angel and Travis came in and dumped another body.

Angel looked at him as he was peeling off his shirt. He smiled.

"That some righteous herb or what?" he said.

Coglin was pulling on the black T-shirt when Aidan came in with a square metal can and began pouring. It was gasoline; the sweet unmistakable cloying smell immediately filled the room. He splashed liberally over the bodies and then along the trailer walls. He looked at Honest Abe, the white of his eyes rolled back into the small remainder of his shattered, open head.

"Lisa," Coglin said, remembering her suddenly. "I left her back . . ."

His uncle slung the dregs of the gas can on the floor and then hurled it out the broken window.

"She's OK. She has your car," Aidan said. "She's gonna meet us. Now go."

Coglin stumbled out the door. The mutant crew's van had been moved into the woods a little farther off the dirt drive and was already in flames. He followed Travis and Angel quickly toward the pickup.

Coglin got in the passenger side and Angel hopped in the back while Travis turned the engine over. There was a loud whump from the trailer, and Coglin turned to see his uncle exit its doorway. He was walking, not even hurrying really, as orange flames suddenly flared up behind him like something angry, the spirits of the slain within perhaps, trying desperately to grab hold of him. They seemed to lick at his back.

The trailer was immediately engulfed. Furnacelike flames were roaring out of the broken windows by the time Travis had brought the truck, tires screaming, halfway up the steep driveway. With his neck craned all the way around, Coglin watched his uncle, backlit by the inferno, walking toward Lisa's small car. Through the haze of shock, he tried to determine what he looked like, and then he realized it.

Like the devil coming out the back door of hell, he thought suddenly.

With his wild hair and blue eyes, soot-smeared face, and the flames raging behind him, he looked like the devil entering the world after a long hiatus to take a little spin.

Chapter Twelve

THE FIRST TIME COGLIN AWOKE, he noticed they were on a highway. The restaurants and businesses alongside the roadway weren't open yet, but their signs were lit. Coglin gazed at them. Tony's Pizza, Little Tykes Karate, Lube-In-A-Minute. Civilization, he thought. Thank god. He'd made it back.

A vague feeling, bad and dark, welled up in him then, trying to erase his relief.

Not for you, it reminded him. He couldn't think clearly, and he prayed without hope that it was nothing, the remnants of a nightmare maybe, nothing real.

He pressed his head against the cool of the door frame below the open window and allowed himself to slide back into sleep.

He woke the second time when the truck stopped. He opened his eyes and looked around, blinking, at the half-full parking lot. There was a huge building in front of them, eight or nine stories high, pyramid-like, with a few lit windows in it and a large, brightly lit entryway. The sky above it was still dark and beyond it, the occasional car shot by on a highway larger than the one that he'd noticed when he first woke up.

"How is he?" he heard his uncle ask Travis through the driver side window.

"I'm fine," Coglin said groggily.

When he turned, he saw that his uncle looked somewhat normal now. The black face paint was gone and he'd changed his clothes.

"Alright then," his uncle said with a smile. "Let's go inside."

The hotel doors opened automatically as they stepped before them. Muzak played softly from somewhere above the bland lobby, an oboe rendition of "In a New York Minute." A small Mexican gentleman in a purple vest and bow tie smiled at them from aside a gleaming brass luggage cart.

His uncle had already gotten adjoining rooms. They took an elevator and stepped down the carpeted hallway of the fourth floor. Travis and Angel went into a door and he followed his uncle into the other.

"Shower. Then we'll talk," his uncle said, opening the bathroom door.

Coglin threw open the faucet, stripped down and stepped under the water. He had put it on cold by accident and the water was so freezing that at first it took his breath away, but once his breath came back, he left it on. He looked at his forearms, the crisscrossing, deep red lines where the wire he'd been tied with had cut into his skin. He closed his eyes.

He didn't need to go over what had just happened. There'd be time for that. He just needed to clean himself up and sleep. Wake early and drive back to the courthouse, as if nothing had ever happened. He'd stepped into the middle of some stuff that had nothing to do with him. Been a victim and a witness to a crime. He'd forget it and deal with his own host of problems. He laid his hands flat against the white tile and pressed his head under the cold water.

Farewell drink, he thought.

Gee, Uncle Aidan. Can I play in traffic now?

When he came out of the bathroom, dripping in his towel, his uncle was sitting in a chair by the bed and there was a room service tray on the dresser. The air in the room was frigid. Coglin shivered.

"I ordered you some food," his uncle said.

It was a steak sandwich and though it wasn't hot anymore, Coglin sat on the edge of the bed in his towel and cleaned his plate. He grabbed the bottles of beer from the tray, handed one to his uncle and moved to the chair facing his uncle's.

"What time is it?" he said.

Aidan checked the cheap digital at his wrist.

"Three-fifteen," he said. "What time do you have to be in court?"

"Nine," Coglin said.

"You'll make it," Aidan said, lighting a cigarette. He passed the pack to Coglin. Coglin lit one up with his uncle's lighter and leaned back, blowing smoke.

"I got you caught up in my business," his uncle said. "I should've told you to leave earlier. I made a mistake and almost got you killed. I'm sorry."

Coglin raised the palm of his hand and shook his head.

"Don't worry about it," he said.

"That big man's name was Thayer," Aidan said. "I knew him . . ."

Coglin put a hand up.

"No need to explain," Coglin said. "You got your business.

Lord knows, I got mine. Far as I'm concerned, nothing happened. We never met. I'm sleeping in my bed right now back in the Bronx, waiting for the prison to open."

Aidan flicked ash on the windowsill.

"Lisa said you left and came back for her."

"I was down the road a little. I saw . . . whoever . . . kill the headlights of their van before they turned into your driveway," Coglin said. "I decided to see what was up."

"She also said you turned yourself into them so she could get away."

Coglin took a drag of his cigarette.

"I was just drunk and stoned is all," he said. "I couldn't think of anything else to do. Just out of curiosity, those bodies you burned in your trailer?"

"Trailer can't be traced back to me," Aidan said.

Coglin took a drag of his cigarette.

"That's good," he said.

"Are you really OK?" Aidan said.

"Shook up," Coglin said. "My first torture."

Aidan smiled.

"How was it? You like it?"

Coglin rotated a palm back and forth.

"I think it's gonna take some time to grow on me," he said. "Might be awhile before I'm ready to try it again."

"If only that were true, John," Aidan said. His eyes squinted sympathetically. "Unfortunately, there's gonna be plenty more opportunities for you in the near future once they stuff you in that cage."

"Gee, Aidan. Thanks for reminding me," Coglin said.

"Reason I bring it up is because, as it turns out it, doesn't have to be that way," the Irishman said. He took another casual pull on his cigarette. "For you, I mean."

Coglin stilled. He could feel the prick of something, like the opening of a small window deep within him. A thin shaft of light cut at the gloom of his mood. He swallowed.

"Yeah?" he said carefully. "How you figure?"

"Been workin' on a little something. It might interest you."

Coglin eyes widened. *No jail?* he thought. No jail. Could he even allow himself to consider it?

"You want to hear it?" his uncle said.

Coglin looked down at the carpet as the image of the bullet-ridden bodies heaped on the trailer floor flashed before him.

Calm down, he thought, blinking it away.

Coglin took a slow and calculated drag of his cigarette. The smoke he exhaled swirled slow and blue in the light from the dresser's lamp.

"Hell, I'm all the way out here," he finally said. "Might as well hear it before I head back."

Chapter Thirteen

"THIRTY-SIX MILLION IN DIAMONDS," Aidan said. "A high-rise in Midtown Manhattan. I have a buyer set up. We walk away with ten."

"Robbery?" Coglin said. "Or burglary?"

Aidan glared at him.

"Robbery," he said. "Armed."

Coglin smoked.

"This high-rise is what?" he said. "An apartment house?"

"An office building."

"Where?"

"Fifty-first and Fifth."

"Fifty-first and Fifth?" Coglin said. "That's fucking Rocke-feller Center."

Aidan smiled.

"Yes it is," he said.

"Are you out of your fucking mind?" Coglin said, his voice rising. "What time of day are you planning this?"

"Lunchtime. Tomorrow at lunchtime. Well, actually today at lunchtime," Aidan said, checking his watch. "If you want to get technical."

"What?! Today? Lunchtime at Rockefeller Center?" Coglin said. "What? Was Times Square on New Year's Eve taken? You know how many cops are stationed around Rock Center?"

"Several," Aidan said.

"Damn straight, several," Coglin said. "Several times twenty. I know I used to be one of them."

"Fuck off," Aidan said, clapping his hands suddenly. "Good luck, man. You could help us then. You could lead us out."

"Good luck, my ass," Coglin said. "What you want to do is impossible."

"Let me finish," Aidan said calmly. "There's this new television awards show. *The Sunset Boulevard Video Awards.* It's gonna take place tomorrow night at Radio City Music Hall. Now apparently, movie and television stars don't like to go to these fuckin' things unless everything is paid for, OK? They get put in designer gowns they get to keep, free limo rides and what have you. Who knows? Maybe they fuckin' pay them in drugs. Who cares?

"The thing is, though, this video company is new and they need stars for publicity to promote their company, so they give them extra perks. One of the perks for this little soiree is lending out luxurious gems. An up-and-coming jewelry company is semi-sponsoring this event by loaning out thirty-six million dollars worth. We know where they're going to be holding the jewels before the event, and it's no fucking vault. Get this. Asshole network executives want the jewels to be displayed in a Rockefeller Center law office before the event for private viewing. So they can show their wives and shit. A fuckin' law office."

"It doesn't matter," Coglin said. "The security is wall-to-wall."

"Security," Aidan said contemptuously. "Listen up. Banks are fuckin' wired. Nothing harder to rob than a bank. Jewelry stores? Fucking fortresses. Armored cars? A real fucking bitch. Office buildings? Boyo, office buildings are a fuckin' walk-through. They might as well leave that shit in a box with a red ribbon wrapped around it, sittin' out on the steps of St. Paddy's across the street."

Aidan stood suddenly. He went to the corner and took some papers out of a bag. He spread them out on the small table before them. There were maps, blueprints, floor plan sketches.

"Where'd you get all this?" Coglin said, flicking through them.

"Lisa."

"Lisa?" Coglin said.

"Lisa," Aidan said, nodding his head. "She works for the phone company in the city. She found it all out."

"That's hard to believe."

"Believe it," Aidan said. "I bunked with her husband, this little Brooklyn mobster, in for aggravated assault. Violent little bastard, he was, but we got along. We had release dates a week apart. Made plans about working together once we both got out, but he got gutted two weeks before his release."

Coglin shook his head.

"Yeah," he said. "I think she told me something about that. Sweet. I guess he didn't get a chance to take some mother-fucker's eyes out."

"Guess not," Aidan said. "There was three of them, story I heard. And it wasn't any sharpened toothbrushes they stuck him with. One who took him down had a hunting knife Rambo woulda been proud of, they said. Fuckin' massacred him."

Aidan shrugged.

"Piss off the wrong person, bad things can happen. Who knows? But two months after I'm out, I get a call. It was Lisa. She told me she took a job with the phone company a couple of years after she got married. Her husband was in and out of jail, and they had a kid, so she wanted something reliable. Then one day, she gets a phone call that her husband is cheating on her with this old girlfriend from their neighborhood. So, Lisa finds out the old squeeze's home and work numbers and decides to tap them."

"Tap them?" Coglin said.

"Phone tap," Aidan said. "She works in manholes where all the lines are. Anyway, she's got a tap on this girl's work phone. The girlfriend was married into a family of Israelis who owned a jewelry company in the city, and she worked there. But Vinny gets popped again for aggravated assault, and she forgets about his little dalliance for a while. Only then Vinny gets shanked, right, and Lisa, all heartbroken, I guess, collects these tapes she'd recorded. On the tapes, she hears about this deal.

"The company doing the award promotion needed to sub-contract in order to get enough jewelry, so they dealt in the Israeli family company. You see? So, she gets the where, the when, how much. Not only that, phone company has the blue-print on the building. She gets her hands on that. Then, God love her, she knocks out a couple of phone lines from the firm where the jewels are gonna be held, and does a walk-through. Cases the place cold."

"She's done this before?" Coglin said.

"Beats the shit out of me," Aidan said with a shrug. "Maybe she's a natural. Anyway, she comes to me with all this stuff, tells me her husband told her I was good at this sort of thing, and asks me to hit it. I looked it over, made some adjustments and now it's tight."

"Why do you think she wants to rob the place? She wants to fuck over the girl who was screwing her husband?"

"I suspect that might have something to do with it," Aidan said, looking over at him. "Fuck why. Sounds like her business to me. You like her, don'tcha? Good lookin' woman, she is."

"I got eyes," Coglin said.

"Now that's fuckin' sweet," Aidan said. "Really. You'd make a cute couple. Can I continue my fuckin' story?"

"How are you gonna do it?" Coglin found himself saying.

Aidan paused.

"Are you in?" he said.

"I haven't heard it all yet," Coglin said.

"'Cause you keep interrupting," Aidan said. He pointed at the building plan. "We're going to knock down the phone lines for the whole building, and go in like an emergency phone crew here. We got ID. Helmets, the whole nine. The service elevator is the only one that doesn't have a camera. When we get inside it, we're going to tie up the porter. Service goes right into the back of the office here," he said, pointing at the blueprint. "And we're gonna come in, take it over, lock the front office door, grab the jewels and run."

Coglin stared at the schematics, nodding.

"The machine guns?" he said. "They really necessary?"

Aidan put out his palms.

"Two guards with handguns are going to be with the gems. You were a cop. Somebody put an assault rifle bead on your chest, how quick are you gonna play cowboy? None too fuckin' quick if you're sane," Aidan said. "Would it make you feel better if we went in with handguns? How about baseball bats? Armed robbery is armed robbery. You get caught, makes no fuckin' difference if it's a BB gun."

"That was what all that shit in the trailer was about? Coglin said, remembering all the M-16s. "A gun deal?"

Aidan nodded.

"Remember that jail story I told you?"

"The guy who was hitting on you?" Coglin said.

"Right, that bald bastard who had you tied up was the head of the white gang, the one who gave me the blade. Out in the world, he did some arms dealing. He turned me on to some weaponry, then thought he could fuck me."

"That firefight was over money?" Coglin said.

"I wish," Aidan said. "I paid half up front, and two days ago when we went to collect, they ambushed us. Friend of mine was killed. What we did tonight was get back what they owed us. That and pay them back for our friend."

Aidan grinned.

"Not to mention saving your drunk ass," he said.

Coglin passed a hand across the blueprint in front of him.

"This other job you did?" he said. "California. Anybody end up shot?"

"Not a soul," Aidan said. "They'da let me out if someone had?"

"What exactly do you want me to do?" Coglin said.

Aidan opened the window a crack and flicked out his cigarette.

"Your old Uncle Aidan got you a tit job," he said, turning back. "You watch the elevator."

"Watch the elevator?"

"You're the getaway elevator man. You don't even go in. You stand next to it, make sure nobody takes it. That's all you do."

"The guy who wound up dead, your friend. That was his job?"

Aidan nodded.

"So when you called me up, it wasn't just to dispense street wisdom," Coglin said. "You had this job offer all lined up?"

"It might've been in the back of my mind."

Coglin shook his head.

"You need an out," Aidan said. "I need a getaway elevator man. It's win-win."

"Not so fast," Coglin said. "There's still too many cops outside. Plus, you're right in the center of Midtown. Fuck the freight car, they'll tow the getaway one."

Aidan put his hands out, urging him to hold up.

"We go in wearing masks and these paper tearaway coveralls," he said. "And under those, we wear UPS and FedEx uniforms. We ditch everything except the diamonds before we get to the lobby, and then we walk out nice and slow and split up into the subway."

Coglin tilted his head and nodded.

"You've been workin' this out," he said.

"Inside and out. Plus, get this. Lisa'll be a block away in her phone truck with a scanner, right, to listen for any police calls that come in. And you know those cameras that they have at streetlights that snap your picture if you run the light?

"I've heard of them."

"Well, Midtown is full of them. They're all not operational yet, but they're set up. Lisa found out about them at work because the phone company takes care of the cameras' underground video feed. She knows how to access the software in order to get a live video image of any corner you type in. She's gonna be sitting in her truck with her laptop a block away, watching us exit. Things get hairy, she'll be able to tell us where to go."

"Get outta here," Coglin said.

Aidan nodded proudly.

"Hi-tech, baby," he said.

"So Lisa stays outside?"

"Yes, Romeo," Aidan said with a smile. "Your girl stays outside. Not even directly outside. A block away."

"Well, it sounds pretty impressive," Coglin said.

"Fucker's wired," Aidan said. "How many cops are there?"

"Twenty, fifteen maybe with people off on vacation," Coglin said.

"You know where their stations are?"

Coglin looked at the map.

"One-man posts on the corners," he said. He pointed down at the paper. "Two here at the entrance to the plaza from Fifth and Fiftieth and Forty-eighth Street. There are at least eight more men scattered around the rink and shops and the lower level concourse where the subway entrance is. A mounted cop or two on the street here. Maybe a motorcycle for the tourists. That's all I did all day. Put my arm around Japanese tourists' backs while their wives or husbands went at it with the Minoltas. We called it the cheese detail."

Aidan was smiling.

"Which way are you planning on going in?" Coglin said.

"Fifty-first Street. Here," the Irishman said, pointing at the side entrance of the building near Fifth.

"I'd come out the same way then," Coglin said. "Fuck the one cop on the corner. He'll be too busy lookin' at the broads. Go to Fifth and head uptown. Maybe to Fifty-second which goes east. Get a taxi or fuck it, cross over and walk. Around lunch, it might be quicker. I'd go over to the East Side, and if you have to catch a subway, do it there. And I'd have on something underneath the UPS shit, too, and throw it down on the run. Let the traffic work for you. If it's clogged, it'll slow down any pursuit to a crawl. Did I just say that?" Coglin said.

He took a drink from the bottle.

"I can't believe I'm even listening to this."

Aidan took a sip of his beer and propped the bottle between his knees.

"Could you believe how you were put on trial for murder?" he said.

"No," Coglin said.

"How about how that fuckin' freak tied you up in the trailer a couple of hours ago?" Aidan said.

Coglin looked out at the lights again and rubbed absently at his wrists.

"It's hard to believe that even now," he said.

"World's a surprising place," Aidan said. "What are you going to do?"

Coglin dragged the last of his cigarette and crushed it out against the glass ashtray. He put his elbows on his knees, held his head in his hands and stared down at the carpet.

He was fucked either way, he knew.

Maybe he should just stop acting like a jackass and cut his losses. His sentence wasn't right. Unjust didn't begin to describe it. But wasn't that just the way shit happened sometimes? Wrong place at the wrong time and you had to take some lumps. Plus he could appeal. He'd be guilty, do some months and win on appeal just like Clarke had suggested.

He didn't need to do this. Some hard-core takeover robbery? Jesus Christ. Waving machine guns around in some network office? That was just too . . . fucked up. He was one of the good guys.

And even if they did get away with it. Even if he had a million dollars, what then? Where the fuck would he go? Mexico? Under an assumed name? Wouldn't he need a fake passport? Sounded like a whole lot of shit he didn't know about.

That's right, he thought, at least getting gutted in prison was simple.

He took a deep breath.

"I need to make a phone call," he said.

Aidan stood. He took a cell phone out of his jacket and handed it down to Coglin. He pushed open the sliding door to the balcony.

"I'll be outside," he said.

Coglin dialed as the door slid shut.

"Huh? What?" his lawyer said groggily after the fifth ring. "What? Who?"

"It's me," Coglin said grimly. "How's it going, Counselor?"

"John," Mulvane said. "I've been beeping you like crazy. Where the fuck are you? I gotta talk to you."

"What is it?" Coglin said.

"They nixed it. The fuckers took it away. The DA. The manslaughter. They called me at six and said it's off the table. Said let the jury decide."

Coglin sat completely still. Out the window beside him, car lights went back and forth on the highway. There were tiny yellow lights of a house in the darkened hill beyond. An image came to him, a house propped on the edge of a sheer cliff with wooden beams, one of the beams cracking suddenly and falling twisting away.

Murder two, he thought. The three syllables like a series of slammed shut doors.

"Why?" Coglin said, his voice suddenly dry, scratchy. "Why did they do that now?"

"Fuckers are confident, I guess," Mulvane said. "But we know better, OK? I wasn't going to tell you to take the deal anyway. Grandma Perez and Johnson that bus driver. They're not gonna let you down. I've been dealing with juries a long time and I got a good feeling. It's gonna come down right."

Twenty-five to life, Coglin thought. Life.

"What about an appeal?" Coglin said quickly, desperately remembering the words of his friend, Lieutenant Clarke. "The media would be gone and things would work out better for us there, right?"

"You don't want to get into all that," Mulvane said. "It's gonna work out tomorrow, John."

No, it isn't, you fucking fool, Coglin wanted to say.

"Why don't I want to get into all that?"

"I won't lie to you," Mulvane said. "An appeal is a process fraught with peril. Though you're entitled to them legally, in real terms, judges always hold it against the defendant as wasting the court's time and resources on a case that was already successfully dealt with. They're just not priority cases, so they keep getting pushed back. Plus, the DA's office pulls every trick in the book to delay them. You're talkin' years before you can set the thing up."

"Years?" Coglin said. He could see the other beam beneath his mental house explode into dust under the pressure. The house hovering.

"Yep," Mulvane said. "Years and even then, who knows? They're just not pretty. But that is not gonna be your fate. The jury is deliberating the fuck out of this one. I'm thinking acquittal, mistrial at the very least."

Really? At the very least, you fucking idiot, Coglin thought. *I'm thinking more like life.*

"Have some faith, John," Mulvane said. "Don't give up on yourself now. Try to get some sleep. See you tomorrow."

"Uh-huh," Coglin said as he watched his house finally go over, dropping soundlessly into a bottomless abyss.

He heard the click of disconnect and sat with his mouth open. After a minute, he knocked on the glass of the balcony door. His uncle slid it open and stepped back in.

Was it still a choice, he thought, *if there weren't any other options?*

"I'll do it," Coglin said as he handed back his uncle's cell phone. "On two conditions."

"Name them," his uncle said.

"I'm not gonna hurt anybody, and if anybody, and I mean anybody, starts shooting people, you guys ain't gonna have to worry about the cops."

Aidan put his phone away and looked out at the lights. He nodded.

"Sounds reasonable to me," he said, smiling widely, extending his hand.

Coglin took it warily.

"Welcome aboard, boyo," Aidan said pumping it roughly. "I knew you'd do it."

"You did, huh?" Coglin said.

"Why do you think I invited you out for a drink?" Aidan said.

Coglin shook his head.

"Listen now," Aidan said, checking his watch. "We leave at five. Get some rest."

There was a soft knock on the door.

Cops, Coglin thought. *No, FBI SWAT.* They'd traced them already.

Aidan raised an eyebrow.

"Stay there," he said, getting up.

Coglin waited for blinding flashlights in his eyes, stomping boots, gunfire.

When Aidan came back, Lisa was behind him. She sat stiffly

in the chair where Aidan had been sitting, her dark eyes wide and glued on Coglin's. Coglin began raising his beer but then stopped and placed it on the windowsill.

"Would you look at the time?" Aidan said, heading toward the door. "Sleep," he called over his shoulder. "You need it."

The door closed loudly behind him.

"You saved my life," she said.

Coglin smiled.

"You gave me a ride," he said. "Least I could—"

Then she was out of her chair. She crashed into him with such force he thought she was trying to knock him down. She opened his cut with her kiss.

For a second, it was like he was drowning, suffocating. The recent series of atrocities that had happened to him began to flash in his mind, one into the other like cars in an interstate pileup. Pieces of a strange and hideous puzzle made no more apprehensible by the fact that they were actual events in his life.

Falling off the roof and shooting the kid. The trial and castigation by the media. His daughter. The verdict. The torture in the trailer and the gunfire. And what he'd just agreed to do.

Then the smooth, flowing heat of her enveloped him. Her perfume washed over him, the clean smell of rain, cool and soothing after a long drought.

Was it possible that his luck, he thought, reaching a hand for the bedside lamp, *could in fact be taking a turn for the better?*

She slapped his hand down.

"No," she said frantically in his ear. "Leave it on."

Yes, he thought. *Indeed it had.*

Chapter
Fourteen

WHEN HER PHONE STARTED RINGING from the chair where her clothes lay, Colette thought she knew who it was. She remained motionless in the bed, feigning sleep, and let it ring. Through the wall behind her head came a high groan: water beginning to shoot through old pipes as the shower went on. She tried to debate the merits of what she should do, but goddamn it, she was too hung over. Without rising, she shot out a hand, thumbing on the Ericsson before it reached her ear.

"Yeah?" she said.

"What the hell?" her old boyfriend, Billy, said. "You're screening your calls now? Get your ass out of bed, girl. You're running late."

From the bedroom window, she could see the lights still lit on the very top of the eastern tower of the Brooklyn Bridge, the sky dark behind it.

"Late for what?" she croaked. She'd smoked last night. Smoked!

"I don't work in a bakery," she said.

"For your run," Billy said. "What? You're telling me you don't do that anymore?"

"I hurt my knee," she lied. "I only go three times a week now."

Week, she thought. *Year. Who was paying attention?*

"Besides," she said into her pillow. "I thought we went over this."

"Went over what?" Billy said. "You said 'friends.' Friends don't call each other?"

"At lunchtime maybe," she said. "Late afternoon."

"You're just pissed I woke you up," he said. "I know how you are before your coffee."

She passed a hand through her blond hair. There was a scuzzy bar film on it. She remembered a place with a lot of tall, good-looking, well-dressed people smoking on her. Flashing lights. She couldn't remember the exact details of the end of the night, but she thought, with a sick feeling, her last memory definitely had her wearing clothes.

Lost control, she thought. Pathetic. No excuse. She was the one who should be in the shower.

"So how was it?" she said, hastily recalling the trip he'd been on, the job he'd been offered.

"Honey," he said. "Honey, you have to see it. It's gorgeous. The house is on Main Street. It's actually called Main Street, OK? Some old dude in a pickup waved at me as I was driving into town. Then some lady on the corner. I had to pull over to see if I'd left my coffee on the roof or something. I think they were, get this, being friendly."

"Does that mean you're going to take it?" she said.

"Well, I think the constable was low-balling me a little on the salary. I asked, and he said he'd have to get back to me. But that's not the only thing."

"Seems to me you got it all worked out. What's the problem?"

There was a pause.

"I want you to come with me."

There it was, she thought. She'd been waiting a while now and—slam drop—there it was on the carpet before her. She pulled herself up slowly, head spinning, and sat up completely with her naked back to the wall.

"Come with you?"

"Yep," he said.

"You realize you called *me*, Colette, right?"

"I'm speaking with Colette Ryan, right? The FBI agent with the fine ass?"

"You are the biggest . . ." she began. "I can't even say what you are. I can't come up with a word. Come with you. See, what did I say? I knew this was coming. Poor Billy, the prodigal asshole, returns. Oh yeah, Billy, I'll go up to some pisswater town in Maine with you and be the Fire Chief's wife. I'll stay home, under six feet of snow, while you go out drinking with your fire buddies. That sounds like fun. Hey, maybe I'll have six or seven kids to keep me company. Whataya think?"

"No, you're right, honey," Billy said. "Better you stay where you are. Things are going so well. Because you have at least another four or five years to safely have kids. There'll be just enough time to plan the wedding. Where are you and good ol' celebrity DA Phil thinking? Some place down near Wall Street? Some place historical maybe. I can't wait for the announcement in the *Times*. White horses pulling the carriage. Rosebuds swirling down Pearl Street. It'll be everything your dad had hoped for."

"Fuck you," she said. "Don't you dare say anything about my father. Fuck you."

Billy whistled.

"Ouch," he said. "Truth kinda stings, doesn't it? Then maybe you can pop a baby out there under the wire and stick her with the nanny just in time to get back to work. Because, Jesus Christ, it is your fuckin' career we're talking about here. God forbid anything gets in the way of that. That's the fantasy right, honey? See, you come off so feisty, and that's what I love about you. But deep down, deep, deep down, you're a princess aren't you, sweetheart? Deep down you're just as deluded as all the rest of those empty, cheap corporate humps you find yourself hanging with. Because you deserve all that's good in this world, don't you? The finest of everything. To be pampered like a queen."

She heard the hinges of the bathroom door squeak and pulled up the sheet, absently covering herself.

"No, Billy. I deserve waiting and waiting and waiting for you and having you never show. That's what I deserve. Well, I got tired of waiting, Billy. The bus never showed. Now it's too late."

"Yeah, lucky for you a limo showed, though, huh? Now you don't have to ride the bus."

"That's right, Billy. Lucky me."

Phillip stepped into the room, rubbing at his black hair with a towel. He wore another towel around his lean, muscular waist and she was thankful for that.

"I left the water on for you," he said. "Who's that?"

"*You're there!*" Billy said. "You're at his place right now?"

"That's right. Get it now, Billy?"

The second after she said, she knew she shouldn't have. He didn't deserve that.

The silence that followed was so profound she thought she'd gotten cut off.

"The water's on," Billy said very quietly. "You better go."

There was a click as the line went dead.

Phillip sat on the edge of the bed, looking at her. She tossed the phone back on her chair.

"You want to talk about it?" he said warily.

She lay back down and stared at the ceiling. It looked recently painted.

"Not right this second," she said. "Is that OK?"

"You know me," Phillip said gently. "Look at the time. I gotta get going. You want coffee?"

She thought about what Billy had said.

"You know what?" she said. "Do me a favor? Put on some tea?"

She felt better, showered and dressed ten minutes later, though she had a little trouble looking at herself directly in the mirror. In the kitchen, she squinted at the overhead lights, gleaming off his stainless steel countertops and tile floor. He was beside the stove, holding the steaming kettle with a potholder, pouring her tea, his crisp pinstripe shirt rolled to his elbows. She couldn't decide whether she should be gladdened by the fact that it looked like he could take care of himself or frightened that he'd cleaned the apartment for this eventuality.

Why don't you dust for prints, Special Agent, she thought. Or better yet, wait till he's gone, then toss the place. Billy would like that.

"Lemon?" he said, opening the fridge.

"Sure," she said, wishing she'd said yes to the coffee. She sat down at the small table.

"So have you decided?" he said.

"Decided?" she said.

"Lunch?" he said. "My parents?"

His parents, she thought. Right. His father just happened to be the senior senator from the great commonwealth of Connecticut. She vaguely remembered him asking her the night before.

"It's too soon, isn't it?" he said. "I'm rushing things."

She looked at him with the words of her old boyfriend still echoing in her ears. What? She *couldn't* like him because he came from money? What about the fact that he was good-looking or that he was the most successful DA in the Southern District. Or that he really was a nice, sweet guy. She couldn't like someone successful, compatible? Fuck that.

"Of course, I'll be there," she said.

He wrote something down on a pad on the fridge, ripped off the sheet and handed it to her.

"Twelve," he said. "OK? I'll meet you out in front."

She nodded.

"I need to get home and change," she said standing, leaving the tea untouched. She leaned over the table and gave him a brief kiss. She registered how quickly his hands danced around the ten-millimeter automatic in the pancake holster on her right hip.

"Your squad might notice you showing up in the same thing as yesterday?" he said with a smile.

"You kidding me?" she said, scanning for the door. "If we spent as much time on our cases as on each other's social lives," Colette called as she stepped out of the kitchen, "they'd be digging up Hoffa right now."

Chapter Fifteen

IT WAS STILL DARK when the city first came into view. Now twenty miles north of it, they topped a highway rise and through the windshield, it was suddenly there, outlined in pinprick, connect-the-dot lights. It seemed tiny and perfect and unreal in the distance, Coglin thought, like the paperweight skylines they sold to tourists down in Times Square.

Wonderland, Coglin thought, sipping the coffee he'd gotten when they'd stopped for gas half an hour before.

Through the looking glass and back.

The SUV they were driving was a luxury one, a new, black Cadillac Escalade that had tinted windows and leather seats. It had been rented with a stolen credit card by one of Angel's associates the morning before and had been left in the lot of the prearranged hotel. When Aidan had laid eyes on it, dark and gleaming in the corner of the lot, he'd given Angel a broad smile and clapped him on the back.

"Class, boy," he'd said. "I knew there was a reason we'd taken you on."

Aidan, Travis and Angel now lay sunken in the dark, creamy leather of the back seat and behind them, under some hotel blankets, were the assault rifles.

There were five of them. The three they'd paid for as well as the two they'd taken off the white supremacists slain in front of Aidan's trailer. Only one had anything wrong with it, a cracked stock where two of Aidan's bullets had ripped through the hard plastic.

The M-16s were military issue, Travis had told Coglin when they were transferring them from his truck to the back of the SUV. They hadn't been modified in any way, he'd said, and when set on autofire, they could empty a twenty-round clip in less than five seconds.

With them were several clips and two rectangular, metal boxes, like toolboxes, brimming with the rifle's .223-millimeter rounds. They were stacked alongside a couple of police scanners and a laptop, some cell phones, black ski masks, black gloves and the thin, heavy layers of three Kevlar bulletproof vests.

Coglin reached out and turned the rearview mirror at himself for the hundredth time.

He was completely bald now. Everyone had agreed that altering his infamous appearance was necessary to the success of the operation, so Lisa had ended up shaving his head with Aidan's electric razor in the hotel bathroom before they left.

Hey, psycho, he thought, shaking his newly shiny head with a dumbfounded expression. *What the fuck'll you do next?*

He tilted the mirror back and turned around in his seat. His uncle was sleeping soundly. Travis was on the other side, his tall, longhaired Viking-like form struggling to stretch out, trying to nap. Between them, Angel was lighting a cigarette, the match illuminating the gold in the youth's grim smile.

He turned and looked over at Lisa driving, her green eyes leveled ahead in fierce concentration, looked at the long, red nails she rested against the steering wheel's leather. The ones that less than two hours ago had gouged the deep scratches he wore now on his back.

"You know I forgot to ask you something last night," he said in a low voice.

She smiled at him, looked back at the road. "What's that?" she said.

"Why the fuck are you doing this?"

"You know about my husband, right?" Lisa said.

"Yeah," Coglin said. "He was killed in jail."

"Ever hear of money smuggling?" Lisa said.

"Drug smuggling?"

"No," she said. "Money smuggling. Let's say somebody living in another country makes money illegally in this country, money that can't be put into an account and wired.

"Money smugglers sneak cash back to those people," she continued. "My husband, idiot that he was, idiot that I was ever to have . . . ughh. Don't let me get into it. Basically, my husband got this offer to smuggle money for these Columbians. Fuckin' Columbians, right? Sounds like a real safe business relationship there. Doesn't tell me anything about this, mind you. He's paying his little girlfriends to fly down to Cancún and drop off packages.

"Well, one of these sluts takes a drunken header off a balcony into the front parking lot of her hotel, and a package never makes it. That's why my husband got killed. Now, get this. *I* get a package in the mail a month and a half later. Photograph of my daughter at her preschool and typed on the back of it, a number, a date and an address. Seven hundred twenty-seven thousand, eight hundred fifteen dollars and seventy-three cents. Don't forget the seventy-three cents. Date for next week, address at this place out in Sunnyside, Queens."

Coglin whistled.

"They're gonna come after your daughter if you don't pay?" he said.

"That's the gist I got."

"That's why you're doing this? To pay them off?"

Lisa looked at him.

"Fuck that," she said. "I'm here to make money I can run with. Killed my husband and I'm gonna pay them? I mean my husband was a piece of shit, but fuck them. I'm gonna run."

Coglin looked at her without speaking for a moment.

"Aren't you afraid they're going to find you?" he finally said.

"Wise up," she said. "You change your name and move to some anonymous city, the fuckin' FBI can't find you. A bunch of crazy Columbian drug dealers are gonna catch up with me? I don't think so. I figure if I stay out of nightclubs in Miami, I'll be fine. Haven't you thought about this? What the fuck are you going to do after?"

"I haven't thought that far ahead," Coglin said.

She shook her head and smiled.

"Got your picture plastered on the front page of the newspaper, and you haven't thought that far ahead, huh?"

Coglin smiled. He laughed for a second. It felt good, cut the tension for a brief pulse.

"I like to live by the seat of my pants," he said, shrugging.

"You and that Irishman back there are related. You're both completely fuckin' brain-dead," she said.

"Yeah," Coglin said, dragging on his cigarette. "That's the core of our appeal."

She smiled again without looking at him.

"How's that back feeling, Officer?" she said.

Coglin leaned back, wincing.

"You're lucky I'm not hauling you in for assault," he said.

They were hitting some traffic now, early-bird commuters trying to zip in before morning rush hour's crushing fall. They blasted over the city line, drove by his old building. When he looked up, he saw a light on in his mother's apartment.

Jesus Christ, he'd forgotten her. She had to be worried sick.

"Lisa," Coglin said. "Let me borrow your phone."

His mother answered in the middle of the first ring.

"Hey," he said.

"Where the hell are you?" she said.

"Mom, listen. Don't go today."

Coglin could hear Angel start to laugh behind him.

"What do you mean?" his mother said. "Get back here now. You have to get ready."

"No, Mom," he said calmly. "It's not gonna happen."

"You have to show, John." She was pleading now. "Don't you listen to my brother. He's nothin' but bad, you hear me?"

Not about to get into it, Coglin thought.

"I'll call you, Mom," Coglin said and hung up.

He put the phone down and thumbed it off. Beyond the windshield, the passing streetlights lining the highway were reflected in the dark hood of the truck, and they flashed quickly over it like pale minnows in a dark pool.

When they sped under the off-ramp for the George Washington Bridge, even in the predawn murk, Coglin could see the rust on its underside, the dark splotches on the painted iron like rotting, open sores. Yankee Stadium loomed large to their left and above it, on top of a hill, was the courthouse where he was supposed to be in a few hours. They shot past it onto the ramp for the Willis Avenue Bridge into Manhattan.

Well, Coglin thought, listening to the pitch of the truck's wide tires rise higher on the bridge's metal roadbed. *At least it was decided.*

Below, the dark, greenish face of the East River seemed still, as if it had come to a dead stop. He put a cigarette in his mouth and pressed down the lighter in the dash.

TWENTY MINUTES LATER, they pulled to a stop in front of a small diner on West Thirty-eighth Street. Huge exhaust-blackened stone buildings lined both sides of the narrow street to the east like a hellish canyon. Against the sidewalk ahead were garbage trucks parked at forty-five-degree angles, their diesel engines smoking and roaring savagely.

Aidan slapped Coglin on the back of his bald head playfully.

"Come on, ya bald prick!" he yelled. "Let's eat."

The warm air outside smelled of bacon grease and exhaust. Coglin glanced back at the truck as Lisa bleeped on its alarm from her key chain.

"It's alright to just leave it there?" Coglin asked his uncle.

Aidan yawned at the entrance to the restaurant.

"John," he said. "You have to learn to relax."

The waiter was a short, white-shirted Hispanic who tended to them with a gracious air of formality that seemed strangely out of place in an establishment that lacked air conditioning and had two duct-tape-covered old car seats for booths. He poured their coffees deftly and bowed after he took their orders.

"And water," Aidan called after him. "With ice."

The slow ceiling fan high above in the dark, tin-stamped ceiling pulled their cigarette smoke up in a blue helix.

"Hey, Lees, great job getting us in here," Aidan said with a wink. "How many months ago did you have to make reservations?"

"Fuck you, O'Donnell," Lisa said with a smile. "At least it doesn't smell."

Aidan looked at Coglin.

"You ready to do this, right? Haven't changed your mind?"

"Nope," Coglin said. "Not yet."

"You just follow me and do what I tell you, everything's gonna work out fine."

Coglin nodded.

"That goes for all of ya," Aidan said. He sipped at his coffee. He looked at them and then around the decrepit room, pleased.

No one spoke for a moment.

"Some pep talk," Lisa said. "You shoulda been like a football coach or something."

They all laughed. Travis pointed a finger at Lisa.

"You just make sure you keep your eyes and ears open, little darlin'. Countin' on you to take us home."

After a little while, the waiter appeared with the water pitcher. Coglin glanced out the plate glass window as his cup was filled. Down the block were all kinds of industrial clothing stores. Klein Zippers. Job One Buttons. Acme Clothing Racks. As Coglin watched, a passing businessman in a suit stopped beside the steel shutter of the button store. He placed down his briefcase, looked around and then, facing the store, began pissing against the steel shutter. After a moment, Coglin watched him adjust himself, step carefully over the stream of his piss, pick up his briefcase and move on.

Get up, Coglin heard an interior voice counsel him. *Just get up and go now. There's still time.*

Coglin looked to see if anyone else had witnessed the outside incident, but no one had. He sipped his water. He patted at his sweating face with his napkin. When he turned, the waiter was approaching with their food.

After his meal, he walked back to the bathroom. He splashed cold water on his face, and dried himself with a paper towel. He was sweating again by the time he opened the door. Aidan was waiting in the alcove right outside.

"I need to talk to you," he said, turning to see if there was anyone behind him.

"Something I forgot to tell you before," he said. "After this is over, I got something set up for the two of us."

"What?" Coglin said in the darkened space. "Fort Knox?"

"Wise guy. Listen," Aidan whispered, taking a step closer to him. "There's a container ship leaves out of Port Newark tonight. Captain owes me a favor. Me and you are gonna be on it."

"Where's it going?" Coglin said.

"Does it matter?" Aidan said. "Out of the country. There's gonna be a little heat on this. Best thing to do is lay low. I still know a couple of people from my younger days. I'll set us both up. Papers, everything. That's what you're looking for, right? Unless you want to stick around."

Out of the country, Coglin thought. Farthest he'd ever been from home was a trip he and Karen had taken to Florida. And how far would he have to go?

Far as it took, Coglin concluded. Last train was already out of the station. No getting off now.

"No," Coglin said. "I don't want to stick around here."

"Anything goes wrong, I want you to meet me there, across the street from parking lot three. You know where the port is?"

"By the airport."

"Right," Aidan said. "Three, OK? Don't forget."

"Just the two of us?"

Aidan nodded.

"What'd you do for the captain?" Coglin said.

Aidan's face was grim as he brushed past him into the bathroom.

"Go back and finish your breakfast, boy," he said. "We'll have plenty of time to talk later."

The sun was coming up in the eastern crack of the horizon as they exited the diner. It was blood red and huge. The dirty, iron grates in the sidewalks brightened suddenly, and their dark metal shone pale in the light, like golden cages buried in the ground. Morning rush was underway now, and at the far corner, people, like dual marching armies, were crossing each other on the street. Their silhouettes were very black and thin in the red of the sun, like figures made of burnt matchsticks. Their shadows fell long to the west down the street and scissored back and forth in front of Coglin and Aidan. The slowly cooking air was oppressive; it seemed to suck at Coglin's strength.

"What is it?" Coglin said to his uncle as they stepped toward the SUV. "Red sky at night, sailor's delight. Red sky at morning . . ."

Aidan had turned toward the sun as well and its red light shone coppery on his tight-lined face, making a strange alloy of his metal-colored eyes.

"Come now," his uncle said, ushering Coglin toward the shiny, black truck. "Never mind that. We gotta get going, or we'll be late."

Chapter Sixteen

S O WE'RE INTERVIEWING THIS WITNESS," Carlos said.

"The Uptown thing? The Chase?" Colette said.

She reached down quickly and leaned on the siren of the Crown Vic, freezing the taxi up ahead to the right about to cut her off. They were crawling up Second Avenue in the forties and, as usual, late morning rush was insane. Double strands of crackle fired from both the FBI and NYPD band radios bolted beneath the ashtray as if amplifying the melting of the sun-flooded buildings around them. Roving car duty, even without a hangover, was always a bitch.

"Right," Carlos said. "St. Nicholas Avenue."

He smoothed the lapel of his gray suit. He was an NYPD second-grade robbery detective who hid his smarts behind his Spanish accent, and he was the youngest member of the FBI/NYPD Bank Robbery Task Force. A lot of the agents only liked to go out with other agents, but Carlos was smart and tough at the right times, and she liked to work with him. Plus, he was married, which always made things easier.

"So, there was ten other witnesses we spoke to, and they tell us the guy's black, right? Tall black guy with a red bandana tied around the front of his face."

"Sounds like a Western fan," Colette said.

"That's what we said," Carlos said with a smile. "But a sawed-off instead of a six-shooter and no ten-gallon hat. So anyway, this one witness says no, the guy was Hispanic and the bandana was blue. So, of course, we want to talk to this guy to see why he saw something so completely different.

"It turns out, the witness is this young black kid on his way to college who was at the bank filling out some financial aid stuff. He was this decent sorta citizen so, of course, Bishop starts leaning on him real hard with the robot FBI routine he's got down so well. And I'm standing behind Bishop, just shaking my head, like every word about the guy being Hispanic is making me personally enraged.

"So after about a minute and a half, the kid cracks and says, 'Please don't make me testify. It's my father. My father did it.' So we get his address, call up Greg and Hunt and go to pick him up. We kick in the door, and he's sitting there in his living room, drinking a tallboy watching Judge Righteous Green. Sawed-off was in the closet, money under the bed. Hunt told him he didn't have to watch Court TV anymore, that we had a ticket for him to be a member of the live studio audience."

Colette laughed.

"Turns out, this kid's old man was a career criminal, but the mother was this decent, hard-working token-booth clerk who made her son study hard, kept him out of trouble. Kid went to Stuyvesant and is headed to Brown."

"Nice," Colette said, sipping the Starbucks she'd insisted they pick up outside of 26 Federal. *Ah,* she thought, blinking at the blast of caffeine. *Nitro.*

"So are you gonna make him testify?" she said.

"What do you think?" Carlos said. "Bishop said fuck him. Little Ivy League fucker could write a memoir about it when he gets out of school and make a million bucks."

"You like working with Bishop," Colette said. "I can tell."

"He's a cheap fuck and he's heartless, but he's good at this, isn't he?" Carlos said.

"That's all that counts," Colette said.

"They say you're better, you know," Carlos said, stretching.

He picked up his own coffee. He liked it black, just like she did. Had to love him.

"Actually, they say you're the best," he said.

"That's not all they say."

"That's true," Carlos said. "Hunt says he thinks you're bootyliscious."

"No, he doesn't," Colette said with a smile. "You do. You say that."

Carlos licked his lips as he looked out the window.

"What the hell is it with this traffic anyway?" Colette said, putting the sedan into park behind a now completely stopped Con Ed truck. She gave it a good dose of her siren as if trying to destroy it with the loud laser blast sound. Nothing. Not an inch.

"Weren't you awake this morning?" Carlos said. "Boss said the prez is in town. Our commander and chief has some vital executive duties he needs to attend to in our fair city."

"Some vital city pockets to pick for his reelection campaign, you mean," Colette said. "Some vital streets to snarl."

"Turn that frown upside down, Special Agent," Carlos said. "It's Friday. Put on a happy face."

"Speaking of which," Colette said. "I'm thinking we do a couple of wire leads before lunch, wait until the banks close at one, and then just chill out and listen to the radio. I got some leg-work to do on a couple of cases, but it'll be there Tuesday. Plus, I got a lunch I have to go to in Midtown."

"Great," Carlos said. "Where we going?"

"*I'm* going to be eating in a nice French restaurant. You, I figure, will probably hit a hot dog stand."

"Oh," Carlos said. "We got a date, huh?"

"The leads," Colette said. "Whatta we got?"

Carlos lifted the clipboard onto his lap and turned a paper over.

"Here's one out of Baltimore. Suspect in an armored car robbery there was reportedly seen at corner of One-twenty-fifth Street and Fifth. One Paul Witherspoon, black male in his twenties last seen wearing jeans and a black leather coat."

"Sounds real solid," Colette said. "Paul's still gotta be wearing that coat with this heat, right? And he's black, so that narrows things down. Hope the Baltimore squad is waiting by the phone, because it'll be ringing any second now."

Carlos smiled.

"Soundin' real into the swing of things today, Special Agent."

Colette sipped the coffee and slipped it back into the drink holder.

"I have what we in the Bureau refer to as a hangover, Officer Alvarez. It's very need-to-know."

"It's Detective Alvarez," Carlos said. "Remember I didn't kiss all that ass for nothing. So, we were hangin' out a little late with the good counselor, Phil, were we? And now lunch? Sounds special."

Colette turned to him. It was her turn to be surprised.

"How did you find that out?"

"I'm learnin', Colette. I'm pickin' things up."

"Everybody knows, huh?"

Carlos nodded.

"Great," Colette said.

"What's the problem?" Carlos said. "I like Phil. Some people think he's stuck up, that he's just in this for his political résumé, but let me tell you something. My uncle was havin' some trouble with his green card, and Phil called somebody in INS for me and straightened it right out. He's a nice guy."

"For real?" Colette said.

"No shit," Carlos said.

See Billy, she thought. *Take that. He is a nice guy.*

"So you guys tailin' me or what?" Colette said.

"Well," Carlos said with a smile. "We all tail you to a certain extent."

"I'm tellin' Inez you said that," Colette said.

Carlos sat up in his seat.

"About Inez. We were up the other night talkin' and open marriage came up, and Inez is all for it. So you better let Mr. Phil know he's got his work cut out for him."

Carlos put an arm up on the seat behind her and leered at her.

"That forbidden love thing we got goin' on just got the green light."

"Now I'm definitely callin' your wife," Colette said, taking her Ericsson out of her bag. "You're gonna get in so much trouble."

She hit some numbers with her thumb and lifted the phone to the side of her head.

"You know, that's illegal to do now while driving," Carlos said nervously. "As an officer of the law of New York State, I can't have you doing that."

"I'm federal," Colette said. "My powers like totally supercede yours. Yeah, hi, Inez," she said into the phone. "It's Colette."

When he reached for the phone, she let him grab it.

"Inez," he said in a perky tone of voice before he realized that it wasn't on.

Colette laughed.

"Cops," she said. "Now pick out a real lead, and let's get at least something done."

Carlos put down her phone sheepishly and shuffled paper on the clipboard.

She put the siren on full at a minibus that was actually trying to double park in front of her, until it decided it wanted to move along after all.

She looked over at her partner.

"'Inez,'" she said in a perky voice.

Chapter Seventeen

THEY WAITED FOR LISA a block farther west of the diner. Through the windshield ahead, the glass office towers of Midtown rose sharp and huge behind the old, brick sweatshops of the garment district like shining mountains behind low, brown hills. From the front passenger seat of the SUV, Coglin looked upon an abandoned tenement beside them as a pigeon darted its head out into the now blinding sunlight from a crack in a cinder-blocked window and then quickly retracted it back in.

I'm with you, little guy, he thought. A definite call-in-sick day.

Coglin lit yet another cigarette, wishing he had something cold and alcoholic to go with it.

Lisa had gone in to work to get her telephone truck and would meet them momentarily. Aidan sat in the driver's seat of the SUV, squinting out at the sun glinting off the glass skyline and smoking a cigarette. Coglin sat beside him silently.

He reached at his belt and pressed off his beeper as it hummed for the eighth time in the last three minutes. It was Mulvane. Court had started at nine, an hour and a half ago. He had to be going completely nuts. The judge, the jury, the reporters. He could see them now looking up and down the Grand Concourse.

Sorry, ladies and gentlemen, Coglin thought. The sacrificial lamb has hopped the fence and is heading for the hills.

He checked his watch.

"Stop that," his uncle said. "Makes me nervous."

"You?" Coglin said. "I'd like to see that."

Aidan leaned to his left and peered into the sideview mirror. He pressed a button, and the electric window hummed down and he flicked out his cigarette.

"Here she is now," he said, opening his door.

Her truck was a Ford Econoline cube that had some years on it. There were deep scratches across its front and electrical tape held together one of its side mirrors. But it had the universally recognized telephone company's big blue bell with the circle around it on its side, and Coglin figured that was all that mattered. He passed a hand across the logo as he followed Lisa and his uncle toward its rear.

The back of the telephone truck was filled with battleship gray steel drawers and steel rails and clumps of colored wire and dozens of imponderable boxes and tools. Within thirty seconds, it also held the assault rifles and vests and police scanners.

Travis and Angel got into the back with the guns as Aidan jogged forward and climbed back into the SUV. Coglin climbed up into the passenger side of the telephone truck next to Lisa. They followed Aidan to a parking garage on the corner. They waited a little ways down the block at the curb while Aidan put the SUV in the lot.

"Don't you guys have partners?" Coglin said.

"I sent mine home early," Lisa said.

Coglin squinted out at the forward traffic, rubbed at his hairless skull.

"Lucky guy," he said.

In a minute, Aidan came back and Lisa got out and let him into the back of the truck. When they pulled out again across Ninth Avenue, a skinny black man was starting off the curb with a rack of plastic-covered clothes. Lisa warned him back and the herd of pedestrians beside him with an extended blast of her horn.

"There ya go, Lees," Aidan yelled forward through the metal grate separating the rear from the cab. "Run the bastards down."

They drove crosstown. Morning delivery trucks lined both busted-up curbs of the narrow, soiled streets. Scores of rough looking men loaded and unloaded them. Traffic, cabs and buses, radio cars, trucks clogged the intersections of the avenues. The cross street they were on could've been wide enough for two cars, but Lisa straddled the lanes, her eyes on both mirrors, swerving periodically to block vehicles from trying to cut her off. Horns wailed behind her.

Coglin dropped his cigarette out the window and took out his box for another. The box was empty and he crumpled it in his fist and chucked it into the dusty footwell. Lisa took hers out and passed them to him with her lighter. In the back of the truck, Aidan was telling some story and Travis and Angel laughed periodically.

They made a left on Sixth and went uptown. Office towers, fifty-story frozen waterfalls of black and green glass flanked both sides of the street. Some of the towers to the right on the east side of the avenue were part of the western end of Rocke-feller Center, Coglin knew. Sunlight lay across the avenue at the side street ahead, and Coglin felt its heat land on his skin like a slap when the truck rattled through it.

They made the right onto Fiftieth beside Radio City Music Hall and drove slowly down the traffic-clogged street. They passed the little pedestrian path that cut north/south through Rockefeller Center's two blocks alongside the plaza and the skating rink. Coglin caught a familiar glimpse of white-hot, bright television light through a plate glass window. The colorful flags arrayed around it hung dead and still in the warm air.

They crossed over Fifth Avenue to the right of St. Patrick's, hot dog carts and the tourists sitting out on the pale, dusty steps. They made the left on Madison and then again on Fifty-first and came back toward Fifth on the other side of the cathedral.

Coglin looked at the windows of the stone rectory, wonder-ing if the cardinal was in there. He'd written an editorial in the *Times* all but congratulating the black community for their anger, all but fully agreeing that Ream had been murdered by him. Had also taken part in a "peace pilgrimage" (run by Coglin's favorite charlatan, Reverend Smalls) on the subway that termi-nated with a candle-lit vigil at the platform where he had fought for his life. He gave one of the ornately carved windows a little wave.

Thanks, Your Heavenly Eminence, he thought. *Appreciate all the help.*

"There," Lisa said, pointing at a wheeled cart that was chained to a no-parking sign on the sidewalk to the left in front of Rockefeller Plaza. The bell with a circle around it matched the one on their truck. Coglin flicked his cigarette out and wiped his forehead with the back of his arm as they pulled to the curb beside it.

Coglin followed Lisa out, and she unlocked the back of the truck. When Aidan and Travis and Angel hopped out, they already had on their white plastic phone company hard hats and blue paper coveralls. Coglin could barely detect the bulky line of their bulletproof vests. They all had on sunglasses as well, and as Aidan passed, he put a pair over Coglin's eyes.

Coglin climbed into the back of the truck and put on the bulletproof vest, coveralls and a pair of boots Aidan had given him.

Lisa and the others went to the tool cart, unlocked its chain and rolled it off the curb onto the street in front of a large manhole. Lisa keyed open the lock on the lid of the cart, threw it up and immediately started chucking out traffic cones and orange, plastic stanchions.

The safety area they roped off around the manhole cover reminded Coglin of a boxing ring. Lisa wedged a hooked crowbar into a little space in the cover of the manhole and levered it up. Aidan slid another hook into the crack under the lip of the cover, and on three, they pulled it, scraping onto the street.

Coglin put on a hard hat that was hanging above the doors and looked out warily. A heavy middle-aged woman in an expensive looking suit walked past without even looking at them. A soda delivery man walked quickly behind her, pushing a handcart full of stacked cases. If they or anyone else shuffling past on the nearby sidewalks thought their activity suspicious, they were excellent at concealing it.

Lisa directed Travis and Angel how to set up the rail around the hole. Coglin glanced into the dank darkness of it, at the cables running like a jumble of giant snakes through the murk.

"You go down there?" he said to her.

"Just this one last time," Aidan said, putting his arm around her. Then he gestured at a plastic-covered package by Coglin's feet on the metal floor of the truck.

"Quick now," he said.

It contained the guns and the bulky blocks of clips wrapped in plastic. He passed them out and in a quick assembly line, they were transferred across the safety area to Angel and then to Travis, who secreted them under a yellow, plastic tarp in the tool cart.

Coglin hopped down into the area.

Aidan checked his watch.

"I'm gonna go help Lisa now," he said, walking back toward the truck. "Be back in a few."

Coglin looked after the truck as it pulled out. They were going over to Madison beside St. Patrick's rectory to open the manhole through which the phone lines of the Rock Center building they were about to enter ran. Aidan would walk back and then Lisa would cut the cable, call them by cell phone, and they would go in.

Coglin looked up at the building before him, the majestic rise of its beige-colored sandstone into the dreamy blue, cloudless sky. It had the same type of classic Greek or Roman figures worked into the base of the building's façade that he'd seen on the face of the Bronx courthouse. Thick, androgynous figures, some with arms extended, some crouching. A female in a toga with a breast exposed was layered in gold leaf and she looked aflame in the harsh fall of the sun.

He stood there in the heat, waiting. A pigeon hopped down off the gray curb of the sidewalk into their area, its pink talons scrabbling.

It looked wrong, Coglin thought, dried out, its gray and white feathers more like scales. It pecked viciously at a cigarette butt, sending it flying, and then turned regarding Coglin suspiciously with one of its strange, blank, orange doll's eyes. As though its predicament was somehow Coglin's fault. Sweat from underneath Coglin's hard hat began to drip down the back of his neck and blot in the paper collar of his coveralls.

"I warned you, little fucker," he said to it under his breath. "You should've stayed in bed."

Down the block across Fifth Avenue, there was a construction site. Men in hard hats were sitting down on the sidewalk in front of it with their lunches, more than a few of them crunching open the liquid variety.

Why had he been so stupid? Coglin thought. He'd been one of those men and could still be one right now. Day's work for a day's pay and fuck everything else. Because what else was there? No, *he* had to do something. *He* had to make a difference. Yeah, you made a difference all right, he thought, glancing at the bulk of machine guns under the tarp.

He gazed across at the sunlight winking off the laborer's beer cans. He needed a drink. If he was sure of one thing, it was that. There was a bar down the block, but he didn't want to go in there. He looked around and spotted a grocery store between a couple of small, modern-looking office buildings across the street on the north side.

"I'm gonna get something," he said to Angel and Travis. "You guys want a drink?"

Travis shook his head stoically. He had his arms folded across his chest and was looking west where the truck had gone.

"Hurry your ass up," he said.

"Orange soda," Angel said. "Big one."

"*Mucho grande,*" Coglin said, stepping carefully out across the street. "Comin' right up."

Coglin stopped at the air conditioning vents just inside the door of the deli, took off his hard hat, and let it freeze his sweat. A sneeze-guarded buffet was set up beyond the counter, but there weren't too many people at it yet. Clerks behind the deli case were rolling their necks and stretching their arms as if in preparation for some vigorous event. The cold drinks were in coolers on the back wall, and Coglin stepped through the gloriously frigid air for them.

He found a liter of orange soda for Angel and picked out an ice-cold tallboy for himself. When he was halfway toward the cashier, he decided it wasn't going to be enough. So he went back and exchanged the sixteen-ounce can of beer for a gigantic twenty-four-ounce one. What do you call this one? he thought to himself, hefting it. A big boy? Super boy? Whatever, he thought. He needed courage: liquid, solid, gas, whatever form. More the merrier.

He was waiting on line to pay for it when he spotted his face on the flat screen of the television set hanging down from the ceiling above the cash register. He put on his hard hat. It was the local New York City cable channel and the sound was off. After a second, his picture cut to a male, Asian reporter standing on the steps of the Bronx County courthouse. It said LIVE in the upper right-hand corner, and the reporter spoke rapidly with a grim look on his face.

Then he looked over his left shoulder and the camera panned to the stand they had set up in the park across the street. There were a lot of people around it, more than Coglin had ever seen during the weeks of the trial, and they seemed much more animated than he could remember. On the bright stage itself, a black man he didn't recognize was yelling something, cords standing out in his muscular neck and the crowd beneath him seemed to move in an even more frenzied manner.

A Teletype message, like a warning for a severe storm, started to scroll across the bottom of the screen. LATE BREAKING NEWS: MURDER TRIAL POLICE OFFICER NO-SHOW AT BRONX COURT-

HOUSE. Coglin looked at the time in the upper left-hand corner of the screen: 11:51 A.M.

"Holy shit," he said.

The picture was showing the Asian reporter again and as he spoke, he kept glancing back at a black man behind him who seemed to be screaming at the camera. The scene cut back to the studio.

Thank God he'd warned his mother not to go, Coglin thought. There were a hell of a lot of protesters now. The ones he'd seen the first two weeks seemed more like the media gang, twenty or so professional protesters who knew how to make things look so it seemed like there were hundreds of them. But now, there actually were a hundred or more. And were there any cops there? He hadn't seen any.

"You no drink in here," the old Korean lady behind the counter chastised him.

Coglin tipped his hard hat at her and took out his money.

"Ma'am," he said, still smiling, "if I've offended you in any way, my sincere and deepest regrets."

When Coglin arrived back at the hot and dusty area, Aidan was already back.

"There you are," he said. "Thought you might have taken a powder."

Coglin handed Angel his soda and took another huge slug of his beer. The coldness of it felt even better out here under the burning onslaught of the sun, like coolant he thought, antifreeze protecting him from within.

"After what I just saw," Coglin said, "I wouldn't miss this shit for the world."

Aidan peered at him curiously with an amused smile.

"What?"

"The news," Coglin said. "The late-breaking news. You know

that cop supposed to get convicted for murder today up in the Bronx?"

"Wise-ass narrowback cop?" Aidan asked. "Taken to drinkin' heavy lately? Got a soft spot for Italian broads?"

"The very one," Coglin said. "Well, get this. He never showed, and now there's a riot starting."

"Get the fuck . . ." Aidan said. "A riot over your arse?"

Coglin shrugged, drank again.

Aidan ripped the can away from him and took a long draught. He held it up over his mouth, splashing some across his cheeks. He put an arm over Coglin's back and gestured with the can at the street, the buildings, the sky.

"You always were me favorite nephew," the Irishman said as a cell phone went off in his pocket. He disengaged from Coglin and pulled it out of his paper coveralls as he stepped to the center of the area. He held it up to his ear.

"Umm hmm," he said. "Umm hmmm. Great, sweetheart. Be talkin' to ya."

Aidan clicked the tiny cell phone shut and put it back in his pocket. He looked at each man with a wild, benevolent expression. He raised an eyebrow comically at them.

"Boys . . . ," he said.

Coglin felt a smile play taut on his face, and when he looked at Angel and Travis, he could see they were grinning like fools, too.

"Let's go get rich," Aidan said, and then he stepped over the softening blacktop toward the open cart.

Chapter Eighteen

THE SIDE ENTRANCE of the majestic building had a heavy revolving door made of brass and glass that made a shushing sound when they pushed through it, as if urging silence. Coglin felt the cool of the lobby on the glass with his fingertips. The floor and walls of the corridor inside were inlaid with several types of book-ended dark marble and beyond opened up into a cavernous space with a gold-colored metal ceiling.

Coglin thought it might be gold leaf, but then realized it was a shade duller and figured it to be brass like the door. People up ahead passed back and forth beneath the chamber, their footfalls soft, distant booms in the vaulted space.

The butterflies Coglin had in his stomach were gone suddenly, poisoned by the adrenaline now injected like rocket fuel into his bloodstream. His saliva tasted of copper. No, he thought, glancing up at the ceiling, not copper, brass.

He took a deep breath, the air-conditioned air sweet in his lungs, as Travis and Angel stepped in behind him. They were carrying the plastic-covered rifles, now divided up and stuffed into two large, brown paper sacks. They'd found tapes and tools in the cart and these now lay stuffed at the tops of the sacks, further concealing the rifles. Aidan took a quick step toward the lobby, and they followed him in their sky blue coveralls and white, plastic hard hats.

The marble of the guard's kiosk in the middle of the corridor was black and shiny as onyx and had thin veins of white streaking through it like lightning in a midnight sky. The wide-shouldered, middle-aged black security guard standing behind it looked as if he might've been carved from it. He glanced at them over a pair of bifocals. Aidan already had out his fake phone company ID card and was wearing a grimmer than normal expression as he pushed it at him.

"Please, God, don't tell me it's true," Aidan said to him, leaning hard on his Irish accent. "But would ya do me a favor and lift up your outside line and tell me if there's dial tone on it."

The guard gave Aidan's ID a brief glance as he lifted his phone.

"Of course there's dial tone, I was just talk . . . Hey! No, you're right," the guard said. "It's dead."

Aidan turned toward Coglin with a look of pure exasperation on his face.

"Cut the wrong fuckin' cable," Aidan said. "I told the bastards, didn't I? This'll be somebody's job."

Aidan put his elbow on the guard's desk and lowered his head as if he had just been afflicted with some life-threatening condition.

"You're down," he said. "All of Twenty-four Rock. The whole shebang. They cut all your cables. The fiber, everything. You're out."

The guard stood. The paper he'd been reading slid off his lap and fell to the floor. "We got two company headquarters in here, mister," he said. "We have a network for chrissake. TV studios!"

"You don't have to tell me," Aidan said. "We need to get down to your phone room, see what we got. See if we can pull some slack at least."

He glanced at Coglin.

"You boys can sign in later," he said, lifting his radio.

"Mark!" he called into it. "Mark, get your ass down to the lobby. We got a situation."

The guard pointed down a side branch of the marble corridor in front of him. There was a door at its end.

"Service is on the right, straight down there through that door."

"They want me up here," a voice called out of the guard's radio in a burst of static. "They want me to wait."

"I ever steer you wrong, Mark?" the guard said. "You do what you have to do. But get down here now."

"On the right?" Aidan asked, starting to lead them down the hallway.

"The right, the right," the guard called after them. He gestured with his hands, frantically urging them on.

They stepped down the shiny, stone-lined hall and passed through the door. The grandeur ended abruptly on its other side, and they stood under bright, fluorescent lights in the beige-painted service area before the wide door of the freight elevator. The air was slightly warmer here and smelled faintly of garbage. A half globe of black plastic hung from the ceiling above. They could hear movement and chains rattling behind the door of the elevator. Aidan leaned on the call bell.

"Pull some slack," Travis said with a smile. His drawl was soft. "What the fuck is that supposed to mean?"

"Mind the camera there, boys," Aidan said under his breath.

He turned to Travis with a smirk.

"How the hell should I know?" he said. "I'm a fuckin' crook."

A moment later, a red-haired man in khaki Dickies pulled open the elevator door. The freight elevator was probably original to the old building and had a folding gate and he slid that back as well with a clatter.

"Oh, phone company," he said. "What can I do for you?"

"They cut the cable," Aidan said, stepping past him. "Everything's down. We gotta get to the telephone room."

They all filed in and the maintenance guy pushed the elevator's manual lever forward and they started to descend.

"What about the fiber? They have redundancy, don't they?" he said.

Coglin took a couple of steps back into the left-hand corner of the car. Travis was already behind the man, opening a roll of tape. It made a ripping sound.

"You hear what I . . ."

Travis had the tape around his mouth, wrapping it around his head. Angel pulled the guy's legs out from under him, and the guy fell to the floor as the car jarred to a stop. Travis dug a knee in the man's back, and in thirty seconds, his legs and arms were trussed together in a jumble of tape. Aidan stepped forward and pushed the black handle of the lever back the opposite way and the car started to rise.

Angel ripped open one of the paper bags, exposing the M-16s. He lifted one out and slapped a clip into it. He pulled back the lever beneath the rear sight with a clack, clicked the safety above the trigger housing all the way forward with his thumb and handed it to Aidan. Aidan draped it over the front of his chest without releasing the elevator handle.

"Four," he said, reading the painted numbers on the inside of the shaft doors that sunk beyond the gate as they rose. "Five."

Travis ripped open the other bag. Angel gave Coglin a roll of tape. He didn't ask what for, just ripped open the paper of his coveralls by his pants pocket and stuffed it in. When he was handed the black cloths, he thought it was to wipe the sweat that was pouring off him now, but then he saw Angel put on gloves and pull a ski mask over his face. Coglin followed suit.

The mask was tight, black cotton that felt soothing for some reason. He breathed deeply through its detergent-scented fabric as Angel passed him his rifle. He brought it in front of him and hung it the same way his uncle had. He thought it would be heavy, but it was actually pretty light. He turned it to the side and double-checked that the little latch was on safety with his thumb.

"Thirteen," Aidan said. "Fourteen."

There was a loud, electric snap and the elevator bounced to a stop as Aidan let go of the handle. Coglin felt his stomach leap into his throat.

"We ready?" Aidan said.

Travis pulled on his black mask, bent and chucked the police scanner at Aidan. Aidan caught it and clipped it to his rifle strap. Armed and wearing their coveralls and black masks and gloves, they looked truly terrifying, Coglin thought. His uncle had definitely been right about that.

"Then let's go," Aidan said, concealing his face with his mask and pulling back the elevator's lever.

They rose slowly. Aidan stopped the car flush with the door of the fifteenth floor and quietly rolled back the inside gate. There was a strap on the inside of the vertical shaft door, and he yanked it down and the two doors yawned open like a mouth.

The loud, metal rolling clack of the two doors had not yet

ceased when Coglin laid eyes on the two men standing, mouths agape, directly in front of them. One was black and one was white, and they were both tall and wide and extremely serious looking in their almost identical dark suits. There were little, flesh-colored devices in both men's ears, and he could see over their broad shoulders four or five others like them approaching down a wood-walled corridor.

Suddenly frozen solid, Coglin glanced at the attractive woman talking on a cell phone in their midst. Famous, he thought. For what his suddenly locked-down mind was not letting him know. But she was.

There was a chatter of radio static from somewhere. Then the look of surprise dropped immediately from the faces of the two men standing directly in front of the elevator, and Coglin found his legs giving out, and he slid down into the corner of the car.

She was the vice president's wife, Coglin's abruptly generous mind informed him as his ass hit the elevator's metal floor. The wife of the capital V, Vice President of the United States of America.

Aidan dove suddenly left as the black man brushed aside his suit coat and swung out something black and metal strapped beneath his arm. The white agent was backpedaling with his head down, yelling something into his sleeve.

The first curt, chopping burst of point-blank gunfire came from the black Secret Service agent's Uzi. In the elevator's enclosed metal box, it was like a series of bombs had gone off. Coglin threw his hands over his ears.

Angel, who was standing directly in front of the black man, took the barrage in his face and throat. Ragged holes ripped open the back of Angel's coveralls and ski mask, and he started to sink in a mist of blue and red. Travis had just enough time to bring his

M-16 up to his shoulder before he was shot through the head and went down. Coglin looked up to see the black agent, one knee down, sighting him down the barrel of his Uzi.

Christ no! he thought, throwing up a futile hand he knew would never even make it to his face before the shot.

Then he heard a click.

The black agent cursed and snatched out his empty clip. Behind him, the other men in suits were tackling the woman, who let out a terrified yelp as one cut out her feet, the other going up top, swallowing her up in their arms like boys at a cruel game.

Coglin remained perfectly still.

The black agent had clacked in another clip and was leveling his machine pistol up again when a second burst of gunfire started up from behind him. Beside the protective scrum of agents, a balding blond Secret Service man was in the corridor shooting one-handed, his face red and sweaty behind his Uzi. He was backpedaling as he shot and Coglin, still sitting frozen, watched amazed, as the agent lost his footing on the hardwood floor. The agent went down backward in a comic pratfall-like sprawl, bullets still spitting unceasingly from his right pinwheeling hand.

One errant round caught the kneeling black agent in the back of the head and the rest splattered into the pile of his comrades beside him before the gun ceased.

The blond agent sat up, his mouth open, amazed himself at what he had done.

"Aww, fuck," Coglin heard him say.

The white agent who had been at the door beside the now dead black one appeared in the elevator doorway then and shot Coglin twice in the chest.

The metal wall of the elevator he lay upright upon gonged twice as he smashed back against it. He couldn't breathe. His chest felt as if someone had tried to open it with a jackhammer. He moved his hands at his chest to stanch the blood but there was none. Then he remembered the Kevlar vest he was wearing.

Fuckers really worked! he thought astounded as his breath came back.

His uncle, plastered against the left-hand wall up to this point, took a step out into the open space, raised his rifle and shot the agent three, eardrum-disintegrating times, in *his* chest.

The agent must have been wearing a vest as well because no blood was visible. The clean-cut-looking young man only took a few steps back, looking down at his ripped shirt. Then he shook his head angrily it seemed, threw down the gun he'd shot Coglin with and turned and began stomping quickly away down the corridor. He passed the pile of moaning agents and stepped over the still, fallen blond agent and walked on.

Aidan grasped the strap of the shaft door and yanked it down with a rolling clank.

Trembling, Coglin watched the twin doors slide up and down toward each other like the mouth of a giant creature seen from the inside.

Bullets cracked through the doors as Aidan banged the brass gate shut. He hit the handle of the elevator forward. The ride, so quick on the way up, seemed interminably slow now. Coglin wondered idly if the overhead motor or the cables had gotten shot through. Without releasing the handle, Aidan lifted his mask and wiped his sweaty face with a sleeve. He looked down at Travis and Angel with disgust as he took out his cell phone.

The layer of blood on the metal floor of the elevator car looked as if somebody was mostly finished painting it red. Burnt, brass bullet casings rolled through the blood. Angel and Travis's blue paper coveralls had turned purple with it. Coglin thought insanely of those little paper strips from high school chemistry class. He wondered what the results of the experiment in front of him proved. He raised himself into a catcher's crouch as the blood sloshed, approached his boots.

"Yeah, Lees, listen. Ran into a little problem," Aidan was saying. "No, listen. We can't come back out through the lobby. We're gonna have to go down into the basement and try to get out through the concourse. Speak up, speak up, girl!" he said. "I'm fuckin' deaf. Forty-ninth on the other side of Sixth? OK, we'll try it. Yeah, that's right," he said. "We're gonna be running."

When Coglin turned, he could see the wide rash of bullet holes in the back wall. He probed one, three inches from his head, with a gloved finger as the car rocked to a stop. His uncle stood above him. Aidan reached down and hauled him up by the strap of his unused rifle.

"Bottom floor!" Aidan yelled at him. "Everybody out."

Coglin leaned against the wall wincing, waiting for more gunfire as Aidan opened both the gate and the shaft door and poked out his head. Coglin looked at what was left of Angel and Travis.

"Fuck it," Coglin said weakly to his uncle. "You go if you want. I'll just turn myself in."

Aidan wheeled around, pulled Coglin by his bulletproof vest and slammed him against the wall.

He poked at the bullet holes in Coglin's coveralls with his finger.

"What are these?" he screamed. "They're not gonna let you do that, ya idgit. Turn yourself into a fuckin' corpse maybe!"

Suddenly, Coglin heard a muffled sound and he turned and noticed, for the first time since everything had started, the red-headed maintenance guy they'd taped up, moaning against the back right-hand corner. The tide of blood had washed on the back of the man's shirt and he was trying to move away from it.

Now there was one lucky son of a bitch, Coglin thought as Aidan pulled him out into the corridor.

Coglin's eardrums felt swollen, as though cottonballs had been stuffed into his ears as Aidan half dragged him down a narrow maintenance corridor. Aidan kicked open a door, and they entered a wider hallway that had marble like the lobby above. Clueless people were crossing in the corridor thirty feet ahead.

When they burst to the left into this main thoroughfare, a young businesswoman, thin and gorgeous in a suit and pearls, was walking down a set of stairs twenty feet ahead. If she thought the machine guns and masks odd, it didn't stop her from continuing her approach. Two tall men in sunglasses and suits, Secret Service agents if there ever were any, appeared behind her a half second later, clattering down the stairs, handguns drawn. Aidan dove to his right into another narrow hall with Coglin almost on top of him.

Strength surged through Coglin as he ran down the hall, an animal instinct that seemed to operate of its own accord, his heart and lungs and legs teaming up and deciding to take matters into their own hands.

At the end of the short corridor stood a family of tourists, obese and oblivious, their wide backs to them, reading a map on a wall. A duo of teenage girls exited the front of a clothing store right beside them. One of the girls nudged her friend with an excited, almost beaming, face as they ran past them.

They bore right, and dropped down a short flight of steps into a plaza filled with metal tables and chairs. Before and all around them, tourists and business people were eating lunch, seventy-five or maybe a hundred people. A cop, stationed in the distance beyond the close tables and chairs, yelled and started at them at a run.

Aidan stopped short; Coglin ran into him.

An old lady at one of the nearby tables let out a high-pitched scream.

There was a windowed restaurant a little left of the seated throng and through it at its opposite end: Daylight, white and bright, streamed through a plateglass window. They headed left toward its entrance, picking up speed.

The observant hostess threw herself back against the wall behind her little podium as they thundered past her. They blasted past waiters and well-dressed people hunched over tables and passed through the swinging door of the kitchen. They skidded along the kitchen's stainless steel countertop and came out the open door of the fire exit.

They squinted for a moment in the bright sunlight.

There was a fountain before them and beyond it the unmistakable famous golden statue of falling Prometheus at the very heart of Rockefeller Center.

Tourists stared down at them from among the flags. A flashbulb popped.

Good fucking God, Coglin thought.

The GE building directly before them looked monolithic and very white in the blinding midday light. Coglin stared, mesmerized, at the electric blue sky reflected in its windows. A whistle blew, and then they began running up stairs to their left, climbing them two at a time.

With his rifle, Aidan cross-body-checked a couple of European men posing for a picture at the top of the steps out of their way. Up the flower-trimmed promenade to Fifth Avenue, more big men in suits and mirrored sunglasses were running toward them.

They ran to the right and across Forty-ninth Street. Patrons at the sidewalk café on the opposite corner crouched comically as Aidan and Coglin ran alongside them, like football fans doing the wave in reverse. As they crossed onto Rockefeller Plaza before the glassed-enclosed TV studio, they almost ran directly into a cop mounted on a huge, brown horse. The horse reared slightly and trotted back in a booming clop of hooves.

Aidan and Coglin crossed the plaza diagonally at a hesitant jog. The cop regained his composure and was swiveling in his saddle, drawing his automatic pistol in a cowboy-like pull when Aidan swung his rifle muzzle, not at the cop, but directly at the oblong shape of the horse's head.

"I'll do that fuckin' nag!" Aidan warned. "Try me!"

The cop hesitated, gun wavering. He lowered it.

The first, tentative crackle of gunfire started up behind them as they turned the corner onto Forty-eighth Street. The blacked-out sheet of plate glass shattered in a cymbal crash and fell in as they passed.

They crossed Forty-eighth at a run through the backed-up traffic and headed west. The block was clogged with people, faces widening as they weaved through them. People began to yell, and Coglin could hear the close hard slap of running feet against pavement and frantic shouting behind them. Aidan darted left into what seemed like a glass-fronted store. Following a half step behind, Coglin realized it wasn't a store, but a type of arcade, lined with shops on both sides, that cut through the whole block. As he ran, Coglin could see there were diamonds in the store windows, rows of silver blue and rainbow winks.

Dread flooded through him as he realized their mistake.

A stocky, black, armed security guard exited one of the jewelry shops. Aidan raised his rifle defensively at him, and the guard put up his hands. A short, balding man in the doorway of the adjacent stall drew a squat pistol and fired a round past Aidan's ear. Aidan twirled around and clubbed him to the floor with a rifle butt between the eyes. As police and agents flooded into the corridor behind them, Aidan dropped and began firing, shooting high at the jewelry store window's glass. Alarm bells went off in an amplified end-of-the-world clatter.

Coglin looked out on the sidewalk from smack dab in the middle of the Forty-seventh Street Diamond District. Armored cars lined both curbs of the narrow street. Up and down the sidewalk, security guards, men in silk suits, and bearded Hasidics in funeral black stood still, staring. Two young, beefy undercover cops in T-shirts and sneakers and jeans were running down the block from the west.

Going to die, Coglin thought, remembering the two shots in his chest. Right here. Right now.

His uncle stopped firing and pointed south across the street.

"Go!" he screamed.

Coglin crossed the strangely empty street quickly and darted into the tight space between the front of a UPS truck and the back bumper of a mail truck. When he glanced over to the opposite sidewalk, there was an instant, clacking barrage of fire from the west, and the headlight of the UPS truck exploded. He blinked glass out of his eyes and turned back around in the direction of his uncle.

"C'mon!" he called.

His uncle rose, crossed the sidewalk and was jogging quickly out into the street when the van hit him. It pulled out of a parking spot in a scream of rubber and grazed him with a loud thump. Coglin could see him lying in the street. Aidan dragged himself to a sitting position, leaning back against one of the tires of a parked truck, and ripped the clip out of his rifle, flipped it over and clicked it back in with the heel of his hand. He glanced at Coglin and made a cutting motion at his throat and shook his head. He took out his cell phone and skittered it across the asphalt at Coglin, like a boy skimming a stone. Coglin caught it with his boot, snatched it up and clipped it to the rifle strap. His uncle pointed emphatically east down the block.

"Get gone, boy!" he yelled before rolling under the trailer and firing again.

Cover fire, Coglin thought, blinking.

Coglin found himself moving, running east down the street side of the parked vehicles. He made it about halfway to Fifth when an unmarked sedan and a white SUV screeched to a stop, blocking the road. Armed men in suits spilled out and took up positions behind the vehicles. The first one fired. The mirror of an armored car Coglin ran past shattered above his head. Coglin dove into the space behind it.

More fire followed, bullets whining off the asphalt, clanging off the steel side of the truck. There was a groan of metal from the truck in front of him, and Coglin dropped to the ground and peeked out beside the enormously wide tires at the passenger side and saw a security guard drop out and run for the opposite side of the street.

Coglin climbed up off the hot blacktop. The yellow-and-black sticker on the back of the truck in front of him read, DO NOT PASS ON RIGHT. No choice, he thought, running out for the truck's open door.

A tremendous fusillade of fire chased him to the armored car's cab. There was a sudden sledgehammer-like blow between his shoulder blades that knocked him forward almost off his feet. Another punch struck above his kidney and he realized with horror that he was being shot again. He dove into the truck just in time to see its driver jumping out on the other side. He slammed the passenger door shut, locked it and then leaned across the gearshift and pulled shut the driver-side door. He passed his hand around his lower back under the vest for blood, but there was nothing.

Shot me, he thought. *Fuckers shot me again.*

The two guards had left the truck running, and Coglin climbed into the driver's seat, crouching, and stepped on the clutch. He put it into drive and stomped on the gas. The truck jerked forward and blasted the back of a FedEx truck, and then Coglin clutched and put it in reverse and slammed into whatever was parked behind him.

It took him two more tries to get the truck out, and by the time he cleared the spot, an agent, the same brown-haired one who'd shot him in the elevator, had made it onto the passenger side running board. He held an Uzi to the window and shot. The lead slugs stuck in the exact center of the spiderweb cracks, but the glass didn't break and Coglin roared forward. The truck jerked violently again as he crashed into the parked vehicles on the other side of the street and his passenger was gone.

"No riders, motherfucker!!" Coglin screamed.

Coglin looked out the windshield for his uncle. Aidan was lying facedown in the middle of the street with the two undercover cops slapping handcuffs on him.

"Fuck," Coglin said as he put it in reverse. He floored the gas. From the sidewalks, security guards and storeowners, even the Hasidics, started blasting away at him, squinting behind pistols they'd produced from somewhere, squeezing off shots. Bullets clanged and thunked into the truck like a thunderous downpour as Coglin picked up speed.

The sound was deafening as he collided broadside with the SUV. It skidded back on two wheels for a moment before it flipped in a skittering metal scrape across the avenue. The heavily armored vehicle followed after it, hardly slowing. The air brakes let out a protesting shriek as he slammed on them. The vehicle stopped finally, and Coglin shifted into drive again and swung the stiff steering wheel to his left, pulling slowly forward heading south down Fifth. It seemed the entire world was shooting at him now as he ground the transmission into second. He blinked involuntarily with every shot.

He sideswiped a parked taxi on the south side of Forty-sixth Street as he tried to turn the chunky truck onto it. Then he overcompensated and slapped into a double-parked soda truck on the other side, sending cans flying in a hissing spray across the street. He barely managed to straighten the truck, and he pressed down solidly on the horn as he approached the intersection at Madison. The light had just turned red when he shot across the avenue, and pedestrians on the far side had to dive out of his way.

Traffic was backed up ahead on Park, and he braked and made a hard left onto Vanderbilt, blasting his horn. He spun the big, heavy wheel to the right, straining to turn the tanklike truck east, the wrong way onto Forty-seventh. A speeding taxi swerved, whining to his left, and he crossed over the southbound side of Park Avenue. He hopped the high cement curb of the grass-filled median as the truck turned into the northbound lane, and the people standing there jumped back and fell onto the grass.

When he looked into the driver-side mirror, he was surprised to see no one in pursuit behind him. Then suddenly, two government sedans followed by a police blue-and-white, screamed through the intersection fishtailing, black smoke from their brakes rising behind their flickering lights.

He made it as far as Fifty-second and was running the red light when the cement truck hit him. He'd sensed it a second before as it emerged giant and metal and unstoppable from the east side of the avenue. He decided to stomp down harder on the gas to try and beat it. Had he been going a fraction faster, he would've missed it completely. But the very left of the cement truck's enormous steel grill nicked the speeding armored car's back bumper, and the world tilted left of center as the wheels of his truck left the ground.

There were several almost musical pops as the armored truck flew sideways effortlessly through the steel scaffolding of a sidewalk shed on the corner. The force of the flying steel roof of the armored car sheared the wooden construction fence instantly in half. There was a mound of excavated dirt on the other side, and the truck passed through it, leveling it table straight before coming to a jarring rest on its passenger side as it struck the caterpillar tread of a crane.

When Coglin opened his eyes, he found himself out of his seatbelt turned around, miraculously unhurt. He was on the other side of the steering wheel, his side pressed into the curved space of the dashboard, his back and ass against the windshield. There was something wedged on the other side of his leg, and he looked down.

It was a huge stack of something. Papers or phone books tightly wrapped in high gauge, shrink-wrapped plastic. But it wasn't papers he saw as his eyes focused.

It was hundred-dollar bills.

It must've flown from the rear of the vehicle through the open grate at the back of the cab during the crash.

Take it? he thought.

Gonna get shot in a second anyway, his adrenaline- and shock-drunk mind told him.

Why the fuck not?

He unwedged himself and grabbed the money. It was heavy, about forty, fifty pounds, and he military pressed it above his head onto the shelf now made by the side of the driver seat by the door.

He could hear the groan of the transmission as he stepped on the now sideways gearshift to open the driver door latch. He threw the spring-loaded handle, put a knee on the steering wheel and threw the heavy driver's side door up. It slammed open across the outside cab like the door of a cellar.

He tossed out the money first, pushing it over the still spinning front left wheel. He heard it thump on the ground as sirens and screeching brakes blared right behind him. He climbed quickly out of the cab, dropping to the dirt beside it.

He took out the rubber tape, still in his pocket, and looked down at the heavy, awkward brick of cash. With a couple of quick, loose wraps, he improvised a handle around the left side of the brick and then made a bunch of quick turns improvising a tape strap on the other side. When he lifted it onto his back, he realized he should've made the wraps bigger, but under the circumstances he decided it was gonna have to do. He jogged, the still strapped M-16 banging against his chest, around the side of the truck.

He'd crashed into a block-long excavation project. Before him, beneath the bulldozer, there was a cavity in the earth with some wooden molds set into it, and on its opposite side, a dirt ramp led to an open, wooden gate that exited onto the next uptown block. A gang of construction workers with sodas and sandwiches stood in the opening, watching him as he slid and stumbled down the dirt embankment. He ran across the tops of the molds and struggled up the slope onto the opposite dirt ramp, a lone, brave, cash-wealthy soldier trying to capture a hill.

The workers scattered when they saw the rifle. A shot cracked behind him and the dirt exploded before the toe of his boot. *Hah, missed me,* he thought, staggering, breath ragged, toward the gate. The second shot tugged at the money on his back, almost turning him around as he reached the street. He threw himself right, down the sidewalk eastward.

People scattered very wisely on the sidewalk in front of him.

A ski mask, tattered blue coveralls, an M-16 and a couple of million in cash Saran-wrapped to your back, Coglin observed, stood out even in New York. He was halfway down the block when the phone Aidan had given him began to chirp. He pulled it off the rifle strap as he ran.

"What?" he got out.

"*Where are you?*" Lisa yelled at him.

"Fifty," Coglin said. His breath ripping out of him with difficulty. "Third . . . heading . . . toward Lex."

"Listen," she said. "There's a big silver building on the southeast corner of Lex."

"The Citicorp . . ." Coglin said. "I see it."

"Go into it. It goes through the block onto Third. Get out on the Fifty-fourth Street side and cross Third. There's a post office garage halfway down the block that cuts from Fifty-fourth to Fifty-third."

Coglin could hear his pursuers on foot again behind him. They wouldn't be able to drive at least because it was a westbound side street. He started to run faster.

"I'll be waiting for you just to the right of the garage door," Lisa said. "The back door will be open. Make sure you got some distance when you make it to the other side of the garage. I'll pull out as you jump in. It's our only chance."

Coglin clipped the phone back onto the rifle strap as a blue-and-white streamed across Lex ten feet in front of him, lights and sirens on high. It shrieked to a stop a block ahead as Coglin made the corner. Two more were screaming from the north as Coglin waded into traffic. He stopped in his tracks as the wall of a bus blew past his nose, and then he turned on the speed, barely beating a taxi and one of the cop cars to the opposite curb.

There was a set of stairs leading down to the glass entrance of the shiny, steel skin of the Citicorp building. People were coming out of the building and sitting around the little plaza as Coglin tumbled down the steps. The clacking pistol fire, following him as he reached the bottom, shattered the glass revolving door in front of him into a million pieces. People were screaming as Coglin stumbled, surfing across glass, into the building.

The security guard in the low corridor stared at him in wonder as Coglin ran past into another wide, high-ceilinged plaza full of tables and chairs. He couldn't find an exit, but there was an escalator leading to the upper part of the plaza and Coglin hit it, two moving stairs at a time.

He was crouching, making as little a target of himself as he could as he ran through the wide doorway of a Barnes & Noble. He flew along the carpeted aisle lined with books and up a couple of stairs into a café. At the end of the café there was no door, just the glass wall of the building. Beyond the window, half a story below, traffic crawled past on Third, the post office building Lisa had told him about on its opposite side.

Coglin lifted the rifle and pulled the trigger without slowing. The sheet of glass exploded with a triple boom and Coglin hurled himself out. He smashed into the tar roof of a sidewalk newspaper stand with his chest, as if he were trying to tackle it. He dropped to the street, gasping.

One of the tape straps had broken and the money dangled precariously from his back. He felt like he was breathing through a straw as he pulled himself woundedly across Third.

A taxi rolled slowly into him, knocking him onto its hood. Coglin pushed himself off and with a skipping lurch, finally made the east side of Third. The wide garage door of the post office loomed fifty feet ahead on his right, and he held his breath, trying to ignore the million requests by his pain-racked body to just stop and drop to the pavement. Five seconds later, he crossed its threshold.

Through the wide door, post office trucks were backed to soiled cement loading docks. The sunlight of Fifty-third Street beckoned at its opposite end like the light at the end of a dark tunnel.

He couldn't see Lisa's truck.

Didn't care.

The money was like a slippery anvil on his back. He felt one of his knees buckle as he trudged, closing the distance. He shrugged the rifle off his neck and let it drop with a clack.

Ten feet.

Five.

One.

He was out in the blinding sunlight again, and Lisa's telephone truck was idling at the curb to his right with its back door open, Lisa waving at him animatedly beside it. He climbed up the steel bumper and collapsed inside to the shadowed metal floor. The door slammed shut behind him, locked. Lisa got back into the front and slowly pulled out.

There was the high scream of a siren and the truck slowed. Hyperventilating in the back, Coglin waited for the command for him to halt and come out with his hands up. But by then the police cruisers had already raced by on Third and the phone truck was again moving steadily, the steel floor humming along comfortably beneath him as Coglin tried to breathe, laugh and cry all at once.

Chapter Nineteen

COLETTE'S CELL PHONE RANG toward the end of lunch. The white-jacketed waiter was pouring coffee when the chirp started from inside her jacket and beeped loudly into the hushed silence of the bistro. She pulled it out quickly and glanced down to see Carlos's number on the caller ID. She'd told him not to bother her unless it was an emergency. She pressed on the phone before it could ring again.

"Hold on," she said quickly into it.

"Sorry," she said to Phil and his parents, rising sheepishly. "I have to take this."

"Please, Colette," Phil's father said, leaning back and smiling his perfectly unreadable smile. "We understand."

Would the Senator's elegant rejoinder have been any different had she suddenly let off a shot into the ceiling? She didn't think so.

The Senator, she thought. *Lunching with an actual senator.*

Phil's gaunt-faced mother adjusted her napkin on the skirt of her designer suit without looking up.

Phil shook his head slightly at Colette in a way to tell her not to worry about it.

As she stepped over the rich carpet toward the front of the restaurant, Colette sensed a general tilt of subtly surgically tightened, middle-aged female eyebrows from the tables around. Silent group admonishment for violating some kind of clubby, no-cell-phone policy from the same lunching ladies who'd instantly evaluated and rejected her when she'd stepped into the fancy restaurant forty minutes earlier. She felt like flipping her creds at them. On the job, petrified snots. On the job.

She stopped by the maître d's podium inside the curtained door and lifted the phone.

"Carlos," she said. "What's up?"

"Multiple shots fired at Rockefeller Center," Carlos said grimly. "Just came over the radio."

"Which one? Mine?" she said.

"No, mine," he said.

"Get outta here."

"They said something about the Secret Service and they're calling in every available ambulance."

President's in town, she remembered with a cold start. Her free hand brushed against her ten millimeter.

"Where are you?" she said.

"Uptown," he said. "Ninety-first and B-way. Stuck in traffic."

"I'll walk," Colette said. "Get your ass down here. Call me when you get close."

"What about the boss man?"

"We'll call when I see you," she said and hung up.

When she turned around, Phil was standing there.

"Have to go," she said. "There's been a shooting at Rockefeller Center."

"A shooting?"

"Tell your father to hang out here for a little while longer, would you?" she said, checking her bag for her extra clip. Had her notebook, pens. Crime scene gloves were in the trunk of the Vic. She'd just wait then. She patted her gun. Unclip the holster? Better wait.

"My father?" Phil said.

"The shooting has something to do with the Secret Service," she said, looking him in the eye.

"The president?" Phil said, wide-eyed.

"I honestly don't know. Apologize for me, OK?" she said. She gave him a brief kiss.

"Going off to a gun fight?" he said, passing a hand through his thick, black hair. "Shouldn't I say, 'Don't go' or 'That's my job' or something gallant and macho like that?"

She shrugged her shoulders and hauled open the door to the hot street.

Jogging, it took her three minutes to get to Fifth. She knew something was seriously up even before she got to the corner, because she hadn't seen one car pass on the avenue south. Turning the corner, she'd never seen so many spinning lights. Ambulances, police cars, federal Suburbans, unmarked police cars. Around them, a crowd was growing larger by the second.

"Excuse me," she said loudly, wading through the bodies. "Federal agent. Excuse me. Out of the way."

Already the crowd was in a frenzy around the flipped SUV, snapping pictures and holding video cameras high. She bent under the tape. A burly, bald police sergeant with a handlebar mustache put out a blocking hand. She put her ID into it.

"How you doin', Sarge?" she said. "Whatta we got? A robbery?"

He double-checked her ID.

"OK," he said, turning, guiding her west across Fifth. She looked up at the two giant diamonds flanking Forty-seventh.

Diamond district, she thought.

Holy Christ Almighty.

"Special Agent, this is it," the sergeant said. "Ten, fifteen minutes ago, two males in black masks with automatic weapons entered the middle of the block through that arcade from Forty-eighth there on the right."

"They hit someplace?"

"It's unclear at this point. They shot up the street. One of the white males was struck by a van. He's in custody. The other one got into one of the armored cars parked on this block and managed to blast through a roadblock and escape crosstown. I don't know if he's been caught yet. They're in pursuit."

"The Suburban? Secret Service?" Colette asked.

"Far as I know. Apparently, the two men were fleeing Rockefeller Center. I was told to hold this crime scene, and that's what I'm trying to do."

"Do you know if the president is there?"

"I don't know," the sergeant said, peering down at her. There was a kind of sick look on his face. "I don't think so, but I don't know."

"Injuries?"

"A couple of people cut with glass. Another guy got a rifle butt in the mouth. A miracle considering the amount of gunfire. I was in 'Nam and it brought me right back. If I'd had the coordinates, I would've called in an air strike."

Colette nodded.

"The one you caught, what did he look like?"

"White male, middle-aged, stocky, black hair, blue eyes, oh, and he had an Irish accent. Believe that? Fuckin' disgrace."

Colette pushed the hair out of her face.

Irish? Black hair? *No*, she thought. Impossible. He was still in jail, right?

"Had a big broken nose?" she said.

"Yeah," the sergeant said. "Face like a lousy boxer, now that you mention it. You know the skell?"

"Maybe," she said. "We arrested an Irishman a couple of years ago on an armored car job in California. Same MO. I'll have them fax a picture over. Where'd they take him? Midtown South?"

"No, North got the call," he said.

"The arcade is where?"

The sergeant extended one of his long arms to the west. "Up there to your right," he said.

"Thanks, Sarge," she said.

Jesus, where to start? she thought, clipping her credentials to her lapel and walking west up Forty-seventh. She looked at the surreal, empty street, the oddly silent spectators behind the tape, the blue police barricades. Who had jurisdiction? The Secret Service? She'd call her boss to confirm that, but he was an asshole, and if he found out Carlos wasn't there, there'd be trouble. She looked up as a low-flying police helicopter slipped into the slot of sky between the office buildings and began to hover. She could feel her heart slap with the thump of its blades.

An old Hasidic man with a long, gray beard walked past her as she stepped onto the sidewalk. He held a silver Colt Python loosely in his age-spotted hand.

"Put that gun away, sir," Colette said firmly.

"I have permit," the man said, ignoring her.

She wheeled around with her badge.

"Well, I have this, sir," she said. "Put that away or I'll have you arrested."

Grumbling in a language she couldn't understand, the old man opened his black coat and stuffed the .357 into a shoulder holster.

The confrontation made her feel better, more focused. Secure the crime scene. Evaluate. Gather evidence. Do her goddamned job. Be in charge until she found somebody who was.

O'Donnell, she thought. Was it really him?

She walked to where the yellow tape seemed most concentrated.

An EMT was tending to a small, old man in a bloody white shirt by some stairs. The ground around them was littered with burnt brass shell casings. Colette went under the tape and lifted up one: .223s. Military rounds. The same ammunition they used for the M-16s they trained with at the army base up in Westchester. She looked at the carpet of broken glass covering the corridor behind the man. Police and slick, nervous-looking men in suits stood in front of the stalls of jewelry stores that flanked both sides of the low-ceilinged gallery.

"The men were shooting from here, were they, sir?" Colette said down to the small, bloody man.

"Shooting and shooting," the man said in an Israeli accent. "I tried to shoot one of them, and he did this to my face."

"You tried to shoot one of them?" Colette said, shocked.

"I have gun for my store. Two years in the army in Israel."

"You missed him?"

"Barely, yes."

"Did he shoot back at you?"

"No, he gave me a face full of rifle butt instead, bastard son of a bitch."

Down through the opening of the corridor, she saw a pack of

shorthaired men in suits pass by on Forty-eighth. She stepped up the stairs, careful of the broken glass.

Out on Forty-eighth, a gray Crown Victoria with five long antennae on its trunk was parked sideways in the street. Two large men in dark suits were standing by its hood.

"Agent?" Colette said, holding her ID out as she approached. "FBI Bank Robbery. Heard the call on the radio. How can we assist?"

"FBI just got here," the larger, curly-brown-haired man with linebacker eyes said into his fist. He looked at Colette, nodding as he received information into his flesh-colored earpiece.

"OK," he told his fist. "Right away, sir."

He held a hand out toward Rockefeller Plaza.

"This way," he said.

"Is the president alright?" was her first question as they stepped across the plaza.

"Yes," the agent said, turning right at the corner.

A black-booted cop with a horse stood in front of a sidewalk café holding his big brown steed, talking into its ear as he brushed its mane.

"He's fine," the Secret Service man said. "It was the second lady. She's dead."

Colette felt a numbness spread down the front of her chest to the tips of her toes.

"The vice president's wife?" she said. "My, God. That's . . . I'm sorry. You guys must be . . ."

"She was on the network morning show earlier," the agent said, gesturing at the studio behind the glass across the street.

There was a screech of brakes from across the plaza as a news van stopped. Colette released her grip on her ten millimeter at her hip only a second after the agent did on the SIG Sauer under his arm.

"Afterwards, she was invited to view some jewelry on display at one of the network's offices on Fifty-first," the agent said as they continued north. "Four men armed with M-16s came up in the freight elevator as the entourage was leaving. There was a gunfight. Two of our agents were killed, and two are on their way to trauma at Bellevue right now, hanging on for dear life. The second lady took several direct hits in the chest and died instantly. She's en route there as well."

"Christ, I'm sorry," she said.

The Secret Service agent's eyes squinted, his face hardening for a moment before he continued.

"Two of the assassins were killed by our men in the elevator. Two managed to get down to the concourse level and escape to the south. One was caught. They're taking him to Midtown North, I believe. The other . . ."

"Escaped crosstown in an armored car," Colette said.

"Did they catch him?" the agent said urgently, showing emotion for the first time.

"I don't know," Colette said. "Police sergeant told me they're in pursuit."

The agent stopped, pointed below at where the skating rink usually was. There was some type of restaurant there now with umbrella tables spread about the space. More yellow police barrier tape snaked down the steps and through the tables into a door.

Follow the yellow brick tape, Colette thought distractedly.

A couple of beat cops were talking to some waitresses just inside the door. They stood straighter and adjusted their hats when Colette stepped through with her guide. They came through the empty interior of the restaurant and went out into a low, air-conditioned corridor lined with stores. They passed through an area with metal tables that reminded her of the food concourse in a mall and followed the tape to the right into another narrow corridor.

"This goes all the way to Fifty-first?" she said, looking around.

"Uh-huh," the Secret Service man said.

They crossed over a wider, marble-lined hall at its end. When they entered a narrow service hallway, Colette looked down and saw footprints, two sets of boots, large and blood red, pointing back in the direction they'd just come.

They pulled open a door into a corridor that was jammed with agents and cops.

As they pushed through the crowd of law enforcement toward the open door of an elevator, Colette caught a thick, unmistakable whiff of blood.

Meat, she reminded herself. Just think of it as butchered meat.

Two men were splayed out in the center of the car. One white, one Hispanic maybe. They'd both been shot in the face and head. The white one had an M-16 strapped around him and by the outstretched hand of the Hispanic, an Uzi lay in a pool of black blood. Black masks sat in the congealed blood beside them. Colette looked at the mess of bloody footprints on the floor in front of the elevator. The agent spit at the white body, his gob landing right on the wound between the man's eyes.

Colette gave him a second.

"You're gonna have to get all these men out until crime scene gets here. They're tampering the hell out of this place."

"Yeah, you're right," the agent said, not taking his eyes off the carnage. Then he turned suddenly and pushed back through the crowd without a word.

"Gentlemen," Colette called. Nobody was listening to her. She leaned toward a black NYPD boss in a white shirt beside her.

"Lieutenant, do me a favor. Secure this place until crime

scene gets here. We all want to know what's going on, but evidence is getting compromised."

"You heard the lady," the lieutenant bellowed. "Move on out."

She caught up with the brown-haired Secret Service man out in the hall. He led her down yet another corridor and up a set of stairs into the building's ornate lobby. Radio crackle from the dozen cops and agents standing around echoed across the gilded dome of its high ceiling. The media was all over the place, crowds of reporters and cameramen pressing against the glass entrance doors of Fifth Avenue like rock fans right before they opened the arena.

At a kiosk to the left of the stairs, a couple of plainclothes cops, city detectives probably, were talking to a guard and a red-headed maintenance guy. Colette looked at the blood painted down the side of the worker's shirt and pants. The Secret Service agent pressed the elevator button.

"Hold up a second," she said to him, stepping toward the men.

"... shut it again and then we went back down," the redhead was saying. The detectives glanced at Colette as she stepped up, and she pushed her lapel at them. She watched them roll their eyes at each other, as she took out her pad and pen. One of them put out a hand at the redhead. "All yours."

"You were in the elevator, sir?" she said.

"I just got through telling them," he said in a whining tired voice. Was he in shock? she thought. No, she decided, you couldn't whimper when you were in shock.

Colette smiled at him sympathetically, phased out the audience.

"You must've gone through hell," she said, touching him on the arm. "I'm sorry for that. But right now is when it gets decided if we catch these people or not, and you can help us more than anyone else."

The redhead blinked, taking in her looks despite his shock. He started nodding.

"OK," he said. "I was upstairs."

He told the story. How he got called down, how they ambushed him.

"How'd they get in the building?" Colette said.

"Phones," the guard interrupted. "Phones went down and a second later, they came in wearing those blue work outfits. They had ID. They had a hole open outside there on Fifty-first. I seen them on my break. Probably still open. Then the phones were down and the Irish one said they needed to get down to the phone room in the basement."

Hole, she wrote, 51.

"The Irish guy did the talking?" she said.

"Yeah," the guard said. "Seemed friendly enough."

Knock out the lines and come in like a phone crew strapped to the teeth, Colette thought. Not a bad plan. What had the Secret Service guy said? Some type of jewels on display in an office. Needed inside information there, but pros, real pros, were good at information. Might have worked if they hadn't bumped into the entourage. If they'd had a good getaway.

It definitely could have been O'Donnell, she thought. Maniac had professional pride in what he did. Hit Rock Center in the middle of the day. This kind of epic shit was right up his alley.

"Didn't you see their rifles?" she said to the guard. "The M-16s?"

"They had a whole bunch a shit in big bags," the guard said defensively. "Tools and stuff. How the hell should I know what it is? All the lines were down. What was I supposed to do? Strip-search them? You know how much I get paid?"

Exactly the same amount you won't be making tomorrow after they fire you? Colette thought.

"Phones out still?"

"Yep," he said defiantly.

"OK," she said, taking out her cards and handing them out to the guard and maintenance guy.

"Thanks a lot, guys. You think of anything else," she said, walking away toward the agent, "let me know."

They took a wood-paneled elevator to fifteen. More cops stood outside the curved glass wall of the office entrance. The interior offices they passed were encased in glass as well, the stainless steel of the chairs and desks inside them glowing mutely in the dull glare of flat-screen monitors. Small groups of stunned, young office workers stood in the corridor talking quietly. A heavy, middle-aged woman came out of a bathroom crying.

Around the corner at the back of the office was the freight elevator. Its door and all around it was riddled with bullet holes, smeared-looking buttons of lead in the pocked painted wood, the craters of plaster. Blood was pooled on the painted cement apron right before it. Colette stopped before another pond of blood, thick and black on the shiny blond wood of the floor. A lone pink high-heeled shoe lay in its center like a strange island.

In front of the elevator, an older Secret Service agent with close-cropped silver hair held a wad of bloody toilet paper to his forehead as he spoke into a cell phone.

Colette turned back the way they had come. She searched for bullet holes from the fire that had come from the elevator into the office, but the hall was surprisingly intact.

Funny, she thought. If the entourage was coming down this same corridor and the fire was coming from the elevator, you'd think it'd be shot to shit.

She looked up suddenly at her large escort.

"What was the deal with the jewelry?" Colette said.

"It was for the award show tonight," the agent said. "Two private armed guards set up with the jeweler in an office back near the front. They left right after."

"What kind of gems were they?"

The agent gave her an angry, how-the-fuck-should-I-know expression.

"Diamonds?" she said.

"Sure, diamond necklaces and shit. Fancy expensive stuff the stars were supposed to wear tonight. What does that matter?"

"How many agents were in the entourage?"

"Six," the agent said. "Standard set-up. Why the third degree?"

Aren't we touchy? Colette thought, holding his heavy gaze. But why wouldn't he be, she realized. This was a massive fuck-up. Just like the security guards' downstairs, heads were gonna roll.

"She's here now," Colette heard the bloody agent by the elevator say. He snapped his fingers and gestured for her to come around the crimson puddle.

She ignored the "here, boy" gesture. Just been through hell. Probably didn't know what he was doing. He handed her the phone as she arrived.

"Who am I speaking to?" the voice from it commanded.

"Special Agent Colette Ryan, Bank Robbery Squad FBI," she said quickly.

"This is Assistant Director Dick Dunlop. What in the hell do we have over there?"

She couldn't say anything for a second.

Assistant director of the Bureau, she thought. And right after lunch with a senator. Turning into a busy day.

"Far as I can tell at this point, Assistant Director, looks liked a botched robbery."

She sensed both Secret Service agents glare at her.

"Robbery?" he yelled. "Nobody said anything like that."

"I think it was an attempted takeover robbery. Apparently, there were diamonds on display here. I think the perpetrators were going for that and bumped into the second lady and the Secret Service by accident."

"Why do you say that?"

"Well, the diamonds and the fact that they knocked out the phone lines. And, I'd have to confirm it, but I think I might know the man they arrested."

"Have you spoken to the suspect?" Dunlop said.

"No," Colette said, "The police have him in custody. But I've heard the descriptions and by the MO I'd bet my paycheck he's an Irish national, an ex-IRA man we caught in California for an armored car heist a couple of years ago. Name's O'Donnell."

"Ex-IRA!" the assistant director said. "A terrorist? That smacks of assassination to me, Agent. What did he do in the IRA?"

"Well, actually, I think he was a sniper."

"A sniper? Jesus Christ. He was probably hired."

"I don't think so, Assistant Director."

"Why the hell not?"

"Well, I'm no expert, but snipers work alone, and they don't have to be five feet away. O'Donnell was a pretty good one, by the files we got from MI5. Confirmed kills at more than seven hundred yards. If he wanted the second lady dead, seems to me, he didn't have to look her in the eye. Besides, I believe he's changed careers. Learned how to be a bank robber in the IRA to raise funds. File suspected him as the principal for eight Dublin banks hit for three million in the late eighties."

And why would anyone want to assassinate the second lady? she held off from saying. They didn't like her cookie recipes in *Better Homes and Gardens*?

She glanced at the bloody pink pump, regretting the thought.

Could she try to stop being such a heartless cunt for thirty seconds?

She waited in the electric silence.

And why, she wondered, was she arguing with the assistant director?

"Why is Bank Robbery on this anyway?" the executive agent finally said. "Where's your boss?"

Well, if it wasn't before, it was validated now that he was FBI, she thought. When in doubt, pull rank.

"I was on roving car, sir," she said. "I was just closest. I'm the first one here."

"And you think you know the one who killed the second lady?"

I think I know the one they arrested, she wanted to say.

But who killed the second lady? she thought, looking at the rash of bullet holes in the elevator door.

Couldn't really say.

"The description of the one they arrested seems mighty familiar," Colette tried. "I'm going to have our office fax . . ."

"Scratch the fax, agent. I want you talking to this terrorist ASAP, and I want a call as soon as you're done. I'm at the Ellis Island reception. The president is grounded here until things are settled. Take down my number."

He recited it to her.

"Have they caught the one who got away in the armored car?" he said.

"Not to my knowledge."

"What does it look like there, Ryan?"

"Look like?"

"The vice president is insisting on visiting the crime scene as soon as he's done viewing his wife's body. What's your call?"

"Um, no way, sir," she said. "This place is a war zone. Better to wait until crime scene can do their job and clean up. Who are they sending by the way? Us or . . ."

"Secret Service director has formally asked our assistance in this investigation. Our guys are en route from 26 Fed right now. Any other questions or do you think you can be on your way?"

"I'm gone, sir," she said and hung up the phone.

"It wasn't a fucking robbery," the older bloody agent said to her as she handed him back his cell.

She ignored him and took out her own phone as she carefully skirted the rim of blood.

OK, she thought as the phone began to ring in her ear, order one: Talk to O'Donnell. See if he wanted to what? Roll over? Sign a confession? Fat chance there. Last time, he'd just smiled at her like the Cheshire cat and asked her real politely if it wouldn't be too much trouble, Miss, to give his lawyer a call. Maybe if she talked death penalty. She'd also have to get Bishop and Hunt to come up and stay with crime scene, check the hole outside. Maybe there'd be a hot dog vendor or somebody on the corner who'd seen something.

She hoped she was wrong, but she had a feeling she wasn't hearing the whole story from her colleagues in the Secret Service. She shook the thought out of her mind. Don't jump to conclusions. Let crime scene do their magic, then they could evaluate later. Whatever happened, they'd be able to figure it out.

This was it, she thought excitedly. *The big league shot. The career maker.*

Or breaker, she thought.

"Yeah, Carlos," she said, brushing past the brown-haired agent who'd escorted her up as she made her way back toward the elevator.

"Where are you, man? I need you."

"Yeah, well, fuck you, too, bitch," she heard the agent call at her back.

Chapter Twenty

FLAT ON HIS ACHING BACK on the low roof of an Eighth Avenue methadone clinic for the last ten minutes, Coglin had worked the recent events over in his shell-shocked, strained mind, and he'd finally condensed things down to a one-word conclusion.

Wrong.

The two tremendous air conditioning units he was hidden behind started up suddenly, their violent humming sounding out in the hot sour air around him like an outraged chorus echoing the thought.

Wrong wrong wrong wrong wrong.

Lisa had driven them carefully away from the East Side pursuit back over here to the West Side garment district to hide. He'd gotten out of his coveralls and Kevlar and she'd led him through an alleyway to a fire escape and left him lying here on this rooftop. She told him to lie still and wait until she got rid of the phone truck.

Or maybe, he thought, she'd just left.

Couldn't blame her.

It hadn't gone half bad, he thought, feeling the numbing soreness at his chest and back where the bullets had walloped into him. It had gone all bad.

Secret Service, he thought. The goddamn actual Secret Service.

How many dead?

The black agent who'd shot Angel and Travis was definitely. He'd seen that guy's fuckin' head explode. There was no fixing that. The pile on top of the woman, correction, the pile on top of the wife of the vice president of the United States, seemed to have been shot to shit as well, but who knew?

Calm down, he thought. Maybe she was OK. Maybe they'd protected her.

Coglin shook his head.

Who was he kidding? That fat, trigger-happy asshole agent with the Uzi had mowed them all down. He remembered the dumb look on the man's face as he sat up. Whoops, huh, you fucking retard? Why couldn't you at least have had the decency to shoot me, too?

He closed his eyes.

Gunfire and blood and death.

There was no rock he could crawl under. No time machine to hop into and go back and make it all right. Dead federal agents. Dead woman.

A copkiller. He'd become a fuckin' copkiller.

He thought of the things they said about him in the paper during the trial. The portrait of him as a blood-thirsty monster.

Maybe they weren't wrong after all, he thought. Maybe they'd been right from the very start.

A full minute passed before he opened his eyes again. Same

sun beating down between the black dusty buildings. Same burning metal box at his side screaming its grating roar.

No more debate, he thought. No more destructive considerations. There was only one thing to do.

End this fucking thing before anybody else who had the misfortune to come into his vicinity got killed.

He jumped as he felt a tug at his foot. Lisa waved him up. He lay unmoving for a moment. He was incredibly tired, wearier then he'd ever been. Then he slowly started pushing himself up, his hands burning imprints into the soft gritty tar paper as he hauled his bruised, aching carcass onto his knees.

Back onto the sidewalk, the world seemed comfortingly normal. Same stained clumps of sweating addicts peering over their thin, dying shoulders, same third worlders rolling clothing racks and hot dog carts up and down the blackened, stinking block. The only thing different was the black SUV parked now at the curb ten feet away.

A minute later, sunk in its soft leather with the solid, metal door solidly shut, Coglin fantasized that it hadn't really happened. That it'd all been some midday nightmare vision brought on by heatstroke and exhaustion. Then he turned and looked down at the huge, brick shape of the money under one of the hotel blankets on the floor of the backseat.

He shook his head.

"What do we do now?" Lisa said, climbing behind the wheel.

Frigid air washed over Coglin as she turned the engine over. The police scanner was in one of the drink holders and Coglin grabbed it, turned its chatter up. There was an awful lot of radio traffic. Foot posts were calling in backup up at Times Square. An angry crowd of protestors was forming.

It was for him, he thought suddenly. The protest from the Bronx courthouse was catching, spreading.

He shook his head.

And why wouldn't it be, he thought. He was on a streak.

More interspersed communication said that ESU and FBI SWAT had just arrived at the post office garage. They must've thought he'd rolled under a truck or something.

Welcome to Ten Ten Lose, Coglin thought, staring at the scanner. All Coglin, all the time. You give us twenty-two minutes, we'll give you one dead, racist, cop-killing cop.

"Are you deaf?" Lisa said. "What the fuck happened? Where is everybody? Where's Aidan?"

"Caught," Coglin said.

"Angel? Travis?"

Coglin looked at her.

"Dead," he said. "Both dead."

"Jesus Christ," Lisa said. "My God. How?"

On the scanner, someone asked dispatch where the first suspect in the Rockefeller shooting had been taken. Midtown North, dispatch said.

Midtown North, Coglin thought. His first precinct. He took a deep breath.

Fine, he thought. Let it be there then. Let the circle be closed. That's where he'd go. Maybe they'd let him see Aidan for a minute. That's where his friend Clarke worked, too, so maybe he could take him in, make sure he didn't get shot on his way to jail.

"Got any cigarettes?" he said.

Lisa threw him a pack. He got one lit with the car lighter. He coughed as the smoke burned his already sore chest.

"When we opened the elevator door, the Secret Service were standing there," Coglin said.

"The *what?*"

"The goddamn federal, take a bullet for the president of the

USA, Secret Service. And before you could blink the shooting started, and Travis and Angel were dead. Then one of the Secret Service idiots slips on a fuckin' banana peel or something and shot the fuck out of his own people."

"The president got shot? You fuckers shot the president?" Lisa said, an unlit cigarette trembling in her hand.

"No, it was some woman," Coglin said. He sucked smoke, coughed again. Was that blood he was tasting? Who gave a fuck? He exhaled.

"I don't know who she was," he lied. "I could hardly see her."

"The first lady?"

"I don't know!" Coglin yelled.

"Is she dead?"

Coglin shrugged his shoulders.

"I didn't wait for the paramedics."

"We're fucked," Lisa said. It wasn't a question. "We are so fucked it isn't funny."

Knock over Rockefeller Center, what do you think is gonna happen, he felt like saying. What the fuck did *he* think?

"Drive," Coglin said. "C'mon!"

They pulled out onto Eighth. They drove north past low, rundown office buildings, past the monstrous green dumpster of the Port Authority Bus Terminal. On a digital billboard above the milling crowd across from it, a man and woman in soaked evening wear were running hand in hand up a white sand beach.

"Listen to me," Coglin said. "Go pick up your daughter and immediately get the fuck out of here. Go through with your plan."

They were coming up on Fiftieth now, a block down from Midtown North.

"Pull over," Coglin said.

"Why?" Lisa said, braking toward the curb. "What the fuck are you going to do?"

Coglin looked at her. The amber in her eyes seemed to glow now, like sparks poured in a green pool.

"I gotta set things straight," he said. "They fucked me over. But this . . . this is beyond . . . I never shoulda done this. I'm a cop. Just like those dead Secret Service guys. I gotta set things straight."

"Set things straight? What, are you crazy?"

He smiled at her, held her hand for a second before he opened his door.

"You made my last night real nice," he said. He could feel the tension sliding off him now. It was gonna be all right.

He got out of the truck into the heat.

"Get your daughter, Lisa," he said, and then he slammed the door.

Five minutes later, Coglin stood at the payphone on the corner of Ninth and Fiftieth, watching the squad house fifty feet down the block. A couple of uniforms stood at the top of the small flight of stairs before the precinct house fucking around, smoking cigarettes and looking out over the line of forty-five-degree parked police cars. Coglin fitted a quarter in the slot, let it drop and dialed Clarke's number from memory.

"Midtown North," Clarke answered on the first ring.

"It's me, Joe," Coglin said. "It's John."

"John!" Clarke said. "Jesus Christ. I just got back from the courthouse. You know there's a riot starting up right now in Times fucking Square because you didn't show up? Three quarters of this goddamn precinct are there right now. Where the hell are you?"

"I fucked up," Coglin said.

"You said it," Clarke said. "What the fuck are you doing?"

"I got scared and I fucked up big time, Joe," Coglin said. "But I want to make things right now, before anybody else gets hurt. I want to turn myself in."

"OK, now you're sounding sensible," Clarke said. "But, c'mon now, kid, it's not that bad. The jury hasn't even come back in yet. As of now, fuck it, you're just late for court. Where are you?"

That's right, Coglin thought, seeing the dead Secret Service guy. He doesn't know my latest sins.

"I'm outside on the corner, Joe," Coglin said. "I'm up on Ninth."

Coglin saw a gap flap open in the yellow blinds of the precinct window farthest west.

"You shaved your head."

Christ it was nice to hear a sane friendly voice, Coglin thought.

"No wonder they made you lieutenant detective," Coglin said. "What do you think? Is it me?"

"If you're gay now," Clarke said.

Coglin laughed. An exhaustive sorrow slammed into him.

No, he thought. No breakin' down now. Get this fuckin' thing over with.

"I'll call down to the desk," Clarke said.

"No, Joe. I can't walk in the front and face everybody. I can't face another cop. I just can't."

"Why don't I meet you around back then? I'll take you up the backstairs, and we'll make some phone calls, and then I'll drive you to the courthouse myself."

"I knew you wouldn't let me down, Joe," Coglin said.

"I'll meet you around back, kid," Clarke said, and hung up.

Chapter Twenty-one

"A IDAN," COLETTE SAID, sitting down at the interview room table across from the Irishman. "You promised me you'd be a good boy, remember?"

Sitting with his wrists handcuffed behind him, Aidan shrugged his shoulders and smiled. The black-and-blue mark on his temple from an "accidental" bump into the top of the cruiser seemed especially grievous, but didn't dampen the man's spirits.

Colette had just arrived at a run from Rockefeller Center and as soon as Carlos got there in a minute or two, they'd take custody and transport him downtown.

The second-floor detective bureau was empty, the whole squad having been called either to assist at the Rockefeller crime scene, or at some riot that was apparently starting in Times Square. The supervising lieutenant, Detective Joe Clarke, was the only man in the office. When he offered to sit in, she'd told him politely that it was alright. She could conduct the interview until her partner got there.

"So, you got your wish, Colette," Aidan said. "Finally got back home to the big city."

"Well, it was actually you who got me back," Colette said. "I'd put my papers in, but it was only after I pinched you, that they went through."

"Who knows?" the Irishman said. "Maybe there'll be a promotion this time."

"With the mess you just caused, O'Donnell," Colette said, "they'll make me the fuckin' director. Before we start, do you want to lawyer up like you did last time?"

The Irishman shrugged his shoulders.

"I haven't decided yet," he said. "You wouldn't happen to have a cigarette by any chance?"

"Don't smoke."

"That's right," he said. "I forgot."

"Getting back to this botched abortion of a fuck-up you just pulled," Colette said. "You want to go over it? Honest to God, O'Donnell. Whacking the vice president's wife? They'll execute you. They think you were hired, and you know that with your international jacket, they might be able to make the case."

"Hired?" O'Donnell said with a smirk. "To snuff her?"

"That's right," she said.

He laughed. He looked down at the tabletop and nodded.

"Of course. It wasn't the big fat Secret Serviceman doing the Three Stooges with his Uzi on full auto. It must've only looked like he took out everyone in a three-hundred-and-sixty-degrees radius."

"You're saying the Secret Service shot her?"

"Are the rounds in an Uzi different than the ones in an M-16?"

"Yes," Colette said.

"Then you might want to pull out the ones in the second lady's body and take a close look at them."

"What would that matter, one of your boys who got himself dead had an Uzi."

Aidan blinked. He shook his head. His smile reappeared wider than before.

"That's fuckin' grand, isn't it. They dropped the Uzi they shot her with to make it look good. Well, why the fuck not. Who wants to hear that? I'd check the numbers on that gun, agent. Unless they filed them off already."

"You're full of shit," Colette said. "You guys were armed to the teeth. You yourself shot up Forty-seventh Street."

"With an M-16, sweetheart. An M-16. And did you notice anybody happening to get hit?"

"I forgot," Colette said. "You're the original William Tell. I did see some old man with a busted up face."

"Geezer almost greased me," Aidan said. "What would you have done?"

"I wouldn't have tried to knock over Rockefeller Center," Colette said.

"Of course not," Aidan said with a grin. "You need to be equipped with a set of nuts to do something like that."

"I hear that a lot. About guys' nuts and my lack of them," Colette said. "Not for nothing, but they seem kinda overrated to me. I mean the only thing they do for you is keep putting you behind bars. Now, tell me again who hired you to shoot the second lady?" Colette said.

Aidan's shoulders hitched as he laughed again.

"Everything's a fuckin' spy novel with you bastards, isn't it?" he said. "OK, I was hired, but it was really this other guy on the grassy knoll who took the shot. This big fat clumsy blond Fed with an Uzi."

He was laughing hard now. Tears in the corners of his strange blue eyes.

"But I guess as with all patsies, I'm the one who has to take the fall because I'm the last one standing."

"Not the last one," she said. "You got one pal still running."

The Irishman's eyes perked up.

"No kiddin'? Good for him."

"Only chance you got is give him up before he's caught," Colette said. "Once we catch him, you got nothing. Cooperate right now, you could make a deal. They say lethal injection is pretty painless, but I don't know. You really want to find out?"

The Irishman smiled.

"You've grown, Colette. You're getting good at this. Which is kind of tragic, if you think about it. How hard-hearted a nice little Irish Catholic girl like yourself has become."

"Who's your friend?" Colette said.

"You know what I'm thinking would go really good with this conversation?" Aidan said, looking up at the off-white tiles of the drop ceiling. "A cup of coffee, light and sweet, and a pack of cigarettes. Marlboro Reds. The kind only real cowboys smoke. What do you say? Then we'll work on your promotion."

"Fine, you win already," she said standing, gesturing for the cage behind him. "I'll get some damn coffee. And cigarettes, too? Jesus, how much are they now? Eight bucks a pack?"

"At least," the armed robber said, standing and backing obediently into the room's closet-sized metal cage. He smiled at her as she clacked shut the steel mesh door.

"If you take the cuffs off," he said, winking out of his good eye, "I'll go out and get them myself."

Chapter Twenty-two

CLARKE'S OFFICE WAS on the second floor, past a low wooden gate and a double row of paper-strewn metal desks that belonged to his squad of homicide detectives. They were out now, Clarke had told Coglin as he led him up the back stairs, half to the Times Square demonstration, the other half to a shooting that had just happened at Rockefeller Center.

If they're any good, both groups will be running back in here at any second, Coglin thought. And tackling his ass to the ground.

Coglin imagined himself sitting in one of the empty chairs, a gold shield on his hip.

Would've made it, too, he thought as they entered Clarke's office.

Right up until the point I truly fucked myself, I was on my way.

Clarke sat behind his messy desk, urging Coglin to sit at the couch under the window.

"John," he said, putting his polished shoes up on his desk. "You did the right thing. Comin' in. You did the right fuckin' thing."

Clarke was dressed in a flowing double-breasted blue suit and had on a blue dress shirt with a white collar and a microdot red and white tie. Like other detectives Coglin had come across, Clarke took the lack of a uniform as a real privilege and liked to dress like a dandy.

Clarke's cell phone chirped. He took the small device out of his jacket, pressed a button, silencing it, and chucked it on his desk.

"Fuckers can leave a message already," he said. "Anyway, like I was saying. I'm really proud of you."

Coglin dropped his gaze at the floor.

"Nothing else to do, Joe. Listen I ah . . . I got something else to tell you."

There was a loud rap on the door frame. A tall attractive ash-blond woman in a severe business suit stood in the threshold. The ID clipped to her lapel said, FBI.

Coglin remembered the female voice on the scanner that had asked where his uncle was. They had to have him in one of the interview rooms down the hall.

"Joe, there you are," she said. "Can I talk to you for a second?"

She gave Coglin a little smile, looked back at Clarke.

Clarke gave Coglin an annoyed look, rolled his eyes. Fuckin' feds it seemed to say. Fuckin' broads.

"Excuse me, John," Clarke said, standing and moving out from behind his desk. "I'll be right back."

FBI, Coglin thought as Joe closed the old-fashioned glass-framed door.

Despair slapped at his chest again like another bullet. He watched his left hand start shaking and he took another deep breath.

Setting things straight, he thought. Nothing to be afraid of, ashamed of. You're setting things straight.

Coglin looked around Clarke's office. There was even more paper on his desk than on the ones outside. Framed pictures on the cracked, snot-green walls. One was a diploma, a bachelor's degree from Columbia.

Ivy League? Coglin thought. Little odd, considering how Clarke always came off like such a man's man, like a street guy.

That's why he'd advanced so high, Coglin concluded. He was smart and tough.

There was more paper along the both sides of his desk, huge stacks of it. Coglin shook his head at the precariously perched mound beside the couch that was all green plastic-bound case files.

He looked at them. Homicides, unsolved probably, lying there gathering dust. Real murders, not the trumped-up bullshit the system had pinned on him. He should be working on one right now, running down leads, interviewing witnesses. Catching crooks instead of being one.

He looked at the numbers written in magic marker on their spines: 010598–2816, 061799–4554. The first six digits were the date of the murder, he knew. He'd seen his own case file when the DA handed it over to Mulvane to prepare his defense.

He peered at one of the files buried halfway down the stack. One of Clarke's homicides had happened the same day he'd shot Ream. He leaned over and tugged out one of the papers. Let's see what kind of real crime went unsolved while everybody was too busy fucking him over.

*Officer Coglin stated that he witnessed an altercation
taking place at the bottom of the stairs on the uptown side of*

Coglin snapped up straight in his seat.
What the?

*the elevated subway platform. He stated he saw one of the
assailants run up the stairs and that he followed in pursuit.*

It was *his* file! The statement he had made in his initial interview.

Coglin's mind reeled dizzily. Why the fuck would Clarke
have the file for the homicide he was accused of? Clarke's jurisdiction was Manhattan, not the Bronx. Was it to try and help
him? Why hadn't he mentioned it?

Through the blinds on the door, Clarke was nodding at what
the FBI woman was saying. Coglin looked back at the file.

That didn't make sense.

Coglin scanned the room. He looked at the framed photographs around Clarke's diploma. Golf outings. Men in tuxedos
around circular tables. Men on the deck of a boat, holding a mar-
lin. Coglin got up quietly to look more closely at them. In each
one, Clarke could be seen at the outskirts.

But that wasn't what stilled Coglin.

What made him feel the beat of his own heart suddenly like a
stereo bass cranked up as high as it would go, was that his lawyer
and the Bronx DA prosecuting his case were standing together in
three of the photographs.

The mayor himself was in two.

And in the center of the one with the huge fish was a tan little man with silver spectacles.

The judge.

Take it to trial, he heard Clarke advise again. *I know the judge, kid. He'll kick it upstate.*

Good god.

Things don't work out, John, you could always appeal.

Again and again Clarke's supposed help had fucked him up. Each time, the hopeful path he'd urged Coglin down had turned into a dead end. Each time, his energy had been wasted until there were no more options.

No, Coglin thought, shaking his head. He was being nuts. Paranoid. Had to be hundreds of people with a picture of the mayor. And the Bronx DA? The judge? That was just a coincidence. Clarke was his friend.

What about the file? Homicide cops don't let anybody see their cases. Why the fuck does Clarke have that?

Coglin looked on Clarke's desktop at his cell phone. He lifted it and pressed the caller ID button, scanned the five numbers that popped up.

He recognized his lawyer, Mulvane's, number right away.

What had he been calling him for? Find out where he was maybe? There were two other seven-one-eight Bronx area code numbers, and Coglin brought the cursor down to the first and pressed dial.

"Bronx DA's Office," a voice said.

Coglin pressed off.

He looked at the picture of the DA on the wall as he pressed down the other Bronx number. It had the same exchange as the DA's office, so he wasn't even surprised.

"Judge Barrett's chamber."

He hung up. Dialed the fourth number.

The New York Times.

And the fifth one was Channel Six.

His lawyer and all his enemies in no particular order.

Coglin felt the guilt in him begin to morph, his despair temper and harden like steel in the rising heat of his anger.

He looked at the picture with the mayor.

Election year, he thought. Election fucking year.

It hadn't been the faceless fucking he'd thought it. Some amorphous liberal bias in the system, the media, in the city itself, that was impossible to fight.

You don't want the union lawyer, John, he heard Clarke say again. *I know a guy, Mulvane. He's the best.*

It had been a righteous, behind-his-back dicking by the only person he'd trusted, by the only one in the department, in the whole city, that he'd thought of as a friend.

Duped from day one, he thought.

He looked out at Clarke, laughing now, flirting with the FBI agent. He remembered the TV camera's lights bearing down on him, and his own angry face staring back at him from the front cover of the paper.

At every turn.

Rage, like a silent electrical fire, began to burn behind Coglin's eyes.

The interview rooms were on the other end of the squad room down the corridor on the left. No, he remembered, the right-hand wall.

The phone was still in his hand, and he dialed Lisa's number.

What had his destruction been worth? Coglin thought, glaring at Clarke as he waited. A precinct command? A trip down south to headquarters? A table at Elaine's and a good laugh with the media vermin who had sliced him to the bone?

"Yeah?" Lisa answered.

"Plan's changed?" he said. "Fifty-one and Ninth. Yesterday."

"I'm there in five. Congratulations," Lisa said. "You woke up."

Yeah, Coglin thought, hearing the click of her disconnection. I'm wide the fuck awake now.

Clarke looked at him quizzically as he came back into his office, wondering why Coglin had his phone.

Coglin distinctly avoided looking at the butt of the Berreta that poked out of Clarke's tailored suit jacket. The poker smile that he gave his old friend was the calmest and easiest he'd ever known.

"Yeah, Mom," Coglin said into the dead phone. "I love you, too. I gotta go."

Chapter Twenty-three

COLETTE UNLOCKED THE DOOR of the interview room and placed the cigarettes and coffee she'd gotten from the squad room on top of the table.

"Sorry. No Marlboros," she said to Aidan as she stepped to the cage and opened it back up.

"For fuck's sake," Aidan said, glancing at the cigarettes as he sat down. "Virginia Slims?"

Colette took out her cuffs, locked one end around Aidan's already cuffed right wrist and the other around the bolted-down table leg. Then she unlocked his original set of cuffs so he'd have one hand free.

"Hundreds. These are bitch smokes," he complained as Colette came around and sat at the other side of the table.

Colette shrugged her shoulders.

"You've come a long way, baby," she said.

She'd just gotten out her tape recorder and notepad from her bag when there was a knock on the door. She turned and saw Detective Lieutenant Clarke's face in the tiny square of the window. She exhaled loudly. She thought she'd done him a favor by informing him what was going on when she'd gone out for Aidan's smokes. Didn't mean she wanted to flirt with him all afternoon. What the hell did he want now?

When she got to the door, through the window beside Clarke, she noticed the forlorn looking man with the shaved head who'd been in the detective's office. She'd made him for a cop, but now she could see him bent against the wall of the outside corridor, hands behind him, head and shoulders hunched in a classic perp walk crouch.

Arrested? she thought. What the hell was this?

When she opened the door, she thought Clarke must've stumbled or something because he kind of flew in. Then she was staring into a black hole of a gun bore as her own Smith & Wesson was ripped away violently from the holster on her hip. She looked at the bald man as the door clicked shut.

"Floor," he said.

He didn't seem so upset anymore, she thought, stunned. Just angry now over the barrel of his gun.

And dead serious.

The absence of her gun was like a weight at her side.

"Now!" he said, stepping at her and raising up her gun as well.

"OK, OK," she said, kneeling and then lying on her stomach. "Just calm down."

When she raised her head, Clarke was in the far corner of the room with his hands, palms out, placatingly in front of him.

"Don't be stupid, John," he said to the bald man. "You'll never make it out."

"That's right," the armed man said to him. "You made god-damn sure of that, didn't you?"

At the table, Aidan had a hand over his open mouth. When he moved it, Colette saw there was a kind of surprised awe on his face.

Pride, Colette thought. He was fucking proud of him.

"John," the Irishman said, laughing. "You goddamn crazy son of a bitch."

"Cuff keys?" Coglin barked.

"Girl's bag," Aidan barked back happily.

Colette watched the bald man empty the contents of her bag, toss Aidan her cuff keys. Aidan caught them and freed himself. He put out his hand and the bald man tossed Aidan her gun as he came around the table. Aidan helped Colette up gently and guided her in through the open door of the cage. Clarke was pushed in behind her and the door clanged shut.

"John," Clarke was saying. "They're just gonna . . ."

"One more word, you Judas fuck," the bald man said from the door, "and, I swear to God, I'll shoot you in the kidneys and watch you bleed out."

Then bald John pulled the interview door open, and he and Aidan ran out and were gone.

The door clicked back shut.

Clarke took out his red silk pocket-handkerchief, sat at the wooden bench and wiped at his sweaty face.

"Help!" Colette yelled, shaking the bars.

"Don't bother," Clarke said defeatedly. "Walls are sound-proof. Somebody will be along."

Took your gun, Colette thought.

Stupid weak woman got her piece taken. She could hear the water cooler talk already. Typical.

She thought of the Rockefeller Center security guard.

I'm gonna be on the employment line right behind you, buddy.

Fuck that, she thought, scanning the room.

There was a dusty window behind bars high in the wall above the bench. It would be impossible to get through the bars, but maybe they could open the window and scream for help. She spotted her cell phone lying on the floor next to the table. It was a little more than arm's length from the bars.

"My phone," she said, pointing at it. "See if you can get it with your belt."

Colette climbed on the bench and jumped up, grabbing the bars.

"I'm not wearing a belt," Clarke said.

If he was staring at her ass, she thought, hauling herself up to rest her elbows on the sill, she was going to drop kick him.

"Use your goddamn coat or something then!" she yelled, trying to hold on and push at the window at the same time. Wasn't budging. Probably nailed shut.

Out through the dusty glass, she could see the cross street at the back of the precinct house, and after a moment, she saw two men, one bald, one black-haired, hurrying across, heading west toward Tenth Avenue. She lost them behind a close building to the left. A moment later, a black SUV appeared in the space between two buildings accelerating quickly up Tenth Avenue heading north.

Getting away, Colette thought. The suspects, her gun, her career.

"I got it," Clarke said from the floor.

She dropped down. He was reeling it in with his suspenders. She grabbed it up through the bars and hit the speed dial for Carlos.

Be close, she prayed, waiting. Please be close.

"Yeah?" Carlos said.

"New black SUV heading north from Fiftieth up Tenth Avenue," Colette screamed. "At least two white males. Armed and dangerous. Call it in. Get on them!"

"I'm at Fifty-sixth and Eleventh," Carlos said. She could hear the scream of his tires in the background.

"On it," he said, and hung up.

Fifty-sixth, Colette thought. He could get them. He really could.

Please, she thought.

She was gonna call him back to have him get somebody up here to let them out, but then decided not to. It was up to him now.

She sat down on the bench and watched Clarke put his red polka dot suspenders back on. She noticed for the first time the huge bruise on his jawline below his left ear. She looked back down at her empty holster and shook her head.

"So tell me," she said. "Who's this John guy anyway?"

Chapter Twenty-four

YOU FUCKIN' MADMAN!" Aidan screamed in the back seat of the SUV as they tore, engine racing, north up Tenth. He grabbed Coglin by his shirt and shook him violently back and forth.

Coglin smiled despite everything.

"What? I'm gonna leave you hangin'?" he said calmly.

"You fucker!" Aidan said. There seemed to be tears in his ice cube eyes.

"You fucker," he said again, pulling himself back in the seat. His feet jammed against the bags of money.

"What the fuck is this?" he said, lifting the blanket. His husky-dog–blue eyes bugged.

His mouth opened to speak. Nothing came out.

"The armored car," Coglin said nonchalantly. "I flipped the

fucker on Park and that son of a bitch just popped right out, so I thought I'd pick it up."

Aidan grabbed Coglin's head in his huge hands and planted a loud kiss on his cheek.

"You savage son of a bitch!" he said.

"Enough," Lisa said. "Where now?"

"Keep going north," Coglin said, looking in the rearview. No pursuit. Thank you, God. Thank you.

As if God was really rooting for him here, he thought. *Thou art welcome my thieving son.*

"We'll stop up in Harlem or somewhere and figure something out," Coglin said. "And slow down. We don't want to attract attention."

Coglin looked forward through the windshield and watched a gray sedan come out across Tenth, two blocks ahead, lights flashing.

"Too late!" Lisa said.

"Go right! Right!" Coglin yelled.

Tires squealed as he was thrown against Aidan beside him. Out the back tinted window, the sedan appeared half a block behind. Aidan leaned over the seat. The two M-16s were still there, and he lifted one up.

"No," Coglin said, pushing the barrel down. "No more."

They came across Ninth, Eighth. The side street was jam stopped at Seventh, and Lisa made a screaming right and headed south. They made it as far as Forty-ninth when the traffic came to a dead stop. Over the red brake lights, Coglin could see a crowd beneath the white glare of Times Square. Whistles screamed from the neon lights. Lisa brought the truck to a stuttering stop. They threw the doors open.

"Da ta da ta da," an amplified voice called.

"DA, DA!" the crowd screamed.

"Da ta da."

"DA DA!"

"We have to go into it," Aidan said.

They got on the sidewalk and moved toward the riot.

"IS IT WRONG TO WANT . . ." the man on the stage said. He pumped his megaphone toward the crowd.

"JUSTICE!!!!" they answered.

"DON'T WE ALL DESERVE . . ." the man said. He held a hand to his ear.

"JUSTICE!!!!"

"IS IT WRONG TO WANT . . ."

"Justice!" Aidan called exuberantly as he jogged half a step ahead of Coglin. He punched the air with his fist.

As they reached the rally crowd, Coglin noticed people at its edges turning, looking at them. They could see cops now, too, at the corners, looking nervous, trying without much success to get ahold of the situation. Aidan crossed Seventh, running directly into the throng. Coglin and Lisa followed right behind.

Young black men began turning angrily at them as they pushed their way through. Coglin could feel the energy of the crowd crackling in the hot air all around him.

Please, God, let no one notice me, Coglin thought. *Please.*

Aidan touched the closest man on the shoulder and pointed back the way they'd come.

"They're coming to bust it up," he said. Behind them the tall male agent or cop from the sedan was running full speed ahead toward them down Broadway, gun naked in his hand.

"Look, they got guns," Aidan said. "Guns. Holy shit! They're gonna come in shooting! *Run!*"

There was a quick, electric movement in the crowd as the word spread. The rear contingent of the assembly turned and seemed to expand facing the agent's approach. A bottle sailed from the crowd, line-driving past the cop's shoulder and he stopped on his heels. Another shattered off the phone kiosk beside him and he began to backpedal. In a moment he was jogging away as the crowd moved at him, running, it seemed, back where he'd left his sedan parked sideways in the middle of Broadway.

Aidan patted Coglin on the shoulder and smiled.

"DON'T WE ALL DESERVE . . ." the megaphone said.

"Justice!" Aidan yelled, as he began to carve a path through the crowd.

Chapter Twenty-five

T HE COMMAND CENTER Colette was summoned to was in an old warehouse on the West Side in the twenties. Two tall men, wearing ATF polo shirts and H&K MP5 submachine guns, stood before a sawhorse at Eleventh Avenue when she and Carlos pulled up. The federal men examined their IDs thoroughly before they waved them through.

"Things are this bad?" Carlos said, glancing back at the ominous checkpoint. They began rumbling down the cobblestone surface of the old street toward an old building with a phalanx of marked and unmarked police vehicles in front of it.

"Oh, no," Colette said, wanting, not needing, a cigarette. "They're much, much worse."

She'd called the assistant director from the interview room cage and updated him on the situation. She gave him a description of the SUV, and he said he would mobilize the appropriate forces to track them down. Then he said he wanted to see her immediately in person down at the emergency command center that was being set up to deal with the shooting and the riot. After she hung up, she'd called down to the precinct desk and asked the sergeant to send somebody up to let them out. By the time she stepped out of the precinct, Carlos had already lost O'Donnell and Coglin and was pulling up in front.

Where would they transfer her for not only losing her suspect, but her gun as well? she thought as Carlos squeezed in beside a van that said NYPD BOMB on its side.

Was there a Bureau office in Zimbabwe?

They had to show their creds again to two city detectives manning another checkpoint just inside the entrance. They heard a host of frantic voices and then stepped through a set of double doors.

Inside was a large, open space. Exposed brick, twenty-foot-high ceilings, a series of huge windows set high in the front wall. The shafts of light that shot down through them fell on uniformed cops snapping open folding tables, slitting open boxes of new computers, pulling them out. Men in telephone company hard hats stood on ladders, strapping a cable along a wall. Centered within this buzz of activity, several separate groups of men in suits stood conversing heatedly with each other and yelling into cell phones. And at the center of the largest group was Assistant Director Dunlop. And beside him was the mayor himself.

Colette ignored Dunlop and just stood there, staring at the mayor.

Knew it would happen, she thought, unable to detach her gaze from the mayor's famous profile.

She knew one day if she tried hard enough and rose high enough, she'd come into personal contact with him. After all, it was the reason she'd gotten into this business in the first place, wasn't it? To one day look that fucker in the eye across some courtroom or table and show that he may have destroyed her father, but he hadn't destroyed her family.

Hadn't destroyed her.

He hadn't really changed from the commission hearings. Though it had to be eight years since he stood ripping her father apart on the stand, he hadn't put on any weight, hadn't lost any hair. If anything, he looked even better. As if all the dark, twisted moves he'd made to get from righteous, backstabbing prosecutor to mayor of the greatest city in the world had nourished him, strengthened him, made him younger.

It was him and the thought of him that had made her quit nursing school after her father's funeral and switch to accounting. Him she thought about when she was tired of running laps at the academy in Quantico, when she was first stationed, scared and alone, in the wilderness of eastern California.

She'd taken that initial feeling she'd had when she'd heard about her father's suicide, the horror and shame and unbearable loss, and she'd snatched it, kept it in a compressed box deep inside her to use as fuel to push her forward, upward. Each successful case, erasing a small portion of that shame. Each small victory closing the distance to her eventual showdown.

And now, finally, she was here. The planets had impossibly aligned to allow her this fateful meeting and she was what?

Disgraced all over again.

She stared a hole into the side of the mayor's head.

When he heard her last name, would he remember? Would he stare at her empty holster as the assistant director chewed her out and told her she was off the case and give her his famous grin?

No, she thought. Walking over there with nothing wasn't an option. She wasn't off the case yet. She tugged Carlos's sleeve.

"C'mon," she said. "Let's go back outside for a second. I need some air."

"Listen up," she said to her partner when they were outside. "I need everything you can find out about this cop Coglin. Record, address, phone number, partner, wife, kids. Call in every favor. I'm at the two-minute warning here, Carlos. I got to find this son of a bitch."

Carlos had his cell out and was already dialing.

"You got it," he said, stepping up toward Twelfth.

She took her cell out and called Bishop. He would still be at Rockefeller Center, and maybe he'd gotten something, some angle she could capitalize on within the next three minutes to somehow redeem herself.

"Yo," he said.

"Bishop," she said. "Give me good news."

"Colette! Honey, you OK?"

"You can rip me from now until you retire, alright?" Colette said, taking out her pad. "I'm dangling. I need something."

"Oh, how the mighty have fallen," Bishop said. "OK. Let's see. Anything interesting. Eh, one thing. Spoke to a guy, sells pictures on the corner of Five One and Fifth, out by the open manhole? He told me a phone truck pulled up and let out our four principals. You know, the two stiffs in the freight and the two who are currently eh . . . parts unknown."

"Am I supposed to laugh now?" Colette said.

"The interesting thing is that he saw a woman. An attractive brunette woman who was driving the truck. I put in a call to the phone company, asked them how many female employees in the area had access to trucks. They called me back ten minutes ago and told me there were four or five, but that one of them hadn't reported back after her shift."

"We got a name?" Colette said.

"Lisa Pallone."

Colette wrote it down.

"You run her?"

"Yep. PD's got a car heading to her place right now. Oh, and I also have a little treat for you that you're going to like. But you have to say something first."

"Anything. What?"

"Bishop, you are the best investigator in the squad, bar none."

"Bishop," Colette said. "You are the best investigator in the squad, bar none. What the fuck do you have?"

"Well, thank you for the compliment, Colette. I do try," Bishop said. "I've discovered that Miss Pallone has a cellular telephone, and I have managed, through my superior deductive abilities, to ascertain the precise digits upon which this aforementioned cellular telephone is based."

Yes, Colette thought. Thank you. Finally: a break.

A cell meant they could track her. The telephone company could triangulate any cellular signal and could tell by the location of the fixed cell sites within three hundred feet where it was being received. And once they had Pallone, they had the rest of them.

She thought about the bald cop, saw again the midnight bore of the gun he pointed in her face.

You're mine, fucker.

"What is it?" she said.

Bishop gave her the phone number.

"I owe you, superior investigator," Colette said.

"Don't worry," Bishop said. "You'll pay me back. Oh, I wanted to ask. Did you see the crime scene?"

"Yeah," she said. "Bullet holes look a little one-sided to you, too, huh?"

"Just a little," Bishop said. "I take it this assassination thing everybody's raving about isn't exactly winning you over."

"Investigation, psychology. Is there a field you're not an expert in?" Colette said. "Crime scene bag that Uzi?"

"They're doing their thing, Lead Investigator Ryan. Don't you fret, and look at the positive. At least you're not in the Secret Service."

"That's true," Colette said, jogging into the entrance of the command center. "Now I feel much better."

Assistant Director Dunlop disengaged from the group when she rushed up to him.

"Agent Ryan, I presume?" he said.

He was a short, fortyish man, wearing round wire-rim glasses, overweight, but well dressed and polished. He smelled like he'd just gotten his hair cut. He held her elbow lightly, guiding her a few steps away from the crowd. She noticed Carlos hanging back, not wanting to interfere in confidential Bureau business. The mayor and a few of his cronies didn't feel so squeamish. Their heads popped up beside the assistant director's. She knew one of the mayor's aides; he was a friend of Phil's that she had met the night before. He winked at her. She blinked.

Exactly how bizarre was this day going to get?

"You lost him?" Dunlop started. "The terrorist?"

Go with the anger she was feeling? she thought. Had to. Nothing else left.

"No! *I* did not lose him," she said. "Truth be known, Coglin came into the precinct interview room already armed with the lieutenant-detective-on-duty's sidearm. He lost him. He lost them both."

"Semantics," the pudgy man said calmly. "O'Donnell is at large."

Is "you banged your wife" and "the milkman banged your

wife" just a matter of semantics, too? she stopped herself from saying out loud. Your wife got banged for sure, but wasn't there a little difference?

"What's the lieutenant detective's name?" the mayor demanded.

Clarke was a dick, she thought, looking into the mayor's heartless eyes. But you couldn't torture any help out of me, you soulless prick.

Colette shrugged her shoulders.

"I forget," she said.

"So O'Donnell is loose," Dunlop said.

"He's still loose," she agreed. "He escaped into the riot. But we have something. We found out there's a woman with them. A phone company employee, Lisa Pallone. And sir, we have her cell phone."

Dunlop's eyes perked up.

"Cell phone?" the mayor said. "What are you going to do? Call her up and trade bikini-waxing secrets?"

His people kept their laughter to a polite chuckle.

"Actually no," Colette said with an icy calm. She took a quick breath, smiled at him. "We're going to track her down, sir. I would've thought that you of all people would be aware of law enforcement's ability to trace cell phones. Maybe I'm mistaken, but isn't that what your campaign signs say? Law and Order or something like that. I could go over the process with you, if you want. It's called triangulation. What happens . . ."

"That won't be necessary, Agent Ryan," Dunlop said, looking at her as if she were completely nuts. "I believe there's a liaison from the phone company here with us somewhere in this mess. Why don't you busy yourself by finding him and starting this trace?"

"Certainly, sir," Colette said. She turned to the mayor. "Any other questions, your honor, I'll be right over there."

Plah. *Plah,* she thought, stepping away. Score times two. Not only was she not off the case, she'd gotten right up in the goddamn actual mayor's face. And shut his pack of mutts right up. Phil's friend?

Bikini wax this, scumbags.

"Ryan?"

When Colette turned, Dunlop was stepping after her away from the group with a tall man at his side. He was triathlete lean and blond and handsome in a weather-beaten way. He might've been a well-dressed, over-the-hill surfer except for his dark brown eyes, which seemed extremely un-laid back. They seemed intelligent and cruel.

"I want you to work with someone," Dunlop said. "Kenneth, this Colette Ryan. Colette, Ken Vaughn."

"CIA," Vaughn said behind an even meaner, small-mouthed smile. He didn't offer his hand. She was thankful.

"President wants the whole arsenal in on this, Colette," Dunlop said. "Every card in the deck."

She thought to ask if it wasn't illegal for the CIA to operate on domestic soil, but left it alone. In enough trouble as it is.

"So you spoke to O'Donnell, hmm?" Vaughn said in a raspy voice. "Briefly?" he added. He looked at her empty holster and smiled his little lizard smile again.

"I want you to keep Mr. Vaughn in the loop, Colette," Dunlop said. "The vice president himself has hand-selected him to help track these men down. I want you to work together."

"Absolutely," Colette said. "I was just about to run a trace on the cell phone of one of the perpetrators."

"Fabulous," Vaughn said. "My men are en route. They should be here any minute."

Men? Colette thought. There were more men here already than at an Elton John concert. Did they honestly need more?

"Oh, Colette, listen to this," Dunlop said. "The agency has found something interesting in O'Donnell's file. Goes against the grain of your hasty little theory. Tell her, Kenneth."

"We think we found a link between the terrorist O'Donnell and the vice president," Vaughn said. "Needless to say, this is classified."

Vaughn paused, looking at her for some response. She tried a somber nod. He seemed satisfied.

"In late eighty-five, after the London hotel bombing in which Margaret Thatcher was almost killed, the agency assisted the UK in an attack on an IRA training camp in southern Libya. We provided satellite reconnaissance and air support on an SAS insertion in which fifteen Irish Republican Army Provos were neutralized. One of the provisionals killed was a woman believed to be O'Donnell's fiancée."

Colette nodded again.

"In eighty-five, the vice president was the director of the CIA," Vaughn said. "This is payback."

Ho-ho-hold on a second, Colette wanted to say. Payback? Hit the vice president's wife, after what, fifteen years, over some nebulous aid to the British in whacking his squeeze?

Question. If the information about our involvement was classified, how the fuck had O'Donnell come across it?

Answer. He hadn't.

It was spurious, six degrees of separation CIA bullshit. They could probably stretch a reason around why she had done it.

Dunlop and Vaughn were looking at her with the same measuring expression. Was she on the team or not?

She'd just gotten a foothold back into the biggest case of her life. She wasn't about to wreck it now by stating the obvious.

They wanted to keep spouting this line about assassination, hey, let them. It seemed to make them happy. In the meantime, she had some armed robbers to catch.

"Wow," she said, shaking her head. "Revenge. That's incredible. The possibility didn't even occur to me."

"Sometimes when things aren't apparent," Dunlop said, grinning at Vaughn, "it's because we don't have all the information."

Thanks, Confucius, she thought.

"You can say that again," Colette said, shaking her head as if dumbfounded. *Pull it back a notch, girl,* she thought. Don't get ridiculous.

She held up Lisa's phone number.

"Let me get this over to the phone company," she said with a renewed sense of urgency.

Chapter
Twenty-six

THEY STOPPED FOR THE FIRST TIME to take a breath of air in a deli half a block from Sixth on Thirty-ninth Street. They'd managed to run miraculously unbeaten through the riot and now stood, panting and sweating, in the back of the store next to the coolers.

They had a small window of time, Coglin thought, hyperventilating and scanning the beer section of the cooler. Portholesized.

And where to go? he thought.

Aidan was coughing. He started punching at his chest, loosening something up.

Lisa was staring off into space.

"I have an idea," she said. "You said they're going to be watching the bridges and tunnels, right?"

"I'd say so," Coglin said.

"What about the subway?"

"If it's not shut down around here right now, they'll be shutting it down in a second. Plus, they'll post people at stations in the outer boroughs, just for the fuck of it. If it was just the city after us, I'd say we had a chance. But the federal government? They can do fuckin' anything."

He couldn't even bring himself to utter the reason why. Too damn depressing.

"Port Authority same thing, right? Cops everywhere. Penn Station, Grand Central."

"All of 'em," Coglin said. "We're cornered like rats. What's your point?"

"What if I told you there's a way to get on a train in Grand Central without coming through Grand Central."

Coglin stared at her.

"What do you mean?"

"There's a phantom Metro North station at Fifty-ninth Street and Park Avenue. They use it as an emergency exit. I know because there's a phone box terminal at the bottom of the stairs. They have access grates on the sidewalk at the corners. What we could do, I'm thinking, is go to Fifty-ninth, open the grate, get down into the tunnel and walk south down the tracks under Park into Grand Central. Those fuckin' platforms are like a mile long each. We hop up on one of them from the tunnel end and get on at the front of a train."

"We don't have tickets though," Aidan said.

"Metro North you don't need a ticket," Coglin said, looking intently down at the scuffed linoleum floor. "You can pay the conductor on the train."

"We get up to Westchester or Connecticut and figure something out from there," Lisa said. "At least we'll be out of the city."

Coglin looked up, squinted at the potato chip rack across

from him, thinking. Would they have cops right on the platforms? If they did, they'd be at the front by the station, he decided. Far away from where they would get on. Would they search the train, though? He didn't think so, because they would've just watched everyone who was getting on from the station.

"What about Penn Station?" Aidan said. "Is there a way to get there through a tunnel?"

"Amtrak's got train yards on the West Side, but they got their shit together," Lisa said. "No way you're gonna hop some fence and start walking around."

"It's nuts enough to work," Coglin said. "Grand Central, I mean. But we're going to have to be careful about opening the grate at Fifty-ninth. Cops notice us, we're fucked. And also be careful about being spotted by any train drivers on the track."

"First things first," Aidan said. "We're going to have to get to Fifty-ninth from here first. Only three or four blocks crosstown and about twenty blocks up."

"We should split up," Coglin said. "And walk. Blend into the crowd. They're letting everybody out early because of that friggin' riot."

"You mean your riot," Aidan said with a grim smile.

Aidan looked out the window.

"Hold on," he said. "I think I see something. One of you buy us some drinks and I'll meet you outside."

Coglin reluctantly passed the beer section and brought three Gatorades up to the counter and paid for them. When he stepped warily into the warm street outside, he could see Aidan under a sidewalk construction shed across the street speaking to a thin black man with a shopping cart.

As he and Lisa approached, the homeless man was pulling off his rancid sneakers. Aidan took them and sized them to his own feet, placing them against the sole of his boot. Satisfied, the Irishman sat down at the curb and pulled off his boots and exchanged them with the homeless man. The homeless man laced up his new boots, flashed his three or four teeth at Aidan and walked off counting money, leaving his shopping cart behind.

Aidan stood.

"Money," he said.

Coglin and Lisa handed over their bags, and Aidan hid them under the cans.

Coglin handed Aidan his drink. He took a long sip and then put the plastic bottle down and took off his brown shirt. He was in formidable shape still, his arms and chest and broad back cut tight with compacted muscle, but his middle-age belly was starting to sag and he was very pale.

"Try to control yourself, Lees," he said, leering at her as he wiped his face with his shirt. He tossed it on top of the bags.

"I'll give it a shot," she said.

Aidan took another sip of his drink and then poured the remainder of it over his head, soaking his black hair. He rubbed at the sticky coif, making it stand straight up in uneven spikes. He stuck out his tongue like a crazy man.

"Aleghhh!" he said at them.

Aidan winked and began mumbling to himself as he pushed the cart, clattering east with its precious cargo down the block.

Lisa looked after him, then at Coglin.

"We're gonna do this," she said. "We're going to do this and get out of here."

Coglin looked out at the passing files of clueless rat racers. A couple of chunky white college girls in vintage bell bottoms and hardworking belly shirts passed holding hand written posterboard signs. They were heading the opposite way through the crowd back toward the demonstration.

"NYPD," one of their posters said. "NOTHER YOUNG BROTHA PRONOUNCED DEAD."

Coglin looked back at Lisa, squeezed her hand.

"We're fuckin' out of here," he said.

COLETTE FOUND THE PHONE company liaison, a stocky, black-haired man in a button-down shirt, at a monitor beneath one of the windows.

"Hi," she said, handing him Lisa's number. "We need a cell phone trace. Are you the person I see?"

He'd already typed the number.

"Lisa Pallone," he said. "Two-two-three Hightower Lane, Brooklyn, New York?"

"That's the one," she said.

"You want real time, I take it?"

"Yep."

"She's a customer. Give me ten minutes."

"Thanks, Arch," she said, reading his name tag.

Arch looked up at her, gravely serious.

"Phone company is here to assist in every way it can," he said.

She tossed off another thumbs up as she stepped away.

She walked into Carlos.

"There you are," her partner said. "Just got off the phone. Coglin's got a place on Thirtieth between Second and Third. Emergency Service is on their way. And he's got a mother in the Bronx who's maiden name is, get this . . ."

"O'Donnell. I know. I heard," Colette said.

"Stole my damn punchline," Carlos said. "That's not nice. PD is already there. They actually had a IAD team on Coglin already making sure he didn't light out for the hills."

"Couple of pros," Colette said. "Did a great job."

"Internal Affairs? C'mon," Carlos said. "You're talking cream of the crop. You know, it's funny. I was looking at Coglin's record and it just goes to show you. You can never tell. He started out as a good, promising cop."

Carlos shuffled through his papers.

"Precinct Rookie of the Year. Merchants Association Award."

"Wait a sec," Colette said. "Precinct Rookie of the Year. My dad won that."

She remembered the shield-shaped plaque on the wall in her parents' bedroom. Remembered wrapping it in newspaper when she helped her mom store his effects.

Carlos tapped his chest.

"Small world," he said. "So did I. This cat also had commendations up the yin-yang. Led his precinct in arrests last year and has no civilian complaints against him. As in none. I think I have three."

"Including mine," Colette said, smiling.

"Four then," Carlos said. "And he was about to get onto the Bronx Task Force, on his way to that golden DT badge. And then, bam. Lights out. Imagine, one night of drinking, you let off your roscoe and down the shitter it all goes."

"That's what happens," Colette said, remembering the ruthless eyes over the barrel of the gun. She was smart not to have made a move. He would've shot her like it was nothing. "You like to get tanked up and play Jesse James with some poor kid, you got it coming."

They both turned at the commotion that started then by the entrance. A contingent of black-clad men entered, carrying black knapsacks and long, black-and-silver boxes. Their leader was a short, intense looking man with a mustache. Colette watched Vaughn step up and embrace him.

"Whoa!" Carlos said. "Who's that? Hostage Rescue?"

Wasn't even, Colette thought, scanning the men as they kneeled in the dusty shafts of light and began unzipping their bags, unclasping their cases. She knew some of the faces of the Bureau's most elite SWAT force, but none of them were present. The men at the other end of the open space seemed too young to be agents anyway. She looked at their shaved heads.

Military, she thought. Had to be.

CIA Special Ops. Delta Force or maybe SEAL Team Six.

Vaughn's boys. Counterterror of world heavyweight class.

God have mercy on your soul, Coglin, she thought, watching the young killers get their gear in order.

Because the supply on your ass, by those here on earth, is rapidly depleting.

"Federal alphabet-soup party in the house!" Carlos said. "And you thought it was going to be a nice, quiet, get-out-of-work-early Friday. Now what else I got."

He went through his papers.

"No college," he said. "Yada yada yada. That's about it. I didn't get his partner, but I got the number of the Bronx homicide detective in charge of his case. He should know. You want me to call him?"

"No," she said, taking the paper with the number on it from him. "You done good, Chuckie. I saw some donuts around here somewhere. Why don't you put your flat feet up for a few seconds and refuel."

"Homicide," a voice said from her phone a moment later.

"Hi," Colette said. "Can I talk to Detective Miller?"

"Crap. Not another reporter?"

"Worse," Colette said. "FBI. I'm Agent Colette Ryan. I'm in charge of the manhunt for your boy, Coglin. How you doing today?"

"Better than him," Miller said. "Did he really bust his partner out of Midtown North?"

"Unfortunately," Colette said.

"He used to work there, you know," Miller said. "When he first got on the job. I heard he kicked Clarke's ass and took his gun."

"Heard right," Colette said.

"Hey, well at least one thing worked out right then."

"You got a beef with Clarke?" Colette said.

"You could say that," Miller said.

Great, Colette thought. An eager beaver.

"Well," Colette said. "We're down here trying to track Coglin down, and I wanted to talk to his partner. I was wondering if you could help me."

"All my notes are in the file," Miller said. He sounded obstinate, almost belligerent.

"Could you maybe pull it out and take a look at it?"

"Sure," Miller said. "If I had it. But I don't. They've taken it away yet again."

"Who? Who has it?"

"Do I get told?" Miller said. "Why don't you ask, Lieutenant Clarke maybe. I seen his name on something. He's involved in this shit somehow. All I know is an interdepartmental messenger came and my boss ordered me to give the file to him. He takes it away. They bring it back. Then they take it away again. Hey, what's a little more bullshit on a mountain of it?"

"What do you mean?" Colette said.

"Where do you start?" Miller spat. "Never seen anything like it in my life. Ninety-nine times out of a hundred you got to put your piece to the punk ADA's head, if you want him to prosecute. You could have a priest decapitated in the middle of twelve o'clock mass and they cry, 'Not enough witnesses.' And if you have a busload of them, they bitch, 'Where's the credibility?' 'Cause these guys are winners. They don't even want to think of the possibility of losing. Because as everyone knows, murder cases are all about them. Victim? What victim? 'Cept in this case.

"When the defendant's a cop, then they suddenly got nuts the size of boulders. They took Coglin to trial with one witness. One. A coke dealer who was the deceased's boss. I put that in the file, too, and it didn't even slow them down. It was like they knew it wasn't gonna matter. Let me tell you, I seen bodies hangin' from meathooks, but nothin' ever made me sicker than this case."

"What are you saying? He was framed?" Colette said. "Gimme a break. I was with your pal, Clarke, when Coglin paid us a visit. He took my gun, too, and . . ."

"Ma'am?"

Colette wheeled around. It was the phone company man. He had a couple of pieces of paper in his hand.

"Hold on a second," she said into the phone, taking it off her ear.

"Yeah, Arch?"

"I got the trace you wanted," he said, handing her the two pieces of printer paper. "I took the liberty of superimposing the last readings on a regular city map. Our maps have a lot of notations and such, makes them hard to read."

Colette looked at the black-and-white gridiron. A red X was marked on Lexington Avenue in the upper fifties.

"Signal was moving northward when I looked at it, and seemed to indicate she's on foot I think," Arch said. "I've done traces where the cell is in a car and the signal jumps all over the place."

"Perfect, Arch," Colette said. "Keep tracking, OK? I'll get back to you."

She put the phone back to her ear.

"Where was I?" she said. "Right. Coglin. Framed my ass. He's an armed robbing piece of crap."

"I don't know about all this shit that happened today," Miller said, "but I will tell you a little something off the record. I took it upon myself to go to Coglin's lawyer with my thoughts on the lack of his due process. Told him everything I know. Told him about Ream's mutt boss being the only witness. You know what his mouthpiece did when he had the skell on the stand? Nothing. I was at the trial.

"So, do I blame Coglin for exiting stage left? Not in the slightest. He finally fucking wised up. And as to that Times Square riot, I will say this. I admire the venue. At least they figured out the true source of the bullshit pipeline this time. Let them smash in the windows of all those hot new network outposts. See how they like it. Us slimy bridge-and-tunnelers can finally have a laugh at you 'real' New Yorkers for a change."

Then he hung up.

Framed? Colette thought, tapping the cell phone antenna to her teeth. No. That wasn't possible, was it? She'd just listened to the ramblings of a man on the verge of total burnout.

Vaughn appeared. He glanced at the papers she held.

"You got the trace? Excellent," he said, taking them out of her hand. "I'll take them over to tactical."

He was walking off with them before she could muster up a protest.

Carlos came over, eating a croissant.

"These butter donuts look weird, but they're awesome," he said. "You talk to the partner?"

Framed, she thought.

What had Coglin called Clarke? Judas, she remembered. He'd called him a Judas. Clarke had told her in the cage that

Coglin was an old friend, how he'd been a like mentor to him. He said that Coglin had turned himself into him. That's the reason he hadn't cuffed him, Clarke had said.

Colette looked over to where the mayor was.

It's not like he hadn't set people up before, she thought. She knew that all too intimately. It was an election year.

She looked next to the mayor at Phil's friend, who was laughing at yet another brilliant witticism of His Honor.

"Listen, I have to talk to somebody for a second," she told Carlos. "Chill here with your butter donut. I'll be right back."

The little man smiled again at her as she approached. She remembered him offering something to her in that bar or supper club or whatever the hell it was, as Phil was talking to another one of his friends from school. A little vial of something or was it a pill bottle? Something. She'd turned him down with the shake of her head, and he'd said, "Oh, that's right, you're a cop," and began apologizing and laughing like an idiot.

Gary, she thought. His name was Gary.

"Gary," she said, shaking his hand. It was smaller then hers. "Small world, huh? *You* work for Municipal Marty?"

Gary smiled. He had nice teeth. Exceptionally nice and white and even. He was a happy guy.

"Oh, I do a little spin doctoring, some speech writing," he said. "All-around trouble shooting. What do they call it in the Mafia? Making your bones? Listen, about last night," he said. He swallowed, his tiny Adam's apple bobbing. "I . . ."

What was it about him? Colette thought. It wasn't a gay vibe. Colette took a step in closer to him.

"Relax, would you?" she said quietly. "Why do you think I came over here?"

Gary looked up at her, his eyes wide, wet. *Not effeminate,* she thought. He was past that. He was actually feminine. Some kind of unfortunate surplus of estrogen. Didn't smoking pot cause male breasts?

"You lookin for, ah . . ."

She nodded, holding his eyes. He swallowed again.

"Aren't you like, in charge of this operation?" he said very quietly.

"Fuck it," she whispered to him. "Can you hook me up or what?"

"I, um, yeah. I, ah, sure," he said.

"Let's go then," she said.

"Right now?" he said, laughing a little. "You're crazy."

"I won't tell Phil," she said solemnly. "If you won't."

He led her out of the warehouse area into a corridor. They passed through a darkened, dusty room that was stacked with wooden pallets and folded cardboard boxes. He pushed through a door. It opened outside to a cramped courtyard and the metal stairs of an old fire escape.

"Put something in the door, would you?" he said, sitting down and taking something out of the inside pocket of his tailored suit jacket. Colette kicked half a brick into the crack of the door and took out her handcuffs.

He was busy taking a snort of whatever the fuck it was when she cuffed the wrist holding the vial. He looked up at her in violent shock as she took the vial out of his hand and bent his other arm behind his back.

"Hey! Oww!" he said as she snapped on the other cuff. "What the fuck are you doing?"

"It's not rough sex, you little weenie, so clear your mind of that. Question. Was the cop they're rioting about now, Coglin, was he set up?"

"Set up? What the hell are you talking about? Have you gone crazy? This a joke right? Phil put you up to this?"

"In three seconds, I'm going to drag you back into that warehouse and place you under arrest for the possession of narcotics. In front of the mayor and whoever else's in there. Then you'll see what kind of joke it is."

"What? What is it?" Gary moaned. "What do you want?"

"Coglin, the cop. You know the dead second lady, the riot. Ringing a bell? Was he operated against in any way by the mayor's office? Were there any favors called in?"

"I'm just a fucking speechwriter. I . . ."

"OK, let's go," she said, pulling him up by his lapels. She could feel the smooth inside lining with her fingertips. *Silk*, she thought. What a wimp!

"OK. Alright. Yes," Gary said. "As far as I've heard, yes. OK? The cop wasn't set up really. The mayor, let's say, took advantage of a situation that had already reached a point. The black vote is his weakest link. He needed to do something to get some support. Show he gave a fuck."

"By making sure the cop was prosecuted?"

"It's all about appearances," Gary said. "Don't you understand that? How things seem, not how they are. Coglin seemed guilty. We didn't invent that. We just helped seem become fact. If he'd gotten off, it would've been assumed by a lot of the black vote that it was rigged. And let me tell you something, the black vote is vital these days. Black people vote now like they never did. They're the key to everything."

"So you decided to rig it the other way."

"Do you have any conception of how difficult it is to govern this city? The amount of interests involved? How they shift?"

"So sacrificing somebody is OK then?"

"Exactly," Gary said. "For the good of the whole. You want the Democrats back in there? You want it to be like the late eighties? Dirt and crime and the Bronx burning?"

"I guess it's a shame Coglin isn't as high-minded as you. Now you got a riot anyway, so what did you prove?"

"But when he's caught and brought to justice, we'll still be OK. See? He's actually helped us getting involved in this other crazy shit. Killing the VP's wife? The whole country will want him to rot in jail now. And what's with this is-this-guy-innocent routine? He took your gun. This proves it."

"You fucked him," Colette said.

"He fucked himself," Gary said. "Session over. Get this off my hand."

Colette looked down at the broken courtyard flagstones. There were little mounded holes in the sandy dirt between some of them. Rat holes, she thought.

"How was it done?" Colette said. "How was the fix put in?"

"Calls were made."

"To whom?" she said.

"Use your imagination. The judge. The police commissioner. The police union. How the hell should I know?"

Colette tapped the coke vial against the rusted banister of the fire escape.

"Yeah, I know," she said, turning him back around and unlocking the cuffs. "You're just a speech writer."

She put her cuffs back in their pouch next to her gun and gestured to give him back the vial. She poured out its powdered contents upon the bird-shit-encrusted concrete of the courtyard just as he raised his hand to take it. Then she flicked the vial at him like a used cigarette butt. It clanged off the rusted metal steps above his head.

"I hate it when that happens," she said, yanking open the door.

"Phil's gonna hear about this," he called after her. "I've known him a lot longer than you, you little tramp."

"C'mon, Gary," she called back. "You promised you wouldn't tell, remember?"

When she came back into the "war" room, something was different. Where the hell was the military squad? Where was Vaughn?

"What happened to the SWAT team?" she said to Carlos.

"They just left."

She passed a hand through her hair.

"What did you find out?" Carlos said. "What the hell are you doing?"

"Hold on a second. I have to think."

So, OK, Coglin really was set up.

By the mayor, she thought.

Railroaded.

Just like dad.

To avoid the sentence, his dear old Irish uncle, the bank robber, offers him a job. Big money heist in order to flee the country, go underground. Job goes ridiculously wrong, and the second lady gets killed.

But not even by him, she thought, remembering the bullet pattern. By the Secret Service themselves.

What could be done about it all, though? Even if he were framed, he'd gone over the line beyond all reproach. There was no coming back for him.

But he was still breathing. At least until Delta Force got within rifle range. She could at the very least do something about that.

The truth has to come out now, she thought, looking over by the assistant director.

All the rhetoric and politics had to stop right now.

You're too late. He's just gonna get killed anyway, a small mean voice whispered to her. *Why fuck things up for yourself?*

No, she thought.

This was a heist case. *Her* heist case. Coglin and O'Donnell and Pallone were her quarry, and she was going to catch them.

Alive.

If it killed her.

Dunlop walked to where the mayor was standing by the phone company liaison's computer terminal. Both entourages were crowded around the screen excitedly, like men at a Super Bowl party.

She waded through them and tapped the assistant director on the shoulder.

"There you are, Ryan," he said before she could open her mouth. "Listen carefully. You're off this case. I want you back at headquarters right now, filling out a missing-gun report."

She stood there astonished.

Used her, she thought. Gotten every little thing she knew, and now she could go home with her tail between her legs. It was already over. Federal government had their version of things sewn up. They had their bullshit assassin's revenge package they could sell to the cameras and that was that. The Secret Service's royal fuck-up was swept right under the rug.

As long as there was no one around to dispute things.

And there wouldn't be, Colette thought. Any second now and the last three witnesses to the shooting would be eliminated.

The mayor was smiling at her again. Gary came up behind him and shook his head at her.

Bastard got his scapegoat safely sacrificed in the process, too, didn't he? His reelection in the bag.

Not again, she thought, looking him in the eye.

Not again.

She turned to Dunlop.

"Yes, sir," she said to him. "I'll report right back downtown."

But already she was remembering the trace map and where the red mark on it had been. East Side. Upper Fifties.

It would take maybe ten minutes to get to Fifty-seventh Street, she thought, turning from the crowd of male faces, walking quickly at the exit. Carlos fell into step behind her.

And then maybe another ten to get crosstown.

When she hit the threshold, she began to run.

Chapter Twenty-seven

ON THE CORNER OF FIFTY-NINTH AND PARK, Coglin looked up from the paper he wasn't reading in his lap. He was on the southwest corner, sitting on the steps of a plaza out in front of an aluminum and glass office building, trying not to look too conspicuous as he waited for the others to arrive. The hatch for the underground railroad tracks was twenty feet away on the sidewalk by the corner, a rectangular metal door outlined in faded, yellow paint.

A drop of sweat rolled down his forehead, hung from the side of his nose for a moment, and then dripped onto the newspaper with a splat.

Where the hell were they?

Maybe they'd come already, he thought, and now were circling the block.

And then again, maybe they're caught.

Or worse.

He flicked the negative thought away with a shake of his head.

After a moment, an NYPD blue-and-white began roaring down Park Avenue, siren blaring.

"Warm, warm, hotter, hot," he said quietly as it got closer.

It sped past, siren blaring.

"Getting colder, colder. Oh, darn. Ice cold."

Coglin snapped his head around as he heard a familiar tinny clattering coming from the north. A moment later, his uncle, still bare-chested, turned the corner across the street, pushing the shopping cart. He had his head down, mumbling to himself. He glanced up once at Coglin and gave him a wink. Aidan continued west on the opposite side of the street to the service entrance of an old hotel farther down the block, and just stood there.

C'mon, Lisa, Coglin thought.

When he turned to his right, a bus was passing east across Park, and when it was gone, Lisa was standing on the grass-filled median in the middle of the avenue, waiting on the light. She smiled.

Coglin stood. When he looked over at Aidan, his uncle was nodding. He began pushing his cart. Lisa had made the far curb and was three steps away from him when there was a tremendous screech of brakes across on Park.

A blue van skidded, sliding sideways in the northbound side across the median. A man in a black ski mask, not unlike the ones they'd used in the robbery attempt, was halfway out its passenger side window. The van hadn't completely stopped before the first barrage of gunfire began spurting forth, the sound of it reverberating violently off the faces of the buildings.

Coglin could only stand and stare idly as the ground-floor glass in the office building behind him shattered with a tremendous splashing detonation. The stone steps he stood upon crackled suddenly around him like a heat gun on old paint, and then he noticed that Lisa was down. She was lying sideways on the steps with her feet higher then her head, and blood was running down the steps into the cracks of the sidewalk.

A stone chip sliced the front ridge of Coglin's brow, and he was on his hands and knees scrambling behind the pillar beside him, cement dust and blood stinging his eyes. On his belly, Coglin pressed the top of his head against the pillar, bleeding face down, nose wedged into a thin break in the flagstone.

The barrage seemed unending. He hadn't even thought to pull the Beretta in his belt. When there was a break in the fire, it was like the whole city had ceased all movement. Then Coglin heard something, an electronic bleating, and he looked up. It was coming from Lisa. When he peeked up, he could see it was her cell phone clipped to her belt, somebody calling.

Nobody home, he thought.

Over her body, at the opposite corner, he saw Aidan, crouched at a payphone kiosk with the shopping cart in front of him, receiver in one hand, the automatic he'd taken off the FBI lady in the other. He made eye contact with Coglin and gestured with the gun at Lisa, nodding his head vigorously.

Coglin kneeled and shot a hand out into space, snatching the phone off Lisa's belt. A stone chip from the almost instant hail of bullets sliced across the top of his hand before he could bring it back safely. Blood dripped off the phone as he pressed it on and brought it to his ear.

"Listen up!" Aidan screamed. "*After I start firing, you run for the grate and open it! When it's open, you put down cover so I can cross the street! Nod if you understand.*"

Coglin nodded.

"*On your mark,*" Aidan said.

Oh, Lisa, Coglin thought, glancing down at her as he got to his feet.

"Get set . . ."

Bullets were ripping at the pillar now, chewing at it, turning the cement to powder. Rusty looking strands of rebar appeared grotesquely from the close side like bone through skin.

Coglin dropped the phone and pulled out the Berretta, holding it in his left hand. The newspaper he'd been pretending to read wafted up in a warm breeze and began to dance as bullets smacked through it.

When he heard Aidan's gun start, Coglin waited until the pillar in front of him stopped exploding, and then he was running, crouched, head down for the grate. Across the avenue in front of him, two black-clad commandos were ducking back behind the blue van as Aidan's bullets punched into its side. Then Coglin was diving headfirst over the sidewalk at the grate.

The heavy steel grate swung up almost effortlessly when he yanked the handle. It stopped upright with a bang and there was another small wire gate inside of it, and he pulled that until it also snapped. There was a little doorway now on the sidewalk, and he ripped the mesh door open. Stairs headed down into the dimness beneath, and then he was moving in a rushing crawl toward the close line of parked cars that separated him from the government van.

He transferred the Berretta to his right hand, stuck his hand up over the hood of the car, and began firing blindly.

The trigger pull was exceptionally light. How many shots were there? he thought, firing off three like they were nothing.

Firing, he glanced to his left to watch Aidan running head down, rolling the cart like a man toward the finish line of a shopping spree. The cart flipped at the curb and the cans and money-filled duffel bags slid across the cement sidewalk. One of the money bags dropped into the hole and Aidan, diving, now pushed the other one in after it.

"C'mon!" Aidan yelled.

The car Coglin was shooting behind seemed to spontaneously disintegrate with the return fire the moment he pulled his pistol down. An entire overwhelming symphony of destruction following his weak solo. The tires blew out with a double boom as he half-ran, half-crawled toward the open hole. Aidan, kneeling beside the opening, grabbed him and shoved him forcibly down into it like one of the bags. Coglin's feet found one of the money bags, and he kicked it down the metal stairs, and he slid, descending after it into the musty dark. Then his uncle was on top of him, yanking both lids of the grate closed on top of them with a twin rusty bang.

Chapter Twenty-eight

COLETTE WAS SPEEDING from beneath the ornate arch of the Helmsley Building on Park Avenue, lights and siren cranked, when she heard the gunfire. She shut off the siren and listened to the distant, snapping chatter. She glanced at the glass faces of the huge skyscrapers and the scared ones of the people standing frozen on the sidewalk before them and stepped down on the gas.

"Jesus Christ," Carlos said, gaze fixed out the windshield. He pulled his Glock out, pointed its barrel at the door. "Jesus Christ."

They ate about nine red lights and twice had to drive on the sidewalk to get around the traffic before they stopped before the blue government van parked sideways in the street before Fifty-ninth Street. It had an almost straight line of bullet holes across its side. Two men in black were sprawled on the grass median in the middle of the avenue, laying down an almost continuous wave of fire on a pickup truck parked across the street.

As Colette got out of her sedan, two other members of their force were sweeping quickly across the street on the left. They threw themselves up against the parked cars and started firing at the pickup, ripping holes in its hood and blasting at the already smashed glass of its windshield.

Carlos grabbed her from where she stood gaping and pulled her around the opposite side of the Crown Vic. He had already popped the trunk, and he handed her one of the heavy bullet-proof vests. She took off her jacket and slid into it. She accepted the Wingmaster twelve gauge that Carlos pulled out of the trunk and opened the breech. She stood and grabbed a box of shells from the case on top of the spare and then crouched again, thumbing the red, double-ought shells into the gun until it was full. She dropped another handful of shells into the pocket of the vest and nodded at Carlos.

Gunfire was still going strong as they clambered out from behind the car and over the median.

There was a sudden cease-fire when they reached the opposite side. Colette poked her head out on the sidewalk from the front of a mail truck they were behind and saw one of the commandos waving a hand back and forth vigorously.

Another three soldiers appeared from three different directions and began turning back-to-back, quickly swinging their weapons in controlled arcs. Colette stepped out slowly onto the sidewalk, shotgun barrel skyward, as submachine gun sights momentarily trained on her and then continued their search.

Vaughn arrived at the corner a second before she did. He was unarmed and still had his jacket on, and he was looking around deliberately, searching over the shoulders of the soldiers.

Colette glanced at the metal grate he was standing on, her mouth falling open.

Railroad? she thought quickly. Subway? Tracks went where? Grand Central?

Vaughn looked down slowly between his feet. He tapped the nearest soldier in front of him and pointed out the grate as he took a step back. Vaughn had his cell phone out before the soldiers had surrounded the grate, guns aimed at it. One of them yanked up the two metal doors and the other three charged with remarkable smoothness through its gate under the street, submachine guns to their shoulders. The fourth one who'd pulled the door followed like a snake down a rabbit hole.

There was a rumble beneath Colette's feet as she got to the hole. Hot, stale air blasted in her face as she looked down.

She brushed her matted hair from her eyes and looked across at the woman, bloodily slain on the office building steps.

When she looked back at Vaughn, he was speaking quickly into his cell phone. His wink was like a camera lens with its shutter speed set on low.

Run, Coglin, she thought, backing up, searching for where she left the car.

Run for your goddamn life.

Chapter Twenty-nine

RUNNING THROUGH THE DARK, Coglin first heard, then a moment later, saw the train blast by on his left. It was a commuter train, the squares of its lit windows sharp against the darkness of the tunnel. It was jammed, a blur of pale, featureless faces. Coglin couldn't decide which he wanted more: to be on it or in front of it. He labored forward with the heavy bag at his side, keeping his eyes trained on his uncle's back.

The station directly beneath the stairs had been dimly lit with emergency lights high along its musty walls. They'd run south along a little cement lip in the wall above the tracks. Single, weak bulbs were set at football-field-length intervals in the wall and between them, it was difficult to see. The tunnel seemed to go on into infinity. Along the ledge, their progress was impeded periodically by strange forgotten objects, a folding chair, some bags of cement, a toolbox. Coglin made sure to place the objects directly into the path behind him.

Coglin looked to his left down at the tracks, the silver blue rails like razor edges against the black.

They came upon some orange reflective vests draped beside some shovels on the rusted railing of the narrow ledge. They put them on as they ran, and Aidan chucked one of the shovels onto his shoulder.

The hot subterranean air made the street feel air conditioned, like running a marathon in a boiler room.

Ahead in the high, black ceiling above the middle of the tracks, beams of dusty sunlight fell through a grate and lay in thin, bright even bars along the trestles. A car horn honked loudly from above, and then a cigarette butt floated down in an arc and lay smoldering on the blackened gravel between the trestles. Coglin kept his eyes on the grate, waiting for it to fly open and for men in black jumpsuits to rappel down on ropes.

They had reached Fifty-fifth Street or Fifty-fourth by now, he guessed. He speculated that the labyrinth of tunnels for Grand Central had to start splitting up soon, in the high forties maybe, another ten blocks or so.

"They're comin'!" his uncle said. "Behind us."

Coglin didn't think he could run anymore. The muscles of his arms and legs and chest and back felt like they were pumping acid now instead of blood, and the acid was on fire. But when he saw the tunnel ahead widen and branch into several directions, he decided he was wrong.

The four tracks under Park Avenue split and replicated, spreading east and west. Four to eight, eight to sixteen, sixteen to thirty-two. Each track had its own arched tunnel and together, they looked like a series of giant mouse holes.

Which one though? Which to choose?

The farthest one on the right, he thought quickly. That had to go down. The ones closest to the main track probably led to the more used upper part of the station with the ornate waiting area. If they were to have a chance of hiding, they'd have to go lower, deeper.

Fuckin' tunnel to the center of the earth.

Coglin tapped his uncle on the back and pointed to the far right tunnel.

His uncle let him take the lead. Instead of following the thin ledge, Coglin flipped over the handrail and jumped down onto the tracks where they widened. Aidan was right at his heels, and Coglin began to sprint over the wooden trestles toward the farthest tunnel, hoping to make it inside before being spotted. He looked at the third rail warily, knowing if he tripped and touched it, he'd be fried.

Coglin slowed just inside the far tunnel, breathing heavily. He switched the bag to his other side. The gun he'd taken from his old boss was digging into the small of his back, and he took it out and shoved it in the bag on top of the money.

"Did they see?" he asked his uncle.

Aidan shrugged.

"Assume they did," his uncle whispered harshly.

There was no ledge here, just little, curved spaces where they might be able to fit were a train to come. The ceiling was a lot lower.

Where were they now? Coglin thought. Forty-ninth? Forty-eighth? Fuckin' thing was a maze. They'd gradually moved west which put them under Madison. He tried to gauge whether the tunnel was sloping downward, but he had no idea. He began to jog. He noticed two rats in the light of the wall bulb skitter across the track ahead. Then a third.

"I've been working on the railroad," Aidan sang lowly a step behind him.

The tunnel began to curve, and off the right, there was a little metal stairway that led to a door. Coglin ran to it, but it had no knob. Probably hadn't been opened in a hundred years. He ran back down and they continued south.

They'd only gotten another hundred feet or so when they heard the barking up ahead.

Coglin stopped.

"Dogs!" Aidan said. "Fuckin' dogs!"

"Back!" Coglin said.

Aidan threw out his hand when they got back to the curve. He looked behind them for a beat or two, and then pulled Coglin toward the stairwell, putting his finger to his lips.

"You see something?" Coglin said.

"They're there," Aidan said.

They crept up the stairs. Coglin examined the door. It was a thick, wooden one, nailed shut along the right side. He grabbed the shovel from his uncle.

It took Coglin four baseball swings with its blade to pop out the pin of the top hinge. The bottom one flew out with only two. He wedged the thin shovel blade between the door and the frame working it in, trying to get some leverage. The door moved out half an inch, the nails on the right side groaning before the shovel blade cracked, and it slammed shut.

"Fuck," Coglin said.

The barking from the south was louder now.

"Come on! Come on!" his uncle urged.

Coglin repeated the process with the cracked shovel and this time when the door opened, he wedged the barrel of the pistol into it, and jammed the handle of the shovel halfway through the space.

"Grab the bottom with your hands," he told his uncle. "Pull when I say."

His uncle fit his fingers around the door. They could hear a dog panting now. A rolling click, its nails, or its collar bouncing as it ran.

"Now!" Coglin said, pushing the handle toward the wall. He felt the old door shift fully with a loud, satisfying creak.

Coglin had pulled it away from the frame enough to get a foot in when the dog burst up the stairs, a huge, black German shepherd. It latched onto Aidan's ankle and Aidan grabbed the shovel off the floor and bashed it between the eyes. It kept biting, and he hit again in the ribs, and it released its grip.

He would've hit it again, but the sound of muffled automatic gunfire started up in the distance. Bullets whined off the brick, and Coglin worked himself through the door crack. Aidan pushed at him until the two fell forward free of the door.

On the other side was a low, stone passage, pitch black and even hotter than the tunnel. The dog was barking so loud at the crack of the door behind them, it sounded like it was tearing its vocal cords. Coglin stepped right into a wall.

Sealed in, he thought. Like fish in a barrel, they'd come up the stairs and just shoot them. Or worse, he thought. For what they'd done, they wouldn't even; they'd just seal the door up!

"Go!" his uncle said, pushing hard.

"Yeah? Where?"

His hands probed the surface of the obstruction in front of him. It was smooth. He rubbed at his fingers, coated in a powdery substance.

Sheetrock, he thought. Thank you, God.

He reared back against his uncle and kicked the wall. His foot crushed through it, and bright light spilled into their little passage. For the first time, he noticed the side walls. They seemed shiny, black.

They were moving. The walls of bugs on both sides shifted upward away from the light. Coglin felt something brush the top of his head. Something fell down the back of his shirt, stuck to the sweat of his back and began moving

"Ahhhhhhhh!!!" Coglin yelled, kicking and punching the wall. Aidan was screaming, going completely batshit behind him, ramming against him, trying to smash him through the wall. It took another minute before he fell to a painted cement floor with Aidan on top of him.

Coglin ripped off his shirt and began slapping at himself, flinging the hand-width-sized, shit-brown water bugs off his back, his arms, out of his hair. Aidan, shirtless, was shaking and slapping wildly, and in a moment, a dozen or more bugs covered the floor, running back toward the hole in the sheetrock, making their escape. Coglin must've said the word motherfucker thirty-six times before he could stop shaking and look around.

They were in a boiler or electrical room of some kind. A half dozen huge, turbine-looking cylinders lay half in and half out of the floor with pipes and conduits running out of them like giant metal hippos on life support. The basement of a building, a small set of cement stairs to the left led to an open doorway.

When the black German shepherd burst through the hole in the wall, Coglin thought, fuck you. That's just not fair.

It went right for Aidan. Teeth bared, shining like porcelain knives, it dove for his throat. He punched it. He must have been primed after the bug attack, because he stood, rooted, waiting for it, and Coglin watched him deck the fuckin' thing in the side of its furry head with a nice right cross. The thing went down, sliding across the cement on its side and then Aidan was running for the stairs, Coglin scrambling up racing him. There was a metal slop bucket holding the door open, and Coglin kicked it out of the way while Aidan slammed the door shut. They could hear the dog barking over the sound of the turbines.

Aidan sat with his back to the door and held his head in his hands.

"C'mon," Coglin said to him in an Irish accent. "This is the fun part."

He looked to his left down the basement corridor. Its dingy walls were dimly lit and pipes and conduits hung low overhead. It went twenty feet long and curved to the left. They could still smell the train tunnel.

"What do you think's down this way?" he said. "Alligators or lions?"

Aidan pushed himself up.

"Let's go fuckin' see," he said.

Around the corner was another fifty feet or so of corridor before another left-hand turn. To the right was an elevator door. They stood, looking at it.

"Fuck it," Aidan said, pressing the button.

The door opened. The elevator was empty and much nicer than the basement, all brushed stainless and cherry-colored maple. They stepped in.

"Go outside again?" Aidan said, pressing "L." "I don't know. I'm out of ideas."

"Don't look at me," Coglin said.

At the lobby, the door opened onto a huge, white room crowded with a couple hundred people walking back and forth through it. At least a quarter of them were cops, and Coglin and Aidan just stood there. Two men in expensive looking suits got on. One of them seemed vaguely familiar, Coglin thought. He was talking on a cell phone. The other one pressed for the top button, fifty-eight.

"You guys getting out?" he said.

Aidan reached out and pressed fifty-seven without answering him.

The door closed. The elevator shot up.

The man looked at Coglin, filthy, and Aidan, shirtless, and their bags.

"What are you guys? Messengers?" he said.

He seemed disgusted.

Aidan nodded at him and then looked at the fast changing number on the display.

"You're supposed to wear shirts, you know," he said. "Didn't the guard tell you that? Who let you in?"

"Yeah?" the familiar looking one was saying loudly into his phone. "Well, I don't give a fuck. What do I pay you for? Excuses? Then you lose it. The pad is there. You better be on it or you're fired."

He hung up and turned to the other one. Coglin recognized him then as the real estate guy who'd run the ad in the paper against him, Decatur.

Well, whataya know? Larry Decatur, International Construction. Jet-setting, media-hogging dickhead in the flesh.

"What did he say?" the other one said to Decatur. His number one bootlicker, Coglin thought.

"Said he couldn't fly that low," Decatur said with a roll of his eyes. "He was gonna lose his license."

Coglin and Aidan exchanged glances.

"Said they'd fine the shit out of me."

"Nice of him," beady eyes said. "Lookin out for you like that. Mr. Vietnam. The fuckin' pussy."

"Like Municipal Marty is gonna have the balls. He does, we'll take it out of my contribution. Closin' the city down. I gotta get the fuck out there. Cindy's already havin' trouble with that goddamn French fag. Now he says he wants to serve flowers for a fuckin' appetizer and . . ."

Decatur turned around then and saw them.

"Hey, what the . . . Who the fuck are they?" he said angrily.

"Messengers, I think," beady eyes said. "A couple of fuckin' mutes."

"Jesus Christ! Look at you fuckin' slobs," Decatur said. "You can't come in here like that. That Bobby let these crackheads in here? He's gone! Hey! Hello? You speak English?"

"Maybe they're Polish," beady eyes said. "They still doing asbestos abatement in the subbasement?"

"That's over on Vanderbilt, you idiot," Decatur said.

"Shit, sorry. I forgot," beady eyes said humbly.

"Hey!" Decatur said, taking a step forward and getting in Coglin's face. "Answer me. Do you speak English?"

Coglin smiled and held up a palm. He knelt then and unzipped the bag slowly, nodding his head as though they shouldn't worry, something inside would explain his presence. When he pressed the barrel of the .38 to the side of Decatur's head, he still didn't look like he was getting it.

"No, asshole. Me no fuckin' hable anglais."

COLETTE SCREECHED TO A STOP on the Forty-second Street side of Grand Central Station and jumped out without turning off the sedan's strobing blue light. She ran down the sloping entryway and came out into the main concourse. Beneath the sprawling majestic green dome were people in the thousands, entering and exiting up and down the various staircases and escalators, standing waiting for trains, crisscrossing over the polished beige stone floor.

Where would Aidan and Coglin be coming out from, she

thought. Dead ahead, she thought, seeing the entryway for the train tracks to the north. Unless, of course, they were heading north. In that case, they'd come out somewhere up in Harlem.

Vaughn blasted past her on the right then, three commandos at his heels. Vaughn gestured at the tracks before them, and the three soldiers split up into three separate tunnel entrances. Christ they were fast, Colette thought, watching them. How could they run so fast in the heat with all that gear?

Vaughn stepped back to where she was standing. He had a hands-free cell microphone on now, in addition to a crackling walkie-talkie in his hand. He put the radio between the knees of his summer weight slacks and took out a cigarette and lit one. He offered the pack to Colette. She shook her head.

A Port Authority cop came up from behind them.

"Can't smoke in here," he said to Vaughn.

Vaughn took out a thin billfold and flipped it at him. Colette made out the FBI on his ID.

"On the job," Vaughn said.

Bust his hump anyway, she mentally told the cop.

"Just keep it low," the cop said, walking away.

Pussied out, Colette thought.

"I've always wanted to say that," Vaughn said.

"So," she said. "You're in the FBI, too?"

"Today I am," he said. "I dig it."

"Why don't you just napalm all the tunnels at once?" she said.

"Don't say that too loud," Vaughn said. "One of the bigwigs might hear you and actually do it. You're one feisty broad, you know that? I like that. Like the fact that you're not supposed to be here. I don't want you to take it the wrong way or anything, but that kind of stuff really floats my boat."

He smiled at her, holding the cigarette between a set of very white, even teeth. He was still wearing sunglasses and with his blond hair, the effect was very striking. Some type of celebrity, lamely trying to avoid his fans.

"How could I take that the wrong way?" she said.

"Listen, I'm just like you, sweetheart," Vaughn said. "I'm just a pawn. I follow orders. They tell me to nail somebody, I don't think about it. I take out my hammer and say, where?"

"You know this thing is trumped-up bullshit," Colette said. "There was no assassination attempt. This was a jewel heist, gone cosmically wrong, I'll grant you, but it was just a heist. The Secret Service is just saying assassination because I think one of her security detail made a mistake and shot her by accident. They're covering this whole thing up."

Vaughn smiled at her again.

"Because I like you," he said, "I'll let you in on something you might not have thought about. The vice president, would you say he's a powerful man?"

"Goes without saying," Colette said.

"I'll give you one guess as to where he worked before he became vice president."

"Holy shit," Colette said. "He used to be the director of the CIA."

"Now you're getting warmer," Vaughn said. "If you were a former director of the CIA, a man who was used to ordering hits on people across the globe with his feet on his desk over morning coffee, and your wife got waxed, wouldn't you be a little pissed, let's say? And if you had the power to kill the ones who did it, wouldn't you be tempted to exercise that power?"

"But it isn't true," Colette said. "Her own people hit her. We're gathering the evidence now to prove that's exactly what went down."

Vaughn laughed.

"Evidence," he said. "Evidence has a funny way of getting lost. And witnesses got funny ways of disappearing. Especially when the stakes are high. And these stakes are as high as you get, Colette. These are no-limit, Las Vegas–level stakes. VP ain't looking for truth. He's looking for revenge."

"That's where you come in?"

Vaughn shrugged, flicked his cigarette.

"It's a tough job, Agent Ryan. But somebody's got to do it."

A chatter of noise came off the radio.

"Awesome," Vaughn yelled into it.

"Your two boys just went into the basement of a building," Vaughn said. "The hunt is about to come to a close."

"Get in there and clean 'em up, boys," Vaughn said. "Remember. If at all possible, we want to make sure we don't have any company. You know what I'm saying. Drop and mop. I repeat. Drop and mop."

That was it, Colette thought. Taken out of her hands.

Never really in them in the first place.

Vaughn was running out of the domed concourse back up the slope for Forty-second Street.

"C'mon, sweet cheeks," Vaughn called down to her. "Don't you want to see the end of the game?"

Chapter Thirty

THE TOP FLOOR looked just like the basement. A cement hall-way with some anonymous looking doors and lots of tubing running overhead. There was a set of concrete steps, and he and Aidan pushed Decatur and his ass kisser toward it.

"You're not gonna get away with this," Decatur was saying as they herded him up the stairs.

Coglin banged him through the door onto the roof.

Outside, it was all machinery, the housings for the elevators along with a whole bunch of other humming metal boxes, and air conditioning units. Although they were outside, there was another roof above them. The sides of the building were enclosed in an open cladding, a kind of mesh. Coglin could see the tops of huge letters affixed upon it and another set of steel stairs.

Coglin pulled closed the door to the roof, thumbed back the

hammer of the old .38 and pressed it against Decatur's forehead. Decatur looked into Coglin's eyes for a moment, searching with his famous deal-making eyes for something he could reason with or some fear that he could use to negotiate. Then a look of nausea overtook his well-photographed face, and he closed his eyes. His hand went into his pocket and brought out a thick wad of hundreds.

"Here," he said, "take it."

It had a gold money clip around it that looked like it was about to snap.

Coglin smacked it away with his free hand, knocking it under a huge duct.

"Thanks," he said, "but we got about all we can carry."

Coglin felt power humming through him like the machines at his back. It felt good, he thought. He couldn't deny it anymore. All of it, too. Getting chased. The gunfire. It had been exhilarating, liberating. He didn't want to fight, but the fuckers had pushed him.

Pushed his ass right off the edge.

He felt all the guilt draw out of his muscles, his body, making him feel lighter, as if he could fly away on his own.

"Strip," he told Decatur.

Decatur started loosening his tie without looking at him.

When both of the businessmen were standing in their underwear, Coglin held the gun on them while Aidan put on the minion's clothes and then Aidan held the gun while Coglin put on Decatur's. The suits were both too big, but at least they looked a little better. A helicopter was approaching from the west.

Aidan had both men taped up from the roll Coglin still had in his pocket. He'd brought them around the other side of the structure above the stairs and made them put their arms around a pipe before he taped their wrists so they couldn't move.

"Tighty whities?" Coglin said, looking at Decatur. "What are you? Fuckin' nine?"

"Jeez, look at you slobs," Aidan said. "Who let you in here?"

They heard the helicopter then, the loud whump of its blades above them.

"Adios," Coglin told Decatur, stepping for the stairs. *"Vaya con dios, mis amigos."*

When they reached the top of the metal stairs, they crouched, watching it come in for a landing, the clear glass and red fiberglass nose shining as it tilted upward on its approach. It did a little fishlike turn with its tail as its skids came down. Aidan's hair was blown back in the rotor wash.

When he stepped onto the helipad, Coglin noticed for the first time how high up they were.

Park Avenue lay directly in front of him, the asphalt tiny pale strings far below. He could make out police lights, tiny as Christmas tree ones, by the grate they'd fled into. On his right was the top of the Chrysler building, and its huge silver dome was blinding in the late sun, molten, shimmering. The lights of Times Square were recognizable through the buildings to the west, but thankfully he couldn't see any people. The roofs of the other Midtown skyscrapers were eye-level now, like the tops of backyard fences down a block. The sky was like nothing he'd ever seen before. Cloudless and endless and so light, light blue.

The pilot had his head tilted sideways, looking at them funny as they approached, but Coglin smiled at him, nodded like, "I know, I know. We look nuts, don't we? Let me tell you what happened."

He and his uncle ducked their heads involuntarily under the spinning rotor and began jogging for their ride.

* * *

COLETTE STOOD AT THE EDGE of the helipad atop the MetLife building and smiled. The sun was starting its descent slowly in the west above Jersey, an almost aqua corona burn in the blue around it.

Beside her, Vaughn, blank faced, was searching the horizon with a pair of binoculars.

Five minutes ago, after they'd searched through the entire building and roof, they'd finally found Decatur. After the magnate told them what had happened, she'd actually heard Vaughn try to get a couple of F-14s scrambled. Apparently, he'd been told no because he seemed kind of pissed.

"Guess we're running into a little overtime here," she said. "You know in that game you were talking about?"

"I've suddenly become sick of you," he said, lowering his binoculars. "Sergeant, have Miss Ryan escorted off this site."

One of the commandos appeared at her elbow.

"That's Agent Ryan," Colette said to Vaughn.

"Not anymore," Vaughn said, beginning again to scan the sky.

Chapter Thirty-one

AIDAN MADE THE HELICOPTER PILOT put them down on the mound of an empty, dusty baseball field beside a project on the outskirts of Newark. Coglin opened the bubbled glass of the door, chucked the money bags out into the infield and followed them out. Aidan came out behind him and through the dust, they watched the aircraft lift up and swing back east.

"What if he tails us or something?" Coglin said.

Aidan pointed up into the northern sky at a very low, slowly approaching passenger jet. Lights of other planes behind it seemed to be lining up in the light blue.

"We're right next to the airport landing path, " Aidan said. "He's not gonna follow us."

At the curb, they hailed the first taxi they saw, a beat-up gypsy with a white body, red hood and green door. Aidan took a look at the scraggly looking driver.

Two minutes later, the driver stepped out, counting an inordinate amount of cash. Aidan had insisted the man's license be included in the purchase of the taxi.

"Because if you feel like calling in that your car was stolen earlier than tomorrow, we can make sure to give the cops your address so they can pick up the stolen money we just gave you and lock your ass up."

Aidan made Coglin drive. He guided him through blighted inner-city streets that were different from the ones he'd patrolled in the Bronx by the fact there were more single-family houses, forlorn, ramshackle rows of them. By the screaming overhead passing of planes, Coglin surmised, they were getting closer to the airport. They'd finally turned down a deserted road with tall grass on both sides when Aidan told Coglin to pull over. His uncle pointed.

Through the grass, there was a channel of black water and at its opposite shore, a huge container ship was being loaded. An enormous dockside crane swung steel truck-trailer-sized containers up from a fenced yard of them and placed them down into the hull of the ship. The container yard went in an L shape around the water and its fence ended in the tall grass a couple of hundred yards behind them.

Aidan turned and pointed back at the fence.

"Twenty feet to the left of the corner of that fence is a small hole," he said. "Directly across from the hole is a locked empty container."

"This," Aidan said, taking out a key on a chain around his neck, "is its key. We go in it and the crane hoists us onto the boat and at midnight tonight, when we're well at sea, we come out and have a drink with the captain."

"What about the crew?" Coglin said. "Won't they notice who we are?"

"We stay well out of sight throughout the voyage," Aidan said. "But it doesn't matter, because everyone of them gets a cut."

"Where we headed?" Coglin said.

"First France, then Argentina, then New Zealand. That's where we're gonna get off."

Coglin looked out to the left of the water. Low factories and chemical tanks stood in the flatland distance like cast-off machinery. Twenty or so miles to the east behind them, the skyline they'd just escaped shone in the evening light like an impossible series of giant golden spikes.

Well, he'd certainly worn out his welcome in the tristate area, he thought.

"They got a police force in New Zealand?" Coglin said with a smile. "They hiring you think?"

"As a matter of fact," Aidan said, "they are. Only thing is, a recommendation from your previous employer is required."

"Your thinking the terms I left under might be a problem?" Coglin said.

Aidan shrugged.

"Give your old boss a ring when we get there," he said. "Worse he could do is say no."

"When are we going?" Coglin said.

Aidan opened the passenger side door.

"Now," he said.

Aidan was bent, pulling one of the bags out of the back seat, when Coglin noticed the bloodstain on the back of his jacket.

"Hey, what the fuck?" he said. "You're bleeding. You got shot?"

"I'm fine," Aidan said, swinging the bag onto his uninjured side. "C'mon."

"You're not fine," Coglin said, peering in at the passenger

seat and seeing the blood all over it. "When did you get shot? In the tunnel?"

"It's nothing," Aidan said. "It bled for a little, then it stopped. It'll stop again."

Aidan started off into the grass.

"We got half an hour to get in that container and on that boat," he said.

Aidan had made it about two hundred feet in the grass before he stumbled. He went down on his knees. He tried to get back up for a moment, then seemed to decide against it. Coglin dropped his bag and ran to him.

"I just need to catch my wind," Aidan said. He was very pale now. Blood was dripping from the blotter of his suit coat.

Bleeding to death, Coglin thought.

Aidan took the key from around his neck, shoved it into Coglin's hand.

"You're a good fuckin' lad, you know that. Nobody ever busted me out of jail."

Aidan smiled. He closed his eyes, seemed to lose his balance, and then woke with a start.

"That was something, you narrowback bastard," he said sleepily. "That was something else. Just leave me the cigarettes, would ya? It's the container right opposite the fence, OK?"

But Coglin was pulling the heavy bag off his uncle, leaving it where it lay in the grass as he pulled him up, rushing him toward the car.

Hospital, Coglin thought. Where the fuck was the hospital? Which way?

Chapter Thirty-two

COLETTE WAS RELUCTANTLY pulling up before FBI head-quarters downtown when she heard the call over the FBI radio. It came from the Newark office. Two suspects, one shot, detained at St. Joseph's Hospital in Newark. A request for positive identification was made to the New York office.

"Newark, this is Special Agent Colette Ryan Bank Robbery Squad. I'm on my way."

She turned down the radio to silence any protest from the New York dispatch.

She was in deep trouble anyway, she thought, gunning past the huge cement planters flanking the government building on Broadway.

"Don't I get even a little tiny say?" Carlos said.

Colette shook her head as they ate the red light.

"Sorry," she said.

Even with the aid of her siren and flashers, it took an hour and a half to get through the tunnel and Friday traffic. The hospital was distinguishable from the grim projects that neighbored it on both sides only by the fact that it had a driveway. She left her sedan beside three Newark PD cars and another just like her own. She stepped through the waiting room metal detector and ran right through the triage area into the back of the emergency room where she saw all the uniforms.

She saw O'Donnell first in one of the curtained areas. They'd already put a sheet over him, but it only half-covered his face. He lay sprawled back on the stretcher, one of his blue eyes staring intently up toward the ceiling as if he could see through it and something fascinating was happening on the floor above.

Colette shook her head.

Too late, she thought.

"That him?" a tall, well-dressed black man asked her. She didn't need to see his credentials to know he was one of her own. She could see his partner chatting up a nurse in a corridor through the glass of a door. She looked back down at O'Donnell.

"That's him," she said.

"We found this on him," the agent said, holding up her gun. He looked down at her empty holster and raised his eyebrow.

"Thanks," Colette said, taking it off him. It was lighter now. She pointed the muzzle down at the floor and popped the clip out. Yep. Empty. She didn't bother reloading it. She snapped the empty clip back in and holstered it.

"Thanks a lot. Where'd you guys get him?"

"We didn't get him," the black agent said, gesturing off to the left with his chin. Beyond the white curtain surrounding O'Donnell, the bald man, who'd pointed the gun in her face, was sitting at a row of orange plastic chairs. His shirt was covered in blood and he had one hand cuffed to the leg of his chair, the other holding his brow as he stared down at the floor.

"His partner brought him in. Stiff took one in his liver. Doctors couldn't do a thing except watch him bleed."

"You get the money?"

"We got half from the inside of the taxi they drove here in, we think," the black agent said. "We asked Mr. Clean over there, but he don't seem to be in a talking mood. Wanted to wait for you guys to do the ID."

Colette stepped up to him.

"Hey, Coglin, remember me?"

Coglin glanced at her, looked back down at the floor.

"Vaguely," he said.

"Where'd he get shot? On the corner of Park?" she said, looking at O'Donnell.

"I'm not sure," Coglin said. "In the tunnel maybe."

"He really was your uncle?"

Coglin glanced at the curtain, looked down at the floor. He shook his head.

"He was my friend," Coglin said.

"What about Lisa? Who was she?" Colette said. "How was she connected? And who were those other two in the elevator?"

Colette turned at the group of men who rushed into the hospital.

It was the Delta Force Team, still dressed in black, still strapped with firearms. Vaughn was at the head of them. He stopped at the foot of O'Donnell's bed. Vaughn's face broke into a smile. He turned and gave the lead man behind him a high five.

"Hey, you fuckin' *assholes!*" Coglin yelled, standing, his shackle clacking loudly as it came taught.

"You missed me," he yelled, pointing between his eyes.

"Didn't you? Didn't you? Shoot an unarmed woman pretty quick, but you know what? You fuckin' missed me!"

"But we got good ol' unc, didn't we?" Vaughn said. He gestured with a hand in the air.

"O Aidan Boy, the pipes, the pipes are callin'," he sang in a thick Irish brogue. "From glen to glen and across the mountain side."

"Special Ops?" Coglin said. "My uncle held you off with a handgun. He didn't even have a fuckin' shirt on. That old man had more balls than all you pussies put together."

"Had is the key word in that sentence," Vaughn said. "Was it sad when the last breath came, little nephew?"

Coglin shook his head.

"He died like the man he was. And did I mention, you missed me."

"I wouldn't talk so soon if I was you," Vaughn said. He turned to Colette.

"Agent Ryan, we're here to take Coglin into custody."

"Custody?" Colette said. "He's already in mine."

"The president has signed a special order giving me the power to operate here. Power that supercedes your own. Now," he nodded at one of the black-clad men who began to step forward, "we're taking him in."

Colette stood there, her mouth falling open, envisioning exactly what would happen next, what would come over the radio in ten, maybe twenty minutes' time.

Suspect escaping. Gunfire. Suspect down.

Last problem taken care of. No embarrassment for the Secret Service, and the vice president's grief succored by revenge. Mayor's reelection sewn up, in the bag.

The soldier was stepping past her when she pulled out her gun and pointed it at Vaughn. The approaching soldier stopped instinctively, swinging up his cut down M-16, the barrel at her chest. Six more machine guns clicked and clanked as they swung up on her. Carlos had his Glock out just holding it, not knowing where to aim.

A passing nurse dropped the tray she was carrying and screamed.

The two black FBI agents appeared, guns drawn as well.

"Put those rifles down!" the agent she'd spoken to first was yelling at the soldiers. "This is a public place, goddamn it. You are putting people at danger. I order you to drop your rifles now!"

"You are making a very big mistake, agent," Vaughn said.

"You better hope they have your blood type in stock, Vaughn," Colette said, squinting down her barrel. "Because you're about to come in need of a huge supply."

Vaughn looked around the emergency room. He seemed to be considering something or counting. Exactly how many people they would have to shoot to settle this thing. Finally, reluctantly it seemed, he waved a hand and the commandos lowered their guns and began to back out.

"You're going to regret this, Ryan," Vaughn said as he backed.

"Deeply," he said, and he turned.

"I don't think so," she said quietly to his back. What's the worst they could do, can her? She'd just get another job. Fuck 'em. She thought of her old boyfriend, Billy. What he'd asked her this morning. How cold did Maine really get?

"We take that jurisdictional stuff pretty seriously? Don't we?" the black FBI agent said to her wide-eyed, holstering his gun.

Colette laughed. She couldn't seem to stop. There were tears in her eyes as she sat down in the plastic chair next to Coglin.

"It wasn't that funny," Coglin said.

Colette dried her eyes on her sleeve. *Fired without a doubt,* she thought. *Ah, who gave a damn?* she decided. She'd done it. Gotten what she wanted. Didn't she? Showed them. The mayor. All the bastards. Her dad. Maybe they didn't even know that she showed them. But she had. She knew it at least.

"I almost forgot," she said to Coglin. "You have the right to remain silent. Anything you say . . ."

". . . can and will be used against me in a court of law," Coglin said with her. "I have a right to an attorney."

Together they recited the rest of his Miranda warning. The nurse who'd screamed came out from behind one of the curtains and began picking up the things she had dropped.

"You want to tell me where the rest of the money is?" Colette said.

Coglin looked at her. Her hair was frazzled and there were bags under her eyes. She looked completely worn and burnt out. Pulling the gun on the leader of the SWAT team, he decided, was the act of a woman on the complete edge. The key Aidan had given him was still hidden around his neck and its brass lay cold against his chest.

"I'll tell you on one condition," he said.

"What's that?" she said.

"We go halves," he said.

She turned to him. Her teeth came down on her lower lip, the jab of something scary and insane and yet wonderful starting in her chest.

"Out of curiosity," she said. "Where exactly were you planning on heading?"

"New Zealand," he said.

"From the airport?" she said.

"No," he said, laying the offer out to her. "From a container ship at the port."

Colette sat there.

"Does it get cold in New Zealand?" she said after a minute.

"What?" Coglin said. *No*, he thought, *that would be too insane.*

"Does it get cold in New Zealand?" she said again. "Like compared to, let's say, Maine?"

ACKNOWLEDGMENTS

THIS WORK COULD NOT HAVE BEEN CREATED without the enormous help, generosity and support of the following people: Mary, Keelan, Cara, Brynna, FBI Special Agent Ret. John Downey, NYPD Officer Robert Peterson, NYPD Officer Brian Mullen, the Midtown Evening Gang, Mike Brennan. Special thanks to my partner Dan Dunning for watching my back, his always erudite insights and giving me a ride home. Tom and Mollie Broussard, Frank the bartender at O'Farrell's.

Special thanks to editor George Lucas not only for extending my deadline without questions but for believing in this book from its first stages and rolling up his sleeves to make it the best it could be. Jim Patterson, Lori Andiman who is just every kind of nice imaginable, Sarah, Katherine and most especially Richard Pine, a very good friend in a very bad year.